OUTCASTS

Kelpies is an imprint of Floris Books
First published in 2019 by Floris Books
© 2019 Claire McFall

Claire McFall has asserted her right under the
Copyright, Designs and Patent Act of 1988 to be
identified as the Author of this Work

The publisher acknowledges subsidy from
Creative Scotland towards the publication
of this volume

 Also available as an eBook

British Library CIP data available
ISBN 978-178250-564-8
Printed in Great Britain
by TJ International

OUTCASTS

CLAIRE MCFALL

KELPIESEDGE

For Ben. Here's to the little book that could.

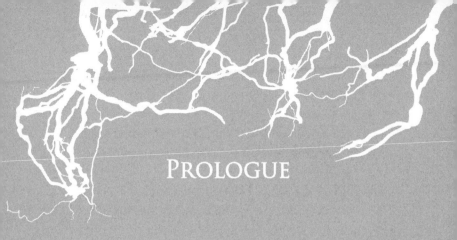

PROLOGUE

Something wasn't right.

The wraiths could feel it. A weakness, a flaw in the veil between the dead and the living. The holes that had pierced it were closed… but it wasn't the same. Not quite.

Driven into a frenzy by the tantalising draw of real flesh, real life, the wraiths pounded the veil again and again. It rippled and warped, but held. Barely.

They renewed their attack, pushing and clawing, thinning the boundary until one creature, snarling and writhing, fought its way through.

The veil snapped back instantly, holding firm against the rest of the swarm, who screeched with frustration, but the damage was done.

Disoriented, the wraith stuttered through the air before steadying, sniffing. Searching through the darkened countryside for the intoxicating lure of blood pulsing through veins. Of life to feast on.

CHAPTER 1

You've got to be kidding me. Dylan stared in horror at her reflection in the full-length mirror. Her eyes were wide, ringed with a thick border of black eyeliner topped with smoky-grey shadow. It had a slight shimmer to it when she turned her head just right. Yeah, her eyes were OK. But the rest…

Her hair had been pulled and twisted and teased until it stood out from her head in what could only be described as a rat's nest. The lipstick that had been smeared across her mouth was a garish shade of red that made her look like a vampire after a quick snack. And then there was the dress. It was taffeta. *Taffeta.* Until Joan had frogmarched her into the 'Special Occasion' section of the big department store at the bottom of Sauchiehall Street, Dylan hadn't even known what taffeta was. She did *not* like it. Especially not in this hideous shade of peach that made Dylan think of over-cooked salmon. There were bulbous sleeves and tight tucks down her mid-section that pinched in all the wrong places. The skirt was apparently meant to swirl in beautiful, graceful swishes around her legs as she walked, and maybe it would, if the tights Joan had shoved at her as she was getting dressed weren't rubbing against the bloody taffeta and creating enough static electricity to power the whole Central Belt.

I look absolutely hideous, she thought, shuddering with enough force that her reflection vibrated subtly in the mirror. She'd been overjoyed when her parents had told her they were getting married, and even more excited when Joan had told her she'd be a bridesmaid.

That was before the dress shopping.

"Oh darlin', you look absolutely gorgeous!" Dylan's Great Aunt Gladys sat in a chair in the corner of the hotel room, a handkerchief clutched in her swollen, arthritic fingers and tears glistening in her eyes. She did have cataracts, which might explain the old woman's assessment. Or maybe this look had been on-trend when Aunt Gladys had been young. Sometime before the Vikings invaded.

"Thanks, Aunt Gladys," Dylan managed to grate out.

"You're the prettiest girl in the whole town, do you know that?"

Dylan grimaced. Heat was rising up her neck, clashing with her gown. She could *not* go out there looking like this, she just couldn't.

A knock at the door made her jump.

"Dylan, you ready? It's just about time." Dylan spun to the door to see the gleaming brass knob begin to turn. "They're waiting for—"

"Just a minute!" she screeched. The knob stopped turning and, mercifully, the door stayed closed. "I'm not quite ready, Tristan. Hang… hang on." Panicking, Dylan turned to Great Aunt Gladys, but there would be no help from that quarter. The old woman was rearranging her walking frame, beginning the laborious process of standing up.

"Come in, boy," she hollered. 'Boy', that's what she called him, despite Tristan introducing himself clearly – and loudly – and Dylan correcting Great Aunt Gladys three times since.

Tristan opened the door and Dylan turned away from him, hoping to spare herself the look on his face when he saw her done up like this. It was a futile effort, because she could see him in the reflection of the mirror as he stood in the doorway, and her eyes instinctively fixed on his face without her permission. He stared at her, his gaze raking up and down her back before looking into the mirror to see the front. He kept his expression carefully blank, Dylan noticed, only his lips twitching slightly.

"Wow," he said.

"Speechless are you, boy?" Great Aunt Gladys hollered. "There you are, young lady. I told you, you look stunning."

"I am," Tristan agreed. "I'm speechless." He gave Dylan a tiny grin. She offered him a wry smile of her own, that widened a little as she took in the gleaming shoes, smart black trousers and bold blue shirt that Tristan was wearing. She'd never seen him so dressed up; it was a good look for him. Especially the shirt, which made his cobalt eyes seem to almost glow, more striking than usual today because his slightly unruly dark-blond hair was swept back from his face.

"You look great," Dylan told him.

"Out of the way, then." Aunt Gladys used her walking frame to manoeuvre Tristan out of her path as she inched step by painful step out of the door. "I'll go and get myself sat down. No, don't offer to help me, boy. It's not as if I'm ninety-two."

"I… uhm…" Tristan shifted awkwardly, clearly searching for an excuse. Dylan bit her lip against the smirk that wanted to break free. It wasn't as if he could tell Aunt Gladys the truth: the large function room downstairs where the wedding was taking place was just too far away. The bond that tethered Dylan and Tristan together would rip and tear at them, leaving them breathless with pain, if they tried to put that much distance between them. It had been bad enough having Tristan get ready in the hotel room next door; she'd known he was there, but she couldn't *see* him.

Luckily, at that moment Dylan's father, James, appeared behind Tristan.

"Tristan." He clapped his hand down on Tristan's shoulder by way of greeting, possibly a little bit too hard, going by the grimaced "hello" he got back. "Hey beautiful, you look lovely." The words came out of James's mouth before his gaze settled on Dylan, but even then, his smile didn't falter. Dylan didn't think there was anything that would remove the grin from his face today. Undeterred by the fact his daughter looked like a giant salmon meringue, he turned to Great Aunt Gladys. "I just came to see if you needed a hand getting to your seat, Gladys. We're starting soon."

"Well." Great Aunt Gladys looked somewhat mollified. "At least *someone* here has manners!" Shooting Tristan a disgusted look, she started shuffling away, leaning heavily on her walking frame but swatting at James when he tried to take her elbow to steady her.

"I don't think she likes me," Tristan confided to Dylan, once they were both sure the old woman was far away enough not to hear. For ninety-two, she had ears like a bat.

"Well, she thinks *I* look good," Dylan replied in a stage whisper, "so I wouldn't rely on her judgement too much."

There it was, Tristan's opportunity to confirm what she knew – that she looked like she'd had a makeover from a hyperactive five-year-old. And she was going to have to go and stand up in front of over a hundred people… dressed like this.

"I think you look…" Tristan ran his gaze over her outfit once more, clearly hunting for something nice to say – and failing miserably. "Well, your eyes are very pretty."

"Great," Dylan snapped, feeling those eyes well up a little, which was even worse. She would not cry like a baby on top of everything else. "I'll just put a paper bag over the rest of it then, shall I?"

"You'll need a big bag," Tristan mused.

For a moment Dylan just gaped at him, aghast. Then she laughed.

Then she thumped him.

"Very helpful," she mock-glared.

"I try," Tristan replied, smirking. He sobered, reached out to take her left hand. "Honestly, I think you'd look beautiful in whatever you wore," he said, "*even* a paper bag. But, I feel the need to remind you that it's your mum's big day, not yours. Everyone will be looking at her, I promise."

"Right," Dylan said, eyeing him dubiously. "I'll just blend in with the background." There was no way anyone could fail to notice Dylan in the Giant Peach. "Maybe I'll get lucky and match the wallpaper or the curtains. If I stand in the right place, I might just disappear."

"That's the spirit!" Tristan grinned, leaning forward to kiss her lightly on the forehead.

Just then, the door across the hall from Dylan's room opened and her Aunt Rachel reversed out of it, appearing unflatteringly ample, peach-covered bottom first as she bent over, fussing with something. A second later she moved out of the way and Joan stepped through into the hallway. Dylan gasped. Joan's normal attire was a starched navy-blue nurse's uniform. At home, she wore comfortable clothes, more often than not smothering her body in an assortment of ugly, woollen cardigans.

Today, she was transformed.

High heels meant she stood several inches taller than usual. Her slim figure was hugged by the satiny cream dress that wrapped around her from cleavage to knee. There was a single thin strap that wound around the back of Joan's neck and disappeared into a wide banding of beautiful, pearl-studded lacework where it met the dress.

In her hands, she grasped a delicate bouquet of roses surrounded by small sprays of pretty white flowers.

"Mum!" Dylan clapped her hand over her mouth and, to her surprise, started welling up.

"Oh no, don't you dare!" Joan pointed a finger in Dylan's direction, the nail glistening with pearl-coloured varnish. "Don't you get me started!"

But it was evidently too late. Joan snatched the handkerchief that Aunt Rachel held out and started frantically dabbing at her eyes.

"This isn't supposed to be a day for crying," Aunt Rachel commented. Her own eyes were tear-free, her lips slightly pursed.

"Oh, please," Joan sniped back. "I remember on your wedding day you locked yourself in the bathroom for an hour, bawling because your hair wasn't sitting right."

Aunt Rachel opened her mouth, her eyes lighting up in outrage, but no sound came out. It was just as well Dylan was used to the little spats that constantly broke out between the two sisters, and knew it wasn't unusual for them to descend into all-out catfights.

The little squabble seemed to have steadied Joan, however, because she sniffed and drew herself up, then beamed at Dylan. "Are we ready?"

Dylan glanced down one more time at her bridesmaid's ensemble and thought she'd never be ready, but, like Tristan had said, this was Joan's day. Not hers.

"Shouldn't you be in your seat?" Aunt Rachel asked Tristan, the sharp tone in her voice giving away her irritation over Joan's well-aimed jab.

"Rachel, Tristan is escorting my daughter," Joan bit back.

She'd softened towards Tristan immeasurably over the past few months, but Dylan knew the comment was more about quieting her sister than defending her daughter's boyfriend.

They were a quiet group as they took the lift down to the hotel's ground floor and then traversed the gleaming lobby to the entrance of the function suite. The double doors were closed, twists of white netting pinned around the doorframe and tied in bows around the handles. A smartly dressed hotel worker waited for them, ready to let them in.

"Perfect timing." He smiled at them. "They're just about ready for you."

Joan nodded and Dylan watched the slightly tense frown melt from her face, replaced by an eager anticipation that made her look years younger. The traitorous tears threatened to burst forth again as Dylan rearranged her grip on her bouquet, a smaller version of Joan's. It was about to happen, she realised. Her parents were getting married; she was going to have a proper family for the first time. Tristan's warm hand on her back, meant to steady and reassure her, almost tipped her over the edge. Because he was there, too. Standing beside her.

Aunt Rachel sighed, and Dylan scowled at her. If she said something to ruin this moment for Joan... But the look on Aunt Rachel's face was wistful. "It's a shame Dad isn't here, to walk you down the aisle," she said quietly.

Sadness flitted across Joan's face for a heartbeat, but then her gaze settled on Dylan and it faded. "It's all right," she said. "I'd much rather be escorted by my baby, she's all I need."

Joan had no idea, no idea at all, how close she'd come to losing Dylan. James understood some of it, but they'd had to keep it a secret from her mum – how Dylan had died, fought her way back to life and then had to fight again to stay here. Joan's words hit deeper than she could have realised and Dylan sniffled, swallowing hard against the lump that had suddenly lodged in her throat.

"Thanks, Mum," she croaked out.

Joan smiled at her, then gestured with one hand. "Front and centre, young lady," she said. "You're leading the way."

Dylan turned, positioning herself in front of the closed double doors just as the first notes of 'Here Comes the Bride' began. Tristan stood beside her, ready to slip into his seat when the bridal party started down the aisle.

Sudden nerves gripped Dylan and she yanked in a deep breath. Then the doors were opening and, as one, the gathered guests turned to stare at them. At her, standing frozen in the doorway, garish in peach taffeta. A hundred pairs of eyes and the long, long stretch of aisle waiting before her.

"Oh God," she whispered, low enough that only Tristan would hear. "This is hell!"

CHAPTER 2

"This is hell." Jack stood at the door of the safe house and glowered at the smattering of wraiths that swirled and swooped outside. The bloodied glow of the sun burning in the sky cast his face into eerie crimson shadow, his eyes dark pits beneath furrowed brows.

"Shut the door," Susanna advised, watching him with the unhappy mix of guilt and responsibility that had plagued her in the seemingly endless time they'd been hiding out here. "Don't look at them."

She sat on a low, lumpy sofa, as far from the door as she could get. That wasn't very far, the safe house resembling a small bothy with stone walls, thatched roof and only one single room. There was no place for privacy, no place to escape each other. In fact, the sofa was the sole large piece of furniture available; a spindly kitchen chair the only other place to sit. When they quarrelled – as was inevitable, stuck in such close confines – there was nowhere to go. A single step outside would mean agony for Susanna as the ever-present wraiths tore into her.

And it would mean something worse than death for Jack.

They'd been living this torturous existence for… Susanna wasn't even sure how many days had passed now since the Inquisitor had banished them back to the wasteland: the real wasteland, where the land burned blood-red and the wraiths were free to hunt any soul foolish enough to step outside.

On the back wall of the safe house was row upon row of neat little lines scratched into the stone. Each mark represented a day that she and Jack had survived within their wasteland prison. She hadn't counted them recently, but there were too many to guess at a glance, and she'd stopped adding new markings some time ago.

"Jack, shut the door," she repeated.

Jack pursed his lips – he still hated taking any kind of orders from her – and leaned forward instead. For a heart-stopping moment, Susanna thought he was really going to do it, was going to step outside and end the stalemate they were trapped in, but he only waited until the wraiths, sensing the movement, snarled and screeched in triumph, before yanking himself back and kicking shut the door.

"You shouldn't do that," she chided as he strolled over and dropped down beside her. "You'll just anger them more."

"I think they're already pretty angry," Jack commented, the frustrated hisses of the wraiths outside attesting to his words. "And it's something to do."

Susanna sighed. That was their problem. Simple boredom.

They didn't need to eat, they didn't need to drink, but at some point soon they were going to have to get out of here – simply to stop themselves going insane.

How many more days would it be before Jack stepped outside the door for real?

She took a deep breath, determined to broach the subject, but Jack beat her to it.

"I've been thinking," he said, staring down at the floor as he spoke. That was enough to snap Susanna's mouth shut. It wasn't like Jack to avoid her gaze. To act so… hesitant. Uncertain.

"About what?" she asked when he fiddled with the hem of his T-shirt rather than continuing.

"I think—" Jack dragged in a breath and then blew it out. "I think we just need to go for it."

"What? You mean—"

He flicked his eyes up and Susanna could see what he was hiding. Fear. It was warring with determination for control of his expression – and losing. Just.

"We can't stay here for ever," he said.

"We can," Susanna corrected.

"No, we can't." He glared at her, daring her to contradict him a second time. She didn't. "We need to just do it. Get it over with. If we don't make it…" He shrugged.

"If we don't make it, you become one of *them*," Susanna reminded him, nodding to where the wraiths could still be seen through one of the small windows.

"And you," Jack countered.

"No." Susanna shook her head. "I won't. I'll end up reassigned, sent to collect another soul. They can hurt me, but they can't kill me. They can't take me and turn me into one of them. But they can do that to you."

Jack gave another little shrug, as if trying to shake off her words. Deny them. Then he sniffed and shifted his jaw. Sat up a little straighter. The bravado he had slowly shed over the long days and nights he and Susanna had been together suddenly snapped back into place.

"So what? If it happens it happens."

"Jack—"

"At least you'll be free."

Susanna blinked, certain she hadn't heard those words.

"What?" she asked.

"You'll be free," Jack repeated. Susanna could feel the tension radiating from his body beside her. "If I make it, well… great. But if not, at least you'll get out of here. Right?"

Susanna didn't know what to say. "I won't be free," she said slowly. "I'll have to go back to being a ferryman, like I was before."

"But you'll be out of here."

"Yeah," she agreed, "I'll be out of here." Out of this cage that was their sole point of safety in the hell of the true wasteland. Away from Jack and the guilt that had her insides twisting every time she looked at him.

And then, every single time she saw a wraith, she'd wonder if it was Jack. If there was any spark of him left inside the creature that was trying to savage her and kill the new soul she was ferrying. She'd wonder if he was suffering, living an endless torment because of her. He'd probably enjoy the chance to get a little revenge, she thought wryly. The idea made her snort out a quiet puff of laughter.

"What?" Jack asked, watching her with a quizzical tilt to his head, looking to share the humour.

It was a good look on him. Made him look younger, friendlier. It softened the harsh, angry lines that so often hardened his face. Susanna couldn't pinpoint when he'd started looking at her like that, but slowly, over the agonisingly long hours, days and weeks that they'd spent together, they'd found a way to coexist. To accept each other. To talk – properly talk – even laugh, and to find their own strange kind of rhythm. To become friends.

That's what she'd be losing if Jack was captured by the wraiths, pulled down and turned into one of them: a friend. But more than that, someone who looked at her and really *saw* her.

"I was imagining you as a wraith," she admitted. "You'd be able to get your own back for everything."

Jack grinned, though it really wasn't all that funny, Susanna knew.

"I'd stalk you all the way across the wasteland," he promised. "Your own, personal wraith to dog your footsteps."

"Thanks," Susanna told him dryly. "I appreciate that."

The small spark of amusement extinguished. They sat on the sofa in silence, watching the sky darken to a deep burgundy as the sun set and the night approached. The noise outside would intensify now. The wraiths would multiply until they were so thick they would bang and thump against the sides of the safe house, jostling and fighting with each other to get closer and closer still. Susanna didn't understand the wraiths' obsession with them – there were other safe houses in the wasteland to terrorise – but she supposed it might be a punishment from the Inquisitor. A way to remind them, nightly, what awaited them if they were foolish enough to make the journey.

"You really want to do it?" Susanna asked as a particularly spine-tingling wail cut through the twilight. "You want to face…" she gestured to the window, "*that*?"

It took Jack a long moment to answer. Finally, he sighed.

"I don't want to leave you…" he said quietly, "but I can't stay here any longer. I just can't."

"When?" Susanna asked.

Another sigh, this one accompanied by a shrug. "Tomorrow?"

"Tomorrow?" she squeaked.

"If not tomorrow, when?"

She shot him a sideways look. "When did you get so sage?"

Jack raised one side of his mouth in a wry half-smile, but didn't answer. Outside, the hisses and snarls started to morph into a low, continuous rumble as more wraiths arrived.

"Light the fire?" Jack asked. He didn't wait to see if Susanna would answer, instead rising and moving to the nearest window. They repeated their nightly routine: Susanna dropped to the fireplace and used her ferryman powers – which thankfully she hadn't lost – to create a blaze among the small pile of wood stacked there, while Jack closed the curtains against the wraiths so that at least they wouldn't see them, shifting in shadowy flickers outside. Tasks complete, they returned to the sofa and, as they did every night, Jack lay down along the back of the cushions and Susanna crawled to lie in her usual place in front of him. He folded his arms around her and they closed their eyes.

It had been horrendously awkward, the first few times they'd done this, but there was nowhere else to lie down, except for the cold flagstone floor. At first they'd spent night after night tense and unmoving, rigidly trying not to touch each other, until Jack had eventually had enough and put his arms around Susanna with a gruff, "I won't bite, you know." It had dissolved any remaining self-conciousness they still felt around each other, and they'd slept this way ever since. Not that they needed to sleep – Jack was dead and Susanna was a ferryman – but it was a way to mark the days. To keep the routine of day and night.

Now, she couldn't relax without it. She was the ferryman, but having Jack hold her made her feel somehow safer, stronger.

She wasn't sure how she felt about that.

When the fire burned down and the room darkened, it was a way for them to grasp a facsimile of privacy, of time alone, as they both pretended the other was asleep.

And somehow, in a perverse twist of fate, or cruel punishment from the Inquisitor, since she'd returned to the wasteland, Susanna dreamed. She didn't know what else to call it. She wasn't asleep, but memories would grab at her, demand her attention in the dark, and she'd be helpless to look away until whatever remembrance that had her in its maw released her back into the relative sanctuary of the safe house.

"You want to talk?" Jack asked, his voice low in her ear.

Susanna shook her head, knowing he'd feel the movement even if he couldn't see her silhouette shifting in the firelight.

"It won't help," she told him.

He squeezed her in sympathy. There was no way to hide the dreams from Jack, not when they often left her trembling or sobbing. Or both.

"Maybe you won't have one tonight," he offered.

"Maybe." She knew she would, though. With their earlier conversation and Jack's decision ringing in her ears, and the wraiths outside singing her to sleep with their nightmare lullaby, she knew she'd dream. It was just a question of which memory would be the one to rip her from Jack's arms and thrust her into the path of pain and fear.

Blowing out a breath through tense lips, she tried to relax her body as she closed her eyes.

The wind was howling, fighting with the wraiths to fill Susanna's ears. She felt dizzy, disoriented.

But she knew exactly where she was. And when.

She should, she'd been here so many times before in her 'dreams'. It was the moment the Inqusitor had sent them back. Back to the living hell of the wasteland.

Jack hollered his opening line. "What is this?" It was still hard to hear him over the whooshing, whirling and screaming, but she knew the words by now. She knew them by heart.

"The wasteland," Susanna shouted back.

"Why doesn't it look like it did before?"

Susanna wished she could stop it, stop the dream now. Just as she'd wished a hundred times before. It never worked.

But the real wasteland waited for her, burning her eyes with a thousand different shades of red. Heat prickled, and sand whipped up by the wind scraped against her skin, a million tiny stings. Rocks burst from the ground in ragged peaks.

It created a maze of shadows. Countless places for wraiths to lurk, waiting to ambush them.

That, at least, was one small mercy. Susanna had memorised where each of them lingered by now. Knew when to expect the attack. Unfortunately, she still had no way to prevent it – the memory would unfold as it always did.

Susanna stared at Jack, guilt bubbling in her stomach. The path the Inquisitor had set before them was impossible; there was no way they could cross the wasteland like this.

It was a death sentence.

"Jack," Susanna said, turning to the soul she'd led too far from his path. The words were already on her tongue, ready to spring forth as they always did, but she'd never meant them more. "I'm sorry. I'm so, so sorry."

"What do we do?" he yelled.

Susanna turned to the safe house. That first time, hunting around the wraiths, she'd been so grateful when she spotted it. There must have been some mercy left in the Inquisitor after all, because it sat there, not a hundred metres from where they cowered, terrifyingly exposed in the empty wasteland. Its door was already open, as if waiting for them.

"Jack!" Susanna pointed with one trembling finger. "Look!"

She turned her head to smile at him, to share the tiny pinprick of hope that was lighting up inside her, and, as she'd known it would, the moment of inattention cost her. A wraith landed on her arm, claws curling round it, like a hawk returning to its master's glove. Only Susanna's arm was bare, and rather than the sleek, beautiful lines of a bird of prey, the wraith was a swirling, writhing mass of darkness, one that began to immediately rake and tear at her flesh as soon as it landed, razor-sharp teeth bared.

"Help! Get it off!" She twisted and thrashed, struggling to present her side to Jack, to give him an opportunity to grab the thing. Then she did... and yet still Jack didn't move. Didn't help her. Glancing at him for a fraction of a second, her entreaty forming again on her lips, she saw it. Indecision.

Should he help her or not? Should he let the wraith just have her? Look what she'd done to him. She deserved it.

The thoughts flickered across Jack's face, as easy to read as if he'd spoken them aloud. Horror had long since stopped dropping like a stone in Susanna's stomach. She didn't have time to plead with him – not that there would be any point; that wasn't how the memory unfolded. Another wraith took advantage of her distraction and tangled itself in her hair, wrenching her neck and scoring gashes across her scalp. Pain shot across her skull, making her cry out.

Pain blazed across her thigh as a wraith scythed past her before circling for another pass. Susanna closed her eyes, ignoring, just for a moment, the wraith attacking her head and the other, attached like a limpet to her arm. *You won't die,* she reminded herself. They can't kill you. Pain is only pain.

Then something much bigger shoved her off balance and she almost fell to the floor. Flinging her eyes open, she saw Jack, a grim, angry set to his face, wrapping strong fingers around her free arm.

"I can't touch them," he hollered at her, his voice almost disappearing under the hissing and screeching creatures. "We need to run."

She couldn't run, not with two attached to her and others trying to take out her legs, but with Jack hauling her along, doggedly ignoring the wraiths that were dive-bombing him, she had no choice. He half-dragged, half-carried her step by step, metre by metre, until the safe house rose up before them: a single-storey stone sanctuary. Their oasis in the desert.

Buoyed by Jack's help, Susanna managed to galvanise herself to tear free of the two wraiths, leaving deep, bloody furrows in her flesh, before they fell in the door.

Quiet. Blessed stillness and quiet as they lay panting on the cool hardness of the flagstone floor. Susanna stared at the doorway a heartbeat longer, assuring herself that, as always, the wraiths couldn't break through the barrier, before dropping her head back, closing her eyes and letting herself sob. Just a little.

Just for a moment.

She felt shifting by her side as Jack detangled himself from her and sat up.

"You're bleeding," he commented.

She was. She could feel the tear on her thigh, and her lower right arm burned and throbbed like it'd been chewed on by a bulldog, which she supposed wasn't far from the truth. The wounds on her scalp weren't bad, she knew, but head wounds always bled more.

"I know," she sighed. "But it doesn't matter. I'll heal. We made it here, that's what's important." Susanna forced her eyes open, blinking away a smear of blood trickling down from her hairline. She ignored it, focussing on Jack, sitting over her almost protectively. "Thank you," she rasped, her mouth dry from fear and the arid air of the true wasteland. "Thank you for helping me."

Jack didn't react to her gratitude. Instead, he looked away. Shrugged. The wraiths flocked round the still open doorway caught and held his attention. "What are we going to do now?"

Susanna stared at the wraiths, too. There were at least a hundred of them out there. Each one ready to tear her apart, to drag Jack below the surface and make him one of them.

She didn't have an answer.

"Susanna!" Jack's voice was low but urgent in her ear. "Susanna!" He gave her a little shake and Susanna jerked, lifting her head and gazing blearily about her.

"What?" she asked stupidly. "What's happening?"

It was pitch-black, the fire having burned out completely. Whatever light might have filtered in from the night sky outside was being blocked by the mob of wraiths who were, as always, doing their best to torment them through the long hours of darkness.

"You were shaking," Jack told her, concern in his voice. "Were you having another nightmare?"

"I told you," she responded automatically, "I don't sleep."

Jack snorted quietly, his arms still strong around her, providing much-needed support. "Call it what you like," he said. "You were dreaming."

Susanna couldn't dispute that, not with the echoes of the wounds she'd sustained that day still tingling, phantom-like, on her flesh.

"Was it a bad one?" he murmured.

"It was… it was when we first arrived." She didn't need to say any more than that. She knew the memories of those first terrifying moments, dumped unceremoniously into the true wasteland, must be even more vivid in Jack's mind. Susanna, at least, had had some idea of where they were, what was happening.

Jack was silent for a long moment.

"You haven't dreamed about that for a while."

No, she hadn't. At first that memory had consumed her every night – all the more terrifying because she hadn't understood why it was happening. She was a ferryman; she didn't sleep, and she didn't dream. Now, she just accepted that the memories were going to come for her – though that didn't make it any easier. But Jack was right, it had been a while since their first, petrifying moments in the wasteland had revisited her.

It didn't take a genius to figure out why.

Jack interrupted her thoughts. "About tomorrow…"

"Yeah?" Susanna replied.

"Well, you know this place better than I do. What's it gonna be like?"

Susanna drew in deeply through her nose and exhaled slowly.

"I don't travel the real wasteland," she told him honestly. "None of us ferrymen do. We collect a soul and guide them across their individual wasteland, then we're taken immediately on to the next."

"So you've no idea?" he ground out, the hard edge in his voice showing his frustration. They'd come a long way together, the two of them, forging a friendship in slow, painful steps, but Jack had never been able stop himself falling back on his final defence when things weren't going his way. Scowl, shout, throw things. Get angry and cold. Sometimes cruel.

Susanna knew exactly why he did it – he was scared, and frustrated – but that didn't make it any easier to deal with.

"No," she said patiently. "I've got a *bit* of an idea. I've always been able to see the real wasteland. At any time, I could drop the veil and see it, but I've never done it anywhere except from a safe house – it was too dangerous."

Jack grunted, a dissatisfied sound, so she went on.

"I imagine it's like travelling the wasteland at night. Normally, the wraiths avoid the sunlight. They stick to very deep shadows, so their opportunities to attack during the day are limited – unless a soul gives in to despair so badly that the weather rolls in enough to create an atmosphere so thick and sunless that they can break free."

Jack considered that quietly. Shifting position on the sofa to release a cramp in her back, Susanna felt how tense he was lying behind her. He was scared, she knew, but trying to hide it. He needn't bother – she was too.

"Have you ever travelled the wasteland at night, then?" he asked at last.

"Lots of times."

"And…?" he prodded.

"It's… well, it's bad." There was no point in lying to him. "Unless we're really, really near a safe house, the soul has pretty much no chance. There are just too many wraiths. You can't fight them at all, and I can't fight them all at once." She thought for a moment. "When I was ferrying Michael—"

"Michael?"

"He was a soul," she explained, "before you. Anyway, when I was ferrying him, I noticed something strange about the wraiths."

"Go on." Jack nudged her shoulder to urge her on.

"They… well, it's crazy, but it seemed like they were working together. Acting as a team, or a pack, to bring me down. Normally they just attack randomly, individually. But with Michael I almost got the impression that they'd thought about how best to go about it."

"What's weird about that?"

"Because wraiths don't think!" Susanna burst out. "They're mindless, savage things. There's nothing left in them of the people they used to be."

"Are you sure?" Jack asked.

"Yes," she replied. "Absolutely. That's why I can't explain it."

"So…" Jack lifted his arm from her side and she imagined him shoving his hand through his hair, angrily grabbing a handful. He did that a lot. "So, you're saying it's impossible."

Susanna nodded. It was dark still, but now that her eyes had adjusted, she thought he'd probably see her.

"There must be a way!" Jack insisted. "Dylan did it – on her own."

Susanna hunched her shoulders, feeling defensive now herself. Was she just imagining the accusation in Jack's tone? They didn't talk much about Dylan and Tristan – what would be the point? But the thought of them was always there, hovering in the air between them. The pair were, after all, the reason they were in this mess.

No, Susanna reflected. They're the reason *I* got us into this mess.

And, unfortunately, there hadn't been time to ask Dylan just how she'd managed to traverse the true wasteland, all alone.

"Well, I'm not Dylan," she said quietly.

"No, you're not," Jack snapped back, and Susanna huddled over a little more. There was nowhere on the tiny sofa to get away from him, from the truth of his words. Especially not when he squeezed her back against him. "You're a ferryman," he reminded her. "You can do all kinds of stuff that she can't."

Susanna blinked, completely taken aback.

"Was that… was that a compliment?"

"Don't get used to it," Jack told her darkly, and she grinned. "But what I'm saying is," another squeeze, "you can do it."

"You mean *we* can do it?" she replied.

"Let's hope so," he said.

They didn't say anything more for a long while, simply lying and resting. Waiting. At one point, Jack got up, climbing awkwardly over Susanna, to open the curtains.

"I want to watch the sun come up," he said, before lying back down beside her.

Eventually, by such infinitesimal degrees that at first it was hard to notice, the sky began to lighten. The wraiths became distinguishable from the night sky, sinuous, undulating blobs of black against a background that started at burnt umber and grew to flaming orange as the red-hot coal that was the sun nudged into the sky.

The noise outside gradually quieted as most – but not all – of the circling creatures outside slunk off to pursue other prey. It was as safe as it was going to get.

Susanna lifted herself up and swung her legs down until she was perched on the edge of the sofa. Jack sat up beside her then stood, stretching. He didn't do his normal thing of walking to the door and opening it, sticking his head outside as far as was safe to taunt the remaining wraiths. Instead, he crossed to the smaller opening of the window, staying far back enough to be out of sight of the wraiths who still bumped the walls and roof on occasion, as if afraid Jack and Susanna might forget they were there.

"You ready?" Jack asked.

No, Susanna thought. She was far from ready. But that didn't really matter, because she was never going to be ready. Honestly, it would have been better if they'd just tried to make the journey straight away. Then, Jack had been her responsibility, had been a source of terrible guilt, but he'd also been bad-tempered and volatile. Now, he was her friend. More than that. She knew him better than she'd ever known anyone – even Tristan. She cared about him, and she knew he cared about her.

Losing him now was a very different prospect.

A lump lodged in her throat and she realised she was on the verge of tears.

"You all right?" Jack asked, catching sight of her expression. "You scared?"

"No." She shook her head, then hiccupped a laugh. "Well, yes. I just…" She took a step forward, grabbed Jack by the hand. "Hang on to me, OK? I'm not going to lose you."

Jack nodded, no smart comeback for once. He gave her fingers a tight squeeze.

"And when we're out there," Susanna said, thinking of all the times she'd been caught in the wasteland after the sun had sunk, all the times she'd dragged souls back from the edge of danger, "don't look at the wraiths. Pretend they don't exist. You can't fight them, it's stupid to try. So just… ignore them and focus on me. On where we're going, or on your feet if you have to."

"Pretend they're like my stepdad, then," Jack said dryly. "No problem, I've had lots of practise at that."

Susanna laughed, Jack's wry humour breaking the tension that had her shoulder muscles in knots, her legs feeling weak and not her own. She sobered quickly, though, and moved to the door, Jack close as a shadow behind her, his hand still in hers.

Susanna paused with her other hand on the doorknob, not looking at him.

"I'm going to get you through this, Jack," she whispered. "I swear."

And then she flung open the door.

CHAPTER 3

"Tristan, are you nearly done?" It was time to just ask outright, because sighing and huffing and twirling around and around in her chair hadn't managed to convey to Tristan that Dylan was bored out of her mind.

"Eh… yeah." Tristan didn't so much as take his eyes off the computer screen, his finger on the mouse click, click, clicking as he scrolled through the website he was looking at.

"Seriously, I think Mrs Lambert is going to kick us out of the library in a minute. Even the cleaners have gone home!" Dylan wheeled her chair over to him. "What are you looking at, anyway?"

They'd been in the library since the end of lunchtime, their History teacher having booked the banks of computers for their afternoon double period to give the class research time for a project on the slave trade in eighteenth-century America. It was now close to 5 p.m., and Dylan was itching to escape the funny smell that seemed to linger in the place, and the oppressive atmosphere created by Mrs Lambert, the world's least friendly children's librarian (she might have been responsible for the smell as well).

Plus, ugly black clouds had been rolling across the sky for the last fifteen minutes, and if they didn't leave soon, they were going to get drenched on the way home.

"Just the news," Tristan murmured. He clicked on another link.

"The news? Tristan, we can do that at home! You know, where there's a sofa and a television and a fridge – and where it doesn't smell weird!" Dylan huffed. "You could have used my laptop. Or your phone. Or my dad's tablet."

"Sorry," Tristan said, not sounding particularly sorry at all. "I'm nearly done though, I swear." He turned to smile apologetically at Dylan as the next page loaded. Dylan returned it half-heartedly then looked at the screen, eyes flickering over the headline and—

"What the hell is that?!"

The image was almost unidentifiable. Dylan could make out four hooved feet, but beyond that, it was just a hunk of shredded skin, hair and muscle. It was repulsive and she leaned away from it as her eyes lifted to read the headline:

HORSE ATTACK LEAVES FARMER BAMBOOZLED

"Well, it *was* a horse," Tristan answered.

Dylan had guessed as much from the shouty title, but apart from the feet, she couldn't make the rest of the bloodied jumble morph into legs, a body, a head.

"What happened to it?" Dylan could have read the article, but she was having a hard time pulling her eyes away from the picture, grisly as it was.

"That's the thing," Tristan said, "nobody knows. *Something* attacked it."

It was impossible to miss Tristan's emphasis, or his choice of words. Dylan looked at him, then back at the picture. *No*, she thought. *It couldn't be. Not another one.*

But her denials didn't stop icy fear from clawing its way into her insides.

"Where did it happen?" she choked out.

"Here." Tristan already had a tab up with Google Maps activated. He pointed towards the little red dot in the centre. "It's just outside a place called Kilsyth."

"Kilsyth?" The cold that had taken up residence in Dylan's stomach melted away as she took in the location and rational thought pushed back against the panic. Kilsyth was a small place near Cumbernauld, it was nowhere near the train tunnel where she'd had her accident – or Denny, where Jack died. She blew out a relieved breath. "It couldn't have been a… *you know,*" Mrs Lambert was too far away to hear her, and there was no one else in the library, but still, she didn't want to say the word out loud, "then, could it? It's too far away – from either of the holes."

And anyway, they'd closed both of those tears. There was no way a wraith could find its way through the veil that separated the world of the living from the wasteland.

"That's true," Tristan said softly. He clicked away from the map, the poor dead horse popping back up onto the screen.

"It must just have been a wild animal, or a pack of dogs, maybe. There are sickos who train pit bulls and mastiffs and dogs like that to attack. That makes more sense, Tristan. It does," Dylan pushed, because while he was nodding along with her, something on his face said that he didn't believe it. "Let's go," she said. If nothing else, she wanted to get away from the picture, the sad remains of what must have been a terrifying attack for the horse. She felt nauseated thinking about how much it must have panicked, tried to get away… "Come on," she pleaded. "It's getting late."

Tristan didn't argue and made quick work of logging off the computer. He was silent as they left the library, silent as they walked through the deserted school building, and silent as they reached the foyer where the lights in the office were all switched off, the place eerily empty.

It wasn't until they stepped out of the front entrance and paused under the overhang to stare out at the pounding raindrops now slanting down from a leaden sky that he spoke. He turned to Dylan, an impish smile on his face. "Oops," he offered.

It was a long walk home. The rain didn't let up and so, even though it wasn't yet 5.30 p.m., it was very nearly dark by the time they arrived home. Or at least, home for now. A big ugly 'For Sale' sign stuck out from Dylan's bedroom window. James insisted that the family needed a new house – an actual house – for their new beginning. Still, until the place sold, they had to troop up the stairs of the tenement building, stepping over the landing where Tristan had collapsed, bleeding heavily from wounds that opened each and every time he and Dylan were separated by any great distance. Though the blood both he and Dylan shed that day had long since been scrubbed away, the spot made Dylan give a little shudder every time she passed it. It was just one of many reasons why she was excited to move.

Neither of her parents were in the flat when they entered. That didn't surprise Dylan. Even though they were married now, they were still 'dating', disappearing off to the pictures or a show, out to a fancy dinner or down to one of the many pubs in the West End for drinks. Dylan wasn't bothered in the slightest – she loved that they were out having fun together, as well as the extra privacy their outings gave her and Tristan. Like now.

"I think I need to change everything down to my underwear!" she complained as she shimmied out of her waterproof jacket. "I'm wet through!"

"I'm sorry," Tristan replied ruefully. His much newer jacket had fared better against the rain than Dylan's had, but she could see huge dark patches on his school trousers where the rain had soaked the material. He toed off his shoes and gave her a wicked grin. "I'll make it up to you, I promise."

And he sauntered right into her bedroom.

Dylan stared after him for a brief moment, but when music started drifting through her open doorway she caught up with herself and frantically tugged at her boots, trying to get them off. They resisted, eventually taking her socks with them when they finally slid free, but the things were wringing anyway so she left them on the hall floor and darted barefoot to her room.

Tristan was already parked on her bed, but what gave her pause was the thing he held in his hands. A large pad of paper, the blue front cover decorated with intricate black swirls. His drawing book, the one he'd never, *ever* let her peek at.

It had driven Dylan near-demented wondering what he was sketching when he'd disappear off to a corner with the thing tucked tight in his grasp, but he'd been shy about her seeing it and, although she'd had a few horribly tempting opportunities, she'd never looked. She wanted to; she really, really wanted to. But she hadn't.

Tristan had never had anything that was his before, had never had any privacy. It was a small gift, but it was something that Dylan could offer him.

But ohh, how it had niggled at her. The pad sitting on her top bookshelf (the one she'd given over to Tristan because she couldn't reach it without standing on a chair anyway), waving at her day after day. Taunting her, tempting her.

Art was a recent discovery for Tristan. Dylan didn't take it at school – she couldn't draw. Or paint. And she'd dropped it as soon as she could – but Tristan had expressed an interest so Dylan had bought him some basic art equipment for Christmas. He'd taken to it like a duck to water... or so it seemed. As she'd never seen any of his drawings, Dylan had no idea if he was any good, but he enjoyed it, and that was all that mattered.

She was curious, though.

He tapped his fingers once, twice against the spiral binding running down the spine, before holding it out to her. "Here," he said. "Your reward."

"Seriously?" Dylan raised her eyebrows in mock astonishment, but in truth she *was* surprised. "You're going to let me see?"

"I am."

Not giving him an opportunity to change his mind, Dylan ignored the cold dampness of her clothes and sat down on the bed beside him. Taking the pad carefully, she flipped the cover over to reveal the first drawing.

Her own face stared back up at her. Her eyes dominated the image, looking out from the page beneath sweeping eyebrows. Her lips were quirked up in a half-smile that made her look teasing, secretive. And pretty. In the picture, she looked pretty.

Glancing up, she saw Tristan was watching her carefully. It was hard to keep her face impassive under his scrutiny but she tried, working to keep her embarrassment in check and off her cheeks.

Slightly clumsy fingers swept the picture away to reveal the next sketch. This one was charcoal, a side-on view of her standing staring at something off the page. Her hair was blowing out behind her in long, sinuous waves.

Another page. Another picture. Dylan in the wheelchair, her face clouded over with frustration as she fumbled with her cast.

The lines of the wheelchair were slightly off, the perspective not quite right, but the mulish look on her face Dylan certainly recognised.

The next drawing wasn't of her. It was her parents, sitting on their ageing sofa. Joan was looking ahead of her – probably at the television – and James was looking at Joan. The expression on his face was… Well, it was just as Dylan had seen it so many times before when she'd noticed the same thing. Longing, loving. Hopeful. Tristan had captured it perfectly.

The next sketch wasn't a picture as such, but six rough pencil sketches of—

"Is that my ear?" Dylan asked, tilting her head in confusion. She didn't necessarily recognise it as her ear, per se – an ear was an ear, wasn't it – but that was her little daisy earring.

"Uhm, yeah." Tristan reached over to take the pad back from her, but Dylan twisted to keep it out of his reach.

"Hold on," she said. "I haven't finished."

She flicked another page over and saw herself, laughing. Her eyes were scrunched up and her chin was tucked in a way that wasn't all that attractive, but Dylan smiled anyway. There was joy in the picture, it radiated out at her.

"Tristan, these are really good," she said quietly, realising that she hadn't said anything bar the ear comment. If it had been her in Tristan's place, she'd be wriggling like she had ants in her pants, wondering what he thought. "I mean, they're really, *really* good. They're so lifelike." The next page was blank, the start of drawings still to come, so she flicked back through the ones she'd seen. "How did you get the details so accurate? You can't have seen any of these for more than a moment!"

"I don't know." Tristan shrugged. He reached again for the pad and this time she let him take it. "I just saw something I liked and then, later, when I was drawing, sketched out what I remembered."

"You're very observant, then," Dylan commented.

"I had a lot of practice," he reminded her. "At night, in the wasteland, there wasn't a lot to do but sit and stare."

"True," Dylan said softly. She didn't like thinking about the long years Tristan had spent ferrying soul after soul, trapped in a never-ending cycle. No, not never-ending, she told herself. He was here now, with her. He'd escaped that life.

She watched as he flipped back to the first picture. The one of just her face, gazing up at them both.

"Why now?" she asked quietly. "Why show me today?"

Tristan shrugged. "I just…" He flicked to another page, the picture of Dylan in the wheelchair. "In the wasteland, it was just the two of us. But here, there are so many people, so many distractions." He closed the pad and set it aside, fixing his full attention on Dylan. "I want you to know that I still see you. This life, this world, it's amazing, but only because I'm living it with you."

Dylan opened her mouth, but nothing came out. How was she supposed to respond to a declaration like that? She'd never been good with words.

"I love you," she managed to blurt.

Tristan grinned, reaching up to tuck a soggy lock of hair back behind her ear. "I know," he said. "I love you, too."

Then he kissed her, his mouth hot against hers as his arms wrapped around her in a tangle of soggy fabric. Dylan closed her eyes and allowed herself to melt into his embrace. The tragedy of the horse was just that, a tragedy, and she let it slide from her mind.

They were safe, and together. Nothing could change that.

CHAPTER 4

Tristan stared up at the ceiling. Beside him, Dylan was sleeping, each breath a warm puff of air against his shoulder. He shifted slightly, trying to get comfortable without turning over and waking her. He shut his eyes and concentrated on deepening his breathing, trying to match his rhythm to hers, hoping that would lull him to sleep.

It didn't.

The same thoughts tumbled round his head and he couldn't stop seeing the ripped and torn carcass of the horse. He imagined the animal as it had been: unblemished chestnut coat gleaming as it wandered aimlessly, cropping the grass. It would have been easy prey for a wraith.

But Dylan was right. It couldn't be. There was no tear in the veil there, and what wraith would bypass a handful of people-filled towns just to snack on an animal? It didn't make sense.

Yet the uncomfortable niggle deep in his chest wouldn't leave him alone.

Giving up on the idea of sleep, he rolled off the bed, careful not to disturb Dylan, and tugged a T-shirt over his head before ghosting out into the hall. Dylan's parents' bedroom door was closed and he tiptoed past it into the living room. He grabbed the television remote from the coffee table before sitting down on the thick pile of blankets that was supposed to be his bed.

According to James, when they moved, Tristan would have a room of his own, but until then his official sleeping place was the sofa. Tristan was pretty sure James knew where he spent each night, but he hadn't said anything so Tristan continued the ruse, waiting until all was quiet in the flat before sneaking in with Dylan.

He turned on the TV, dialling down the volume until the music on the advert was barely audible. Squinting against the sudden flare of light from the screen, he scrolled through the digital guide until he reached the 24-hour news channel. He turned it up a little, just enough to hear the cultured voice of the news anchor as he interviewed a guest – some author trying to pimp his latest novel. Tristan had to wait through a sports bulletin and then the weather forecast (more rain) before at last the presenter moved on to the headlines.

Nothing.

No murders, violent incidents or unexplained deaths in Central Scotland. In fact, there was no news from north of the border at all, the main stories about an earthquake in South America and a famous footballer who'd been arrested for drink driving.

Unable to rid himself of the feeling that something just wasn't right, Tristan grabbed James's tablet from where he'd left it, balanced haphazardly on the arm of the sofa. He trawled through news sites, even looking at smaller, local newspaper websites, thinking they might catch something not considered important enough news for the main news providers.

Still nothing that fit the pattern.

Tristan blew out a breath, releasing the tension that was keeping him on edge, keeping him from sleep. The relief was temporary, though. If it had been a wraith, or even a small group of them, who'd slaughtered the horse, it would be sated. Sluggish. It might not resurface to eat again for days.

He'd need to keep a close eye out, be ready to investigate anything that looked even the slightest bit suspicious. It was part of the bargain with the Inquisitor that allowed Tristan and Dylan to stay in the real world, together. The stakes were too high to fail. He knew if he ever saw the Inquisitor again, it would be for the last time.

He'd be lucky to be returned to the wasteland, returned to his duties.

And if that happened, Dylan would die.

"Can't sleep?" The deep, slightly gruff voice was pitched low, designed not to startle, but Tristan jumped anyway. Turning on the sofa, he saw James in the doorway.

"No, I—" Tristan offered a small smile as he muted the TV. "Sorry, I didn't think it would be loud enough to wake anybody."

"It didn't." James waved away his apology. "I was just headed to the bathroom and saw the light." A quick flash of teeth in the light from the screen. "En-suite in the new place, I reckon."

"Right," Tristan agreed.

"And you'll probably sleep better on a bed rather than that lumpy sofa." James's tone said he knew fine well that Tristan wasn't fighting a nightly battle with the uneven cushions and rogue springs on the ageing piece of furniture. Well, not after the first half hour anyway.

Tristan nodded, trying to look innocent in the face of James's knowing look. The older man's face suddenly sobered and became watchful.

"Something on your mind, son?"

It was an opening, an opportunity for Tristan to share. But it was more than that – it was James offering him a chance to shift their relationship into something other than the father-and-slightly-troublesome-boyfriend dynamic they'd been warily dancing around.

For a heartbeat Tristan considered it. James knew some of what he and Dylan had been through, understood that there were things beyond the world they lived in. And it would be a relief, Tristan thought, to be able to pass the burden to someone. But almost as soon as the idea had taken root, he dismissed it. James's knowledge was scant, and the reasons they'd kept the details from him when he first discovered the tie between Tristan and Dylan held just as true now. The more he knew, the more danger he was in from the Inquisitor.

This burden was Tristan's to bear. If he shared it with anyone, it could only be Dylan.

"I'm fine," Tristan said. "Just… thinking."

"All right." James looked disappointed, and Tristan could tell he didn't believe him, but Dylan's dad didn't push any further. "Try to get some sleep, though, eh? You've got school in the morning."

"Yes, sir." Tristan replied. He switched off the television, made a pretence of lying back among the blankets. "Goodnight."

"Goodnight, Tristan."

James disappeared down the hallway and a minute later Tristan heard the toilet flushing and the quiet sounds of doors opening and closing as James returned to the room he shared with Joan.

It was a long time before Tristan crept back to Dylan's room, thoughts of wraiths still heavy on his mind.

CHAPTER 5

"Don't look."

"I'm not looking."

"I know, just…" Susanna squeezed Jack's hand. "Don't look."

Sweat was dripping down her forehead and her clothes were sticking to her skin. The heat was unrelenting; there wasn't so much as a puff of wind to give them relief. Susanna knew that was a blessing, however. Earlier the wind had swirled and howled, snatching up the tiny grains of sand coating the floor of the wasteland and hurling them against Jack and Susanna, scraping their skin and getting in their eyes and mouths.

Though it had been easier to ignore the wraiths with their eyes scrunched shut.

It was midday, Susanna thought, judging by the height of the sun in the sky. She hoped this was as hot as it was going to get, but with the ground absorbing heat all morning, the afternoon had the potential to become even more stifling once the baking sand started radiating up at them.

There was no shade. Nothing but the dry and cracking ground, undulating just enough to obscure the road ahead, and jagged rocks and tumbled boulders that somehow cast no shadows. In the 'normal' wasteland that Susanna was used to, shadows were a danger, a place for wraiths to lurk. Here, the demonic red sun freed them – and denied any kind of shade that would give Jack and Susanna a chance to hide from its punishing rays.

"I need water," Jack croaked beside her.

"You don't," Susanna reminded him. "You're dead. Your soul doesn't need things like food or water any more."

"All right then," Jack griped back, "I *want* water. Is that better?" His breath came out in harsher, more ragged gasps as the hill they were ascending steepened, causing all the muscles in Susanna's legs to cramp and pull. "Bloody hell," he rasped. "I've never been this hot in my entire life."

"Try to remember that it isn't real," Susanna advised.

"Huh?"

"It's not real," she repeated. "Your skin isn't really burning, you're not really thirsty. And no matter how much you feel like you're overheating, the sun won't kill you." She barked out a breathless laugh. "Heatstroke doesn't exist in the wasteland."

"Well, it *feels* real," Jack replied. "And I *feel* like I'm going to die."

You can't die if you're already dead, Susanna thought, but she refrained from stating the obvious. "You won't," she said. "Just focus on that and keeping putting one foot in front of the other. And don't look at the wraiths!"

She added the last bit because she could see, out of the corner of her eye, Jack's right hand clenching into a tighter and tighter fist. He wanted to grab or slap down one of the wraiths that were diving and swooping round their heads.

"I'm… trying…" Jack ground out. "But it's instinct. They're like wasps. I just want to grab a newspaper and batter them to death!"

"You can't," Susanna said. "React, acknowledge them, *look* at them – and they'll get you. If you can keep ignoring them, then they're just like your wasps. Harmless."

"You've obviously never been stung by one," Jack muttered quietly, needing to have the last word as always.

But Susanna was just as hot as he was, and cross with it. She was in no mood to let him have it.

"Well, maybe not," she snapped, "but I have been attacked by wraiths, more times than I can remember, and it's not pleasant. So ignore them."

Silence from Jack. Then, so quietly it might have been a figment of her imagination, he murmured, "Sorry."

Susanna reached out and took his hand, giving his fingers a quick squeeze before letting go. She understood.

Long minutes later, they reached the crest of the hill. The slope dropped away, steeper on this side, and Susanna winced as she saw the scree that littered the sheer descent. They were going to slip and slide and skid all the way down. Terrific.

A wraith lower down the hill suddenly started making a beeline for them and Susanna slammed her eyes closed, not trusting herself not to follow its progress. She felt the air stir gently – along with a sharp but shallow slice across her cheek – as the wraith passed by. It would likely join the small cloud of its kin that had followed them all morning.

Why not, Susanna thought wryly. *Join the party.*

"Is that how you survive it?" Jack asked, the question surprising Susanna enough that she turned to look at him, found his grey eyes searching hers. Was that sympathy she saw there?

"What do you mean?"

"When the wraiths are hurting you, is that how you survive? By telling yourself that it isn't real?"

A wraith darted between the two of them, daring one of them to acknowledge its presence, but Susanna couldn't tear her gaze away from Jack's and he was watching her intently, waiting for an answer.

"Yes," she said, seeing no reason to hide it from him. "It hurts, but I won't die. And it'll end eventually; I just need to keep breathing." She looked back to the drop before them, finding it hard to hold his gaze. "That's what I tell myself. Over and over."

"Does it help?"

Susanna smiled grimly. Jack was very, very good at asking questions that got right to the heart of things.

"No," she said. "It doesn't help."

She waited for him to say something caustic about her advice – now that she'd admitted it was bad advice – but he didn't. Instead he sighed.

"That's going to be a bitch to climb down, isn't it?"

Susanna wanted to laugh – Jack had hit the nail bang on the head – but it wasn't at all funny. It *was* going to be a bitch.

"Yeah," she agreed.

Jack let out another sigh. "OK then. Let's go."

That was his way. Push on, push back. Keep fighting. But she knew he was just as exhausted as she was, mentally and physically. And that was a sure-fire way to make mistakes.

Mistakes here would see him dead.

"Wait." She reached out, pulled him to a stop. "Let's take a break."

"A break?" Jack laughed harshly. "Did you bring a picnic basket?"

"*No*," Susanna said with exaggerated patience. "But let's just have five minutes of not concentrating every second. I think it'll help. Here." Using her grip on his arm, she manoeuvred him to his knees and then knelt directly facing him. Leaning in, she rested her face on his shoulder, eyes closed. It took a moment, but eventually Jack relented, mimicking her posture.

"There," she said quietly. "Now, even if you open your eyes, you can't see anything. You can relax, just for a minute. They'll still swipe at us, but they won't do anything more than that."

She consciously relaxed her muscles, stretching her shoulders to try and loosen the tension there. It wasn't comfortable, kneeling on the hard-packed earth with tiny stones digging into her shins, but not having to constantly police her gaze loosened the vice gripping her skull and that was blissful.

"How did Dylan do this alone?" Jack asked after a long, quiet minute.

"I honestly don't know," Susanna said. "I guess..." She thought about what she'd seen between Tristan and Dylan, the bond that held them together, the love they shared. "I guess her motivation was strong enough."

"Well, I'm pretty motivated not to die, so I reckon maybe there's hope after all."

Susanna didn't correct him. She knew what he meant. Becoming a wraith would be a death of his self, not just his body.

Guilt wracked her for, oh, maybe the millionth time. Crossing Jack's original wasteland would have been a piece of cake compared with this.

"Jack—"

"If you're going to apologise again, save it."

Susanna yanked in a shocked breath. Hurt punched her low in the belly, solid enough to feel like a wraith trying to batter through her. Forgetting herself, she stupidly made to draw back, but Jack held her there, his hand firm but gentle on the back of her neck.

"I agreed to it," he said, his voice still as harsh, as gruff. "It's my fault as well as yours, so stop beating yourself up about it. Just..." He broke off and squeezed her, turning the grip into a hug. "Just promise me you'll get me out of here."

She couldn't promise that. Not here, in the burning desert with the wraiths so free to torment them. With days and days of this still ahead. She could not promise that. But she did anyway.

"I promise, Jack. I'll get you through this. I swear it."

They stayed there longer than they should have. Susanna knew it, but she couldn't seem to make herself move, and Jack didn't complain. They'd fought all morning, each step, each moment requiring them to keep laser focus: their eyes on the ground or dead ahead, staring into the distance and avoiding glancing, even for a heartbeat, at the wraiths doing everything to catch their attention.

Susanna didn't understand how it worked, why the wraiths wouldn't attack them unless they looked at them – she was only grateful for the chance, however small, to get Jack through this in one piece.

One morning had utterly exhausted them, physically and mentally. She didn't understand how they were supposed to survive the afternoon, never mind days of this. Especially when she couldn't even muster the energy to lift her head. Jack's breath was warm against her shoulder, his hold strong and comforting. Susanna couldn't bear to tear away from him. *Just another minute*, she promised herself. *One more.*

At last, reluctance lost the battle against the instinctive panic of still being out in the open when darkness fell. "All right, let's go." She took a deep breath. "Are you ready?"

"No," Jack mumbled into her shoulder. "But let's do it anyway."

They clambered to their feet awkwardly, still facing each other. Susanna didn't know about Jack, but she kept her eyes shut. Anything to buy another few precious seconds of not controlling her gaze, her every blink.

"Susanna," Jack said at last. She opened her eyes and Jack's face was directly in front of hers, close enough that a wraith couldn't squeeze its away in between them and draw their attention.

She found his eyes and drew strength from them. Slate grey, they were slightly narrowed and ready for battle. As his ferryman, she had Jack's memories in her head, knew he'd fought pretty much every day of his adolescence, and he was ready to fight this, too. He just needed her to lead the way.

"Right then," she said, feeling her own determination rise to meet his. "Let's do this."

The slope was as awful as Susanna had predicted. She found it easier to relax her eyes and focus on nothing, so she couldn't see the bigger stones ready to trip her, the rivers of loose pebbles ready to give way beneath her feet and send her sliding. Each time she lost her footing – and the twice she ended up on her backside – it was a struggle not to sharpen her gaze, to look about and get her bearings, search for something to help her back on her feet or steady her balance. At these times, she just closed her eyes and waited for a hand to reach out and help her. And one did.

And when the roles were reversed she did the same for Jack. Because that was the only way they were going to get through this – together.

CHAPTER 6

"Steven! Steven, please, I can't go any faster!"

The soul was scared. The ferryman knew that, but he couldn't do anything about it. He was concentrating all his efforts on dragging her along. Her legs, limbs she'd cursed her whole life, he knew, because they couldn't run, or jump or dance, worked just fine here in the wasteland. The problem was in her mind. She hadn't had enough time to adjust.

And if he couldn't get her to the safe house, she'd never have the chance to.

"Just a little further," he coaxed.

"Steven, I can't!"

He wasn't called Steven, not really, but a name was a name, and he knew the souls felt better when they had something to call him. It didn't make any difference to him.

"You're nearly there," he urged. "Come on, run. You can, I promise you."

Her only response was to sob.

The ferryman gritted his teeth. He liked this one, and he wanted her to make it. She deserved it. It was his fault, he knew. He'd gone too easy on her this morning, letting her take extra breaks and going at a slower pace to help her get used to the landscape, to walking without the crutches she'd leaned on all her life.

She wouldn't pay for his mistakes.

"All right, hold on."

Letting go of her hand, he grabbed her arm and lifted it, then he bent down and tucked himself into her side. When he stood up, he had her over his shoulder. Her weight centred, he started to run.

It wasn't easy. She was light, but it was cumbersome carrying her. She blocked his sight on the left-hand side, and keeping her balanced required both his hands. The sun was moments from setting, and the chorus of hissing and snarling that seemed to echo all around them in this basin nestled between hills told him the wraiths were ready. Waiting.

Still, the safe house wasn't far away. Just across this short length of boggy marshland, on the first section of high ground, a low platform at the base of the next hill. The mud sucked and pulled at his feet with every step, but he maintained a steady jog. Almost there.

The sun dropped down out of sight.

There was very little difference in light, but the whistling and shrieking escalated as the wraiths were set free. Daring a glance about, the ferryman saw them barrelling down towards him on all sides. Some were smarter, hovering around the safe house that he could clearly see now. It was so close.

So. Close.

He put on an extra burst of speed, though he knew he wouldn't make it before the first of the wraiths reached him. He'd have to fight – but that was OK. The ferryman was a match for the wraiths, for a little while, at least.

"What are those things?" Anna, the soul, had obviously spotted the wraiths, because she went rigid over his shoulder. The sudden change threw him off balance and he almost fell, catching himself at the last second before he tumbled them both into the muck.

"It's all right," he soothed, gripping her more tightly.

His words didn't help. She started shifting and twisting, probably trying to see the creatures racing towards her. He didn't blame her, they were terrifying to behold.

"Steven, what *are* they?"

"Wraiths," he panted.

The safe house was close, but the wraiths were closer. Deciding he'd bought them as much advantage as he could, Steven dropped Anna back down into the marshland. Her feet disappeared into the mud with a squelch.

"You'll be safe in there," he told her, pointing. "Run!"

Anna froze, likely disoriented from bouncing about upside down, but they didn't have time for her confusion. The ferryman grabbed her by the shoulders, spun her to face the right direction, and shoved.

"Go! Run!"

Anna ran. It was ungainly and stumbling, like a foal first finding its feet, but as Steven followed close on her heels, tearing away any wraiths that got too close, slinging them to the side so they'd spin and crash into the water, he felt a surge of triumph.

They were going to make it.

A wraith decided to change tactics, go for him instead. It gouged his arm, but he ignored the pain, flinging it away and batting at another that sought his eyes, to blind him.

"Just keep running," he hollered to Anna. She was less than a couple of metres in front of him, but with the cacophony coming from the wraiths, he worried she might not hear him. "Go straight through the door."

It stood waiting for them, already ajar. All Anna would have to do was barrel right through it and cross the threshold into safety. The remaining wraiths would have an opportunity to tear into the ferryman, but he'd heal by morning. It was nothing unusual.

The ground firmed up beneath their feet. Boggy marsh gave way to grass, then cracked and uneven paving stones. Anna's feet pounded on the path, her hands reaching up to shove at the door. The ferryman smiled, relief coursing through him.

Then the muted greens and browns of Anna's wasteland flickered and stuttered, flashing red for a heartbeat before bouncing back, then red again. At the same time, the ground bucked beneath the ferryman, sent him skidding across the floor, pebbles ripping into his palms.

Undeterred, he lifted his head to see Anna run through the door – and to see the wraiths follow her right on inside.

That was impossible.

Shocked, he stilled, sprawled on his front on the ground. A handful of wraiths immediately descended on him, clawing and hissing as their teeth sunk into his flesh. The ferryman paid them no heed, unaware of anything except the blood-curdling sounds of Anna's screams.

As the world began to fade to white around him, he closed his eyes. He didn't understand it, but there was something very wrong in the wasteland.

CHAPTER 7

"I think we have a problem."

"What?" Dylan looked up at Tristan from the styrofoam container of cottage pie that she was just about to tuck into.

"I'm pretty sure it's a wraith."

"What?" Her plastic fork dropped into her lunch, spattering gravy onto her school shirt. She didn't notice.

"The thing that killed the horse."

"*What*?" Click, click, click, the pieces slotted into place as she finally caught up with the conversation.

"Is that all you're going to say?"

Dylan leaned forward and scowled at him as he dropped into the seat opposite her.

"What do you mean, you think it's a wraith? It happened miles away from the tears Jack and I made. It *can't* be a wraith!" Dylan's voice came out sharp and shrill. Wincing, she looked around the crowded cafeteria, but no one was paying her any attention. "Why do you think it's… one of *them*?"

Tristan took a deep breath. "There's been another attack, at the same place."

"A person?"

"No, sheep."

"A sheep?"

Tristan shook his head. "Not one, a whole herd of them. At the next farm over, just last night. It was on the BBC regional news page. The police are warning people about a possible dangerous wild animal."

"A wild animal? This isn't Africa – there aren't lions and tigers wandering about!"

"The news suggested it might have escaped from somewhere, like a zoo or a private collection."

"There is a safari park somewhere around there," Dylan agreed. She considered Tristan. "But you don't think that's what it is."

"No."

"I just…" Dylan shoved her lunch tray away, her appetite gone. She felt sick now. Though she wasn't convinced, Tristan's worry was palpable and hard to ignore. "I don't see how it can be a wraith. There, in the middle of nowhere. You definitely haven't felt another ferryman coming through?"

Tristan shook his head with strained patience – Dylan had asked him this before.

"Then it makes sense for it to just be something normal. Well, as normal as a panther stalking around Central Scotland! It does, Tristan!" she repeated. "How else would a wraith get here? They can't just come through, not on their own."

He didn't look convinced. "I know, but I feel it… Something's not right."

"I thought you said you couldn't sense a wraith until they were really close?"

"I can't. Not—"

"Not without Susanna," Dylan finished, when Tristan wisely didn't. She heaved out a breath. She knew where this was going. "You want to go out there. Investigate."

He nodded, shrugging apologetically.

Dylan pursed her lips but gave in. If Tristan was right – and she didn't see how he could be – then their deal with the Inquisitor demanded they go and deal with it. Kill the wraith, work out where the hell it came from and stop any others from coming through.

If Tristan was right, and they didn't go and check it out and the Inquisitor stepped in…

"All right," she said, sighing. "Tomorrow's Friday so it's a half day. We can go then. Will that do?"

Tristan made a face, likely chafed by the delay, but jerked his head once in a nod.

"Tomorrow," he agreed.

"You'll see," she said, picking her fork up and forcing herself to scoop up a mouthful, "we won't find anything."

She said it with confidence, and hoped that she was right.

⌒

"I still think this is daft," Dylan griped. She stood shin-deep in mud, her feet freezing in her wellies. She was pretty sure one of her socks was about to slide off as well. In her left hand she gripped an umbrella, big fat raindrops pelting down and creating an uneven drumbeat around her head. She'd pulled her other arm out of the sleeve of her waterproof entirely and had it wrapped around her stomach, numb, frozen fingers tingling against her skin. And every time she exhaled, her breath steamed before her.

March in Scotland was neither the time nor the place to be traipsing round the countryside. To be honest, Dylan really didn't think there was ever a time to do that. She hadn't been an 'outdoorsy' girl before she'd died, and her experiences in the wasteland – and beyond – had done nothing to change that.

Tristan ignored her. She supposed he'd given up trying to placate her after the first five attempts failed to make an impact. Instead, he was peering into the next field, fingers tense around the top string of a barbed-wire fence. Dylan stood a good few metres back from him because, well… beyond was a grim sight.

Really, really grim.

It was like something out of a slasher movie. Countless bodies had been piled one atop the other, limbs contorted at odd angles, more flesh than skin on display. They'd been burned, and the fire still wasn't quite out, the heat creating a swirling mist that rose and coiled like a departing ghost.

The fact that the bodies were those of sheep and not people did little to detract from the horror.

"Tristan, honestly, I don't see—"

"I want to get closer," Tristan interrupted her.

"What?"

Rather than answering, he swung his leg over the fence and dropped down into the field with the smouldering heap of carcases.

"Tristan!" Dylan hurried forwards, squelching through the mud-mire, but she couldn't go any further than the barrier between fields – and that wasn't just because there was no way she'd be able to get over it in her size-too-big wellies. This close, she could see much more detail, her gaze more easily penetrating the smoke, but also, the smell that had been merely uncomfortable in her previous spot was now close to overwhelming. Dylan gagged, wriggling her hand up through the neck of her jacket to cover her face. She breathed through her mouth rather than her nose, but that just meant she could taste it. Soot and burned wool and, underneath, the more familiar flavours of lamb, of mutton.

She liked lamb, normally. After this, she thought she might never eat it again.

In front of her, Tristan seemed unperturbed by the stink, or at least determined enough to ignore it. He was right up at the mound, close enough to touch. As Dylan watched he reached out, as if he was actually going to stick his hand into the huge pile of grossness, but he held back, his hand hovering over what, from Dylan's viewpoint, looked like a charred hoof.

She didn't see why they were here. They had closed both holes through to the wasteland; there was no way for wraiths to get through.

And even if one had, what would it be doing here, far from either of the two sites: the tunnel where she'd died and the alleyway where Jack's life had trickled out through a stab wound in his stomach? And this time it wasn't even people who had died – it was sheep! A lot of sheep, and she admitted that it was odd... but surely it couldn't have anything to do with her or Tristan?

"Tristan!" she called. "It's getting late and it's going to be dark soon."

"All right," Tristan replied, tucking his phone back into his pocket after taking several snaps. "I'm done." He jogged back to her, typically having no difficulty with the deep, sucking mud.

"What do you think?" Dylan asked. Despite her own scepticism, she knew she was no expert. Tristan was.

He grimaced, glancing back at the burned bodies of an entire flock. "I don't know," he said. "I mean, the bodies are scratched and torn just like I'd expect to see in a wraith attack but…"

"But it's sheep," Dylan finished.

"Yeah."

"Isn't it more likely that it was just an out-of-control pack of dogs?" That was what the angry farmer had blamed when he was interviewed on the news, his eyes red-rimmed beneath his weathered bunnet. "Or a wild animal, like the police said?"

"It could have been," Tristan mused.

"I mean," Dylan went on, "we're not even near either of the two breaches. Any wraith that came through would have had to have passed dozens of places with tasty humans in them before it got here."

"Tasty humans?" Tristan quirked an eyebrow.

"You know what I mean!" Dylan rolled her eyes and nudged him with her shoulder.

"You're right," Tristan agreed. "It's probably nothing. I just…" He looked back once more at the pile of carcasses, a long, lingering look this time. "I just have a funny feeling that something's not right."

"Can you sense a wraith?" Dylan asked. Despite her misgivings, Tristan's gut feeling and the low chill now invading her own stomach told her she was beginning to take the possibility of a breach a little more seriously.

"Not really," Tristan wrinkled his nose. "I mean, I don't think so. Without Susanna here it's a bit harder to—"

He bit his words off and Dylan clenched her teeth. Susanna, again. She'd be much more helpful than Dylan was in this situation, and didn't that just rub her up the wrong way.

"Right," Dylan said, more sharply than she'd intended.

Trying to pretend the sheep weren't there, Dylan perused the landscape. They were just a couple of miles outside Kilsyth and the land was all neatly divided into fields. Some, like the one they were in, were grassed over, clearly used for grazing. Others were nothing more than furrowed brown earth, turned to bog after all the recent heavy rain. Up on a hill, about a mile away,

Dylan could see a large house surrounded by a cluster of outbuildings and a barn, probably the farm that owned these fields. She hoped whoever lived up there wasn't in; she didn't want an angry farmer descending on them, shotgun in hand.

Lower down the same hill, on the narrow country road that led out towards the main route back into town, was a row of neat little cottages that probably at one time belonged to farm laborers. The high hedges were hopefully working to keep Tristan and Dylan hidden from the houses, but still, Dylan felt exposed and vulnerable. Irrationally, she was more concerned about being caught here and shouted at than she was about a wraith springing from the hedgerow and trying to punch a hole through her.

"Priorities, Dylan," she muttered to herself.

"What?" Tristan asked. He, too, was gazing at the landscape, but Dylan doubted angry locals were on his mind.

"Nothing," she said. She made herself focus. "Do you know what field the horse was in?"

"No." Tristan shook his head. "The news report only said it was less than a mile from the sheep attack, and we can see more than a mile in either direction from here, I reckon, so it must have been really close by."

"OK." Dylan turned slowly on the spot. There wasn't much to see. "Apart from the houses, I don't see many hiding places."

"If the wraith had found its way into the houses, it would have been a much bigger story," Tristan said.

Well, it was hard to argue with that. Unexplained dead bodies did tend to cause a splash. A fleeting image of the house in Denny, the one where they'd found the nest of wraiths, flashed in her mind. She still had nightmares about the brief glimpses she'd caught of those blood-soaked walls.

"So, what do we do?" she asked.

"Hunt for the wraith," Tristan said simply. "Although…" His forehead scrunched up in a frown. "It would be better if we could find where it got through."

"*If* one got through," Dylan amended, not willing to give up on the possibility that there was no wraith quite yet.

"Right," Tristan said distractedly, his gaze on the landscape.

"How do we do that?" Dylan asked. "We won't be able to see it, will we?"

"Not unless we're close enough to fall in it," Tristan answered wryly. "And I'd prefer that not to happen. If a soul ripped a hole, the other side of the veil should look just like this. It'd be like trying to spot a mirror with no edges, nearly impossible to see. It's almost a shame you can't feel it pulling at you, like in the tunnel. It would make our lives a lot easier."

"Well, I'm not sad about that," Dylan said. The feeling in her chest in the tunnel when they'd revisited the spot where she'd died had terrified her. It had been like something reached inside her, grabbed her heart… and yanked.

"No, I'm not either." Tristan reached out and squeezed her hand in silent apology. He took a deep breath. "Look, let's just concentrate on trying to find out for certain whether there is a wraith or not. If we find one, well, then we'll worry about where it came from."

"OK, that sounds like a plan." Dylan turned slowly in a circle and then stopped. "You're thinking over there, aren't you?"

"I am."

"Of course." She sniffed disdainfully. "The dark, creepy wood. Where else?"

It wasn't really a wood. A copse, maybe. It was halfway up a hill, wedged in on all sides by fields. Really, apart from the houses, which Tristan had already discounted, it was the only place that could hide a wraith during the hours of daylight. If it wasn't there…

Well, they'd have to hope that Tristan was mistaken, because if the wraith had already moved on, it could be anywhere.

It didn't take long to reach the trees. The rain, at least, petered out to nothing and Dylan was able to dump her umbrella on top of a low stone wall that ringed the trees before Tristan gave her a boost over it. They took their first steps beneath the dark canopy. Made up almost entirely of spruce trees, the needles grew just as thickly as they would midsummer, and with the overcast day, it was as dark as twilight amongst the tree trunks.

It was a small copse, and before they'd taken more than a dozen steps towards the centre, Dylan could already make out the light filtering in from the other side.

"Careful," Tristan said, picking up a stout chunk of fallen branch. "A hidey-hole for a single wraith doesn't have to be very big. A fox or badger hole would work just fine, or even a deep gap between tree roots. In here, where there's not much chance of direct sunlight getting through, it wouldn't need to be entirely enclosed."

"Great," Dylan muttered. She continued forward, gingerly placing each foot amongst the mulch of damp leaves and fallen needles that carpeted the ground.

Off to her left, Tristan seemed to be walking in some sort of grid pattern, methodically checking every square foot of the copse. Dylan's approach was more haphazard: she wandered here and there, investigating anything that looked unusual or oddly shaped. She found nothing, and by the time she was bored and cold and about to give up, Tristan had finished his systematic search and was standing with his hands on his hips, looking distinctly discouraged.

"Shit," he said. "It's not here."

"Shouldn't we be glad of that?" Dylan suggested. "No wraith means no hole in the veil. Which means no possible visit from the Inquisitor."

"I know," he said, "But… I was so sure."

"Sorry to disappoint you." Dylan's mouth quirked into a relieved smile. "I'm just glad we haven't been eaten by an escaped tiger."

Tristan barked out a laugh, throwing his head back. And stopped dead.

"What?" Dylan asked, watching him. "What is it?"

He didn't answer her. Instead, he just pointed.

Dylan came over to stand beside him and looked up, following the direction of his finger. There, at least six or seven metres up in the trees, a precarious-looking platform had been strung together. Squinting through the gloom, Dylan could just make out the blue rope that had been used to lash it to the tree trunks and into an irregular triangular shape. It was hard to tell, but she could see some sort of lumpy covering turning it into a little treehouse. From the dilapidated state of it, Dylan reckoned it was a child's secret den that had long been grown out of.

It was her turn to swear.

"Bugger." She heaved a sigh. "Please tell me wraiths don't like heights."

Tristan grunted and dropped his branch. It hit the ground with a quiet thud, cushioned by the leaves on the ground.

"You stay here," he said. "I'll go up and check."

He walked over to the tree and jumped up, grabbing a knotted section of trunk. Dylan watched his feet scrabble for purchase on the slick surface – and fail. He slipped back to the ground and rubbed at the sticky sap now coating his palms.

"Done much tree climbing, have you?" Dylan asked.

"No," Tristan admitted. Undaunted, he jumped again, hauling himself up onto the first branch. "But if whoever built this can make it up there, I can too."

"Yeah," Dylan mumbled to herself, walking around to the other side of the tree and reaching for the first hand-hold nailed into the widest trunk. "Although I'm guessing they put his handy ladder here for more than just decoration."

It wasn't easy – the wood was damp and Dylan's upper-body strength was limited, probably because she avoided any and all forms of exercise. Still, the little rungs were close together and in less than a minute she was pausing, level with Tristan.

He stared at her and she offered a cheeky grin.

"All right," he said at last, "climb back down and I'll go that way."

Dylan shook her head. "No. We're both going. We'll check together."

Tristan was shaking his head vehemently before she'd even finished speaking. "Dylan—"

Ignoring him, she started climbing again.

"Dylan!" He hissed her name, not wanting to shout in case there really was a wraith up above them, but Dylan ignored him and kept going. After a moment, she heard a quiet curse then the creaking of the tree shifting as he started climbing quickly, trying to catch up.

Dylan let him. Her bravery only extended so far – she had no intention of checking the treehouse alone.

She paused just beneath the platform; Tristan appeared beside her almost instantly. He put his finger up to his lips, before holding his hand out in front of him in a 'stay back' gesture. Dylan shook her head. She wasn't staying here and letting him take all the risks. He made a face but seemed to realise he couldn't stop her.

Instead he held up three fingers, then two, then one. A beat after the last, both he and Dylan started creeping up. One step, then another. The platform was just a handsbreadth above Dylan's head when the tree starting swaying alarmingly under her weight. Clutching at the handholds, she pressed herself against the trunk and stupidly looked down.

They were *high*.

Like, break-both-her-legs-again high. Tristan had been right, she should have stayed on the ground, but she couldn't stand the thought of sending him into danger alone. Which was dumb – exactly what help did she think she was going to be?

A gust of wind swept through the copse and the tree swayed once more. Dylan gripped tighter and allowed herself one more moment of cowardice before she drew back and reached up to the next rung, ready to climb again.

Out of the corner of her eye she saw Tristan watching her, concern drawing his features tight. She tried to smile reassuringly at him, but it came out more of a grimace. When he saw she was climbing purposefully again, though, he hurried to overtake her once more.

Dylan's head peeked up over the top of the platform. Empty. At first glance, anyway. Towards the back, the lumpy covering she'd seen was indeed a roof made of old, frayed tarp, but it had long since collapsed, lying in a tangled heap.

Anything could be lying under there.

Or nothing.

Seeing Tristan clamber awkwardly onto the platform, Dylan did the same. The wooden planks were thick and sturdy, but they'd been out in the elements a long time, and Dylan didn't trust the ropes and nails to hold. She got her feet beneath her, then hunkered down with her back against the tree trunk.

Seeing a short length of wood within arm's reach, she grabbed it up and held it, ready to smash at anything that might fly loose as Tristan crept slowly, carefully, towards the bundle of tarp.

Dylan watched him crouch down, tentatively reach out and grasp the frayed edges of the thick material. He paused, the tarp in his hand, and looked over to Dylan. She nodded and shifted her weight, getting her feet balanced beneath her. Tightening her grip on her makeshift plank, she took a deep breath.

Tristan was obviously the type who believed in tearing a plaster off in one go. Instead of easing the tarp aside, he hauled it back, exposing whatever was inside to the dim light. Dylan half jumped, her legs already primed to leap into action, but then she stilled.

The platform was empty.

But there, gouged into the wood, were deep scratches, and the surface itself gleamed a stomach-churning shade of dark red. As Dylan watched, Tristan reached his hand out and stroked his fingers along one of the grooves etched into the platform. His fingertips came away wet.

"A wraith," Dylan whispered. Tristan had been right.

"We're too late," he said quietly. He looked out, towards the sweeping countryside that could only be seen in brief glimpses through the trees. "It could be anywhere by now."

Dylan's heart pounded in a frantic rhythm in her chest, each thump almost painful.

"What do we do now?" she asked.

Tristan didn't have an answer.

CHAPTER 8

The ferryman, Eve, stood knee-deep in the long grass, the soft breeze pulling tangles of hair out of her sensible braid. She smiled down at the little face before her, the girl's expression open and trusting even as trepidation widened her eyes.

"Don't be afraid, Ruby. You're here now, you've made it."

Ruby's lower lip trembled and the sun disappeared as a flurry of low-hanging clouds skittered over the mountainous crags to their left. It didn't matter now, though, the ferryman thought. They were at the line. They'd made it through the wasteland.

"I want to stay here with you," Ruby lisped. "Can I?"

Ruby moved forward to take Eve's hand and, though it almost broke her heart, she stepped back out of reach to prevent it. Ruby's lip wobbled again and Eve knew tears were coming. She steeled herself. Put on the stern face she imagined a teacher might adopt when faced with a stubborn child. That was the role she was playing, after all. Ruby was very fond of her teacher. She hadn't balked at all about walking away from the piles of shattered tile and splintered wood that was all that remained of the old school gymnasium roof, brought down by a violent gust of wind, and out into the countryside for a nature walk, side by side with Miss Higgins.

"You don't want to stay with me, Ruby," she said firmly. "The bad creatures live here, remember? Besides, we came all this way to visit your grandma. Don't you want to see her?" Ruby looked like she was going to burst into tears and say that no, she didn't want to see her grandma. That she wanted to stay with Miss Higgins – or worse, that she wanted her mum. Sympathy twisting a knot inside her chest, the ferryman softened her tone. "She'll be ever so disappointed if she doesn't get to see you. I bet she's even made your favourite treat. What did you say it was, fudge?"

"Tablet," Ruby whispered. "She likes to make tablet."

"She's probably got some waiting for you." Eve forced herself to smile.

Her grandmother was the only person Ruby had lost in her short life. Eve didn't know what was beyond the line, but she hoped that Ruby's grandmother would be there to watch over her until her parents could join them.

She tried not to consider that Ruby's grandmother hadn't made it, that she was one of the wraiths who had wailed and moaned outside their safe house, frightening Ruby into Eve's arms. She'd cuddled and rocked the little girl until she'd fallen asleep every night – her child's mind unable to comprehend what was happening to her, slow to understand it didn't need things like sleep any more.

Surely the world couldn't be so cruel as to steal Ruby from life at such a young age and then give her nobody to offer comfort in the afterlife?

Eve held firm to that belief, even though she knew, first hand, just how harsh and cruel life – and death – could be.

"All you have to do is take just a few more steps that way," she said, her voice tight with emotion, "and your grandma will be there." Ruby didn't move. "Go on, now."

Haltingly, uncertainly, Ruby turned away from Eve and started walking. She took one, two, three steps before looking back over her shoulder as she lifted her foot for the fourth. The last image Eve had of her was the frightened, vulnerable look on her face, a single tear tracking down her cheek, before she vanished across the line.

Though she knew souls never came back through, Eve lingered. Just for a while. She imagined Ruby could still see her and, though she felt foolish, she found herself lifting a hand to wave to the empty air. She hoped there was someone there for the tiny soul; she hoped she found her grandmother somehow.

Knowing she'd done everything she could for the child, the ferryman turned away. Ruby's wasteland began to fade even before she started walking, as though chastising her for remaining there when there were other souls who needed to be ferried. But there was always another soul, and another. The cycle was never-ending – and few were as innocent and sweet and undeserving of their fate as Ruby. Eve was in no hurry.

As usual, the colour leached away from the ground and the sky, the mountains to her left and plains on the right melting away into nothingness. Eve kept walking, waiting for the next world to form. Would it be a city this time? Or the desert? A war-torn landscape showing the scars of decades of hate and violence? She hoped not.

Step after step. White mist swirled around her feet and the sky seemed to drop down on top of her, as if, should she reach out, she'd be able to touch it. On a whim, Eve lifted her fingers and skimmed what should have been nothing, and instead felt like smoke. Heavy, colourless smoke. It swirled around her fingers playfully.

This was definitely not normal. Something, *somewhere*, should have appeared by now. What was happening?

"Hello?" Eve called. "Is anyone there?"

No voice answered. No wasteland appeared.

Instead, the smoke thickened, pressing in at her from all sides until she felt she might suffocate. Eve tried to push it out of the way, to force herself through it, but it just slipped and slid round her form, coming closer again as soon as she stopped.

"Hello?" she called again, louder this time. "Hello?"

She turned left, then right, but she'd lost all sense of direction. In a blind panic she started running, relieved when the smoke gave way to let her through. She ran and ran and ran, until sweat poured down her forehead and exhaustion drove her to her knees.

The scenery didn't change. Nothing but endless, fog-filled white. A sob burst from Eve's lips, followed by another until she was gasping and crying, tears running down her face.

"Help!" the ferryman screamed. "Somebody please help!"

CHAPTER 9

"Just stay here. Just stay in here, Jack, sweetie. OK?"

Jack's mum's face was tight and drawn as she pulled the door closed behind her. Susanna heard the snick as the door locked, then Jack's mum's footsteps pattering on the wooden floor as she rushed away.

Susanna watched Jack's hand reach out and trying the doorknob, rattling it when it refused to give on the first attempt.

"Mum!" he hollered. "Mum!"

He sounded different, she realised. It wasn't just the fear and panic making his voice high like that, this was a much younger Jack. The wallpaper surrounding the door wasn't the cool grey she'd seen during her stay, but sky-blue, with an aeroplane pattern. Susanna was dimly aware of toys littering the carpeted floor nearby, but it was hard to concentrate on anything other than the terror and desperation that led Jack to twist and rattle and yank at the doorknob that wasn't going to budge.

"Mum!" he yelled again.

Jack fell silent and stopped trying to get the door open, instead pressing himself close to it and listening, hard. Muffled, as if coming from several doors away, Susanna could just make out a voice shouting. It was a man's voice, and though the words were lost, the angry tone wasn't.

A sharp bang was followed by a woman's scream, quickly cut off.

"Mum!" Jack pulled away from the door and started kicking at it.

Thump! Thump! Thump!

Susanna felt the jolt rattle up her knee but Jack didn't stop, kicking it again and again. The Jack Susanna knew today would have turned the door into a pile of useless splinters, but the Jack in the memory had only a child's strength and no matter how hard or how many times he threw himself against it, it wouldn't budge.

Eventually admitting defeat, Jack dropped to the floor, leaned against the door, and wept.

"Susanna! Susanna, come on, it's just a dream. Wake up!" A hand shook her shoulder with enough force to rattle her teeth and Susanna jolted into consciousness.

"What?" she said stupidly. "Jack?"

"I'm here." The hand that had been on her shoulder wrapped around her to draw her into a hug and Susanna found herself sagging into Jack's chest. Instinctively, she inched her arm around his back, trying to still the little tremors still wracking her frame.

All too quickly, Jack shifted away, and a moment later the muted glow for the hearth intensified as he poked and prodded at the logs, making fresh flames dance there. Susanna grimaced, watching him butcher her carefully arranged tepee structure, but she knew he was giving her a moment of privacy to get herself together, so she didn't complain.

"I'm sorry," she said, embarrassed. "I don't know why this keeps happening."

"Another memory?" Jack asked.

"Yeah."

"What was it about?" Jack turned back to her but the fire threw him into silhouette and she couldn't see his face.

"I… nothing. Just a soul I lost. An old woman."

There was no way she was admitting that the memory she'd relived this time hadn't been her own, but one of Jack's. He'd want to know which one, and she knew with absolute certainty that he would die before he'd voluntarily agree to her witnessing what she had.

Carrying the memories of her souls was nothing new to Susanna – it had happened with every soul she'd ever ferried – but it was different, now, with Jack. She knew him, and her heart broke to witness the things he'd endured in his too-short life.

"You were shouting 'Mum'," Jack told her, suspicion lingering in his words.

Susanna didn't miss a beat. "That was the role I was playing. I pretended to be her daughter."

"You seemed pretty upset."

Susanna couldn't deny that. Jack's pain and helplessness still tore at her, and she was struggling to keep her emotions in check.

"Yeah, well," she said quietly. "Some souls, they get to you."

Jack didn't reply. He stayed by the fire, staring into the flames.

"I'm going to keep my promise to you, Jack," Susanna whispered, quietly enough that he might not have heard her. He didn't react if he did. "I will. I'll get you there."

CHAPTER 10

"Where do we even start?" Dylan stared at the giant map spread across her bed. It was her dad's, from the days before satnav, and it was ancient, the paper yellowed and slightly torn at several of the folds. Still, a map was a map, and the area it detailed hadn't changed that much over the years. Plus, given its condition Dylan doubted her dad would care that Tristan was scribbling all over it with felt tip-pen. Large blue dots identified the tunnel where Dylan had died, Jack's alley in Denny and the wraith attacks in Kilsyth.

Tristan stood back from the map, assessing it. "We're going to search for any unexplained deaths – people or animals – over the last month—"

"Month?"

"We don't know when the wraith got here," Tristan reminded her. He grimaced. "Or how."

"All right." Dylan took a deep breath and grabbed her phone; Tristan already had her laptop open on her desk. "Let's do this."

Tapping away at the screen, her stomach tightened and twisted. She didn't know if she wanted to find anything or not. On the one hand, they needed the wraith to leave clues for them... but the more they found, the more likely it was the wraith had already snagged the Inquisitor's attention, or would do soon.

A frustrating hour later, she flung her phone aside. Twisting up on her knees, she looked at the map, where they'd marked everything they'd found so far in red. All four of them – and they weren't anywhere near the blue dots.

Oh, there were plenty of deaths. Dylan had found car crashes, stabbings, a drowning. Some poor woman had even died plugging her kettle into a dodgy socket. But a death, animal or human, that couldn't be explained? Almost nothing.

"Well, that didn't help," Dylan muttered. She gazed down at their work, the dots that refused to organise themselves into any kind of pattern that could be connected, and felt panic paralyse her. They didn't know how the wraith had got through, or where. They didn't know where it was now.

They didn't know anything.

"It could be that some weren't reported, if they were just animal deaths. A dog, or a few chickens," Tristan offered.

"I suppose," Dylan replied doubtfully. Then she shook her head. "A wraith that only eats animals, though?"

"I know. It's more likely that it's only been here a few days, that it's responsible for the two attacks we know about. Which is good."

"It is?"

"Yeah, it means that it's likely that the farm in Kilsyth is where it got through."

Dylan nodded. "And it means it hasn't had time to do anything really bad, anything that would bring the Inquisitor."

"Exactly." He offered her a small smile. "Something to be thankful for."

"But what do we *do*?" Dylan pursed her lips and went back to glowering at the map. "We know it's already moved on. How are we supposed to find it now?"

"We need to wait," Tristan replied, sounding as uneasy as Dylan felt. "I don't like the idea of it being out there, looking for prey, any more than you do, but the wraith will kill again, it can't help it. When it does, we'll know where it is."

"We'll know where it *was*," Dylan bit out. "It could be gone again by the time we get there. And it could kill someone this time, Tristan. A person. And that would be on us."

Tristan didn't argue; he knew she was right.

"We can't afford to chase it from death to death! What are we going to do?"

He sighed. "I don't know."

That was the final nail in the coffin for Dylan. If Tristan didn't know what to do, they were lost. And if they weren't able to find the wraith, find it and kill it, then—

"The Inquisitor will come." Dylan glanced around the room, as if saying the being's name might somehow make it suddenly appear.

"It won't," Tristan vowed.

"It will!" Panic was beginning to spread through Dylan's body now, and she could feel herself spiralling. "We promised it we'd deal with any wraiths that came through. Tristan, if we can't deal with this one—"

"Dylan!" Tristan grabbed her face in both his hands and forced her to look at him. Dylan tried, but it was hard to focus, to keep still.

She wanted to run.

"Angel, calm down. Breathe." Tristan kept his voice low, his eyes leaving hers briefly to cast a quick glance at the door. Dylan realised she'd been shouting.

Joan was in bed, sleeping after a twelve-hour night shift, and her dad was in the living room, just a few more feet away, watching football on the television. They didn't want either parent to overhear their words and start asking questions they couldn't answer; Dylan's dad already knew too much.

"Sorry," she murmured. "But Tristan—"

"It's all right," he assured her.

"How is it all right?"

"It *will* be all right, then. How about that? We'll work out a plan. Before the Inquisitor comes looking."

Dylan threw him a dubious look and Tristan forced out a smile.

"Trust me," he said softly. "It will be all right. We have time."

She didn't share his optimism, but he was right about one thing: they didn't have any leads to chase, so there was nothing to do but wait.

"I hate this," she told him. "I feel helpless."

Tristan smoothed her cheek, gently tucking a loose tendril of hair behind her ear. "I know, Dylan. I know."

<hr />

He did know how Dylan felt, but he didn't know how to help. They needed to be patient, to let the wraith reveal itself. It didn't sit well with Tristan, at all, but it was the only option they had.

He had lots of experience with waiting. Dylan didn't; it was going to be hard for her.

Tristan would just need to keep her distracted, to make sure she didn't have time to dwell on their precarious situation. Taking in the wild look in her eyes, the tension in her shoulders, he knew he needed to stop her growing panic.

"Let's leave it for now." He slid his palms down her arms until he gripped both her hands. "Let's do something else, take our minds off it."

Dylan shot him a look. "Are you serious? Nothing is going to take my mind off it! Tristan, this is *bad*!"

"Is that a challenge?" He arched an eyebrow, then went in for the attack. He grabbed the icy cold can he'd been drinking from off the desk and snuck it under Dylan's T-shirt, pressing it against her bare skin. It took a fraction of a moment for Dylan to react, but then she gasped and squealed loudly, twisting violently away from him.

They both waited breathlessly, but there was no sign of movement from Dylan's parents.

"That was cruel," Dylan whispered once they were sure the coast was clear.

"Want me to do it again?"

She responded by snatching the can from him and shoving it against the sensitive skin of his inner arm – the closest she could get to his body with his arms outstretched to fend her off. Unable to hold in a little yelp, he reacted by tickling her until she was wriggling and gasping helplessly, up against the wall in an attempt to evade his fingers.

"No, no, no," she wheezed, "I'm sorry! I'm sorry, Tristan. *Stop*!"

He did, getting rid of the can and pulling her close. He kissed her softly, tugging her up onto the map-covered bed. "Giving up already?" he asked when he drew back.

"It's not fair!" Dylan complained. "You're not ticklish."

"Nope," he agreed.

"Not here…" Dylan ran a finger down his throat, the touch achingly ticklish on his sensitive skin – not that he'd ever tell her that. "Or here…" She softly ran the back of her fingers up his arm, raising the tiny hairs there. It was all Tristan could do to keep still. Or keep his breathing even. "Or even here…" Dylan said quietly. This time her fingers snuck under his T-shirt and she slowly skimmed her fingernails down his side. Goosebumps erupted over Tristan's entire body and he grabbed her hand, not quite sure what he was going to do with it.

They were entering dangerous territory and—

The door opened.

"Tristan," James said quietly.

"Dad!" Dylan sat bolt upright, launching herself away from Tristan. "We were just…"

She tailed off, blushing furiously, and Tristan winced, knowing what James would now assume they'd been up to. That thought was confirmed when Dylan's dad held up his hand to ward off any further comments, a pained look on his face.

"I don't want to know," he told Dylan. Then he looked at Tristan. "I need to talk to you. Now."

Tristan raised an eyebrow at James's blasé attitude. It was one thing to suspect your daughter's boyfriend was sneaking into her bed at night, quite another to come face to face with what they might be *doing* in that bed. He expected James to be… angry. Uneasy. *Something*. But then Tristan realised he held a tablet in his free hand, the screen glowing against the white fabric of his T-shirt. There was something else going on.

"Now?" Tristan asked.

James gave a brief nod then jerked his head in the direction of the living room. "This way."

It had been clear that it was Tristan James was looking to speak to, but Dylan slithered out of the room behind him and he made no move to stop her. He kept no secrets from her – he'd learned the harm of that the hard way – and whatever James had to say, he could say it to both of them.

James must have understood that, because he made no complaints when Dylan followed Tristan into the living room, sitting close beside him on the sofa. James muted the television and then ignored the armchair he usually sat in, instead perching on the coffee table, the tablet in his hands. Tristan tried to peer at the screen, but Dylan's dad kept it tilted away just enough that he couldn't make anything out.

"All right," James said quietly. He paused, flicking his eyes towards the doorway, but it was empty. He obviously didn't want Joan to know about the little chat he was about to have with them – which meant it could only be about one thing.

"If this is about what I think it's about… we can't talk about it," Tristan said, wanting to get that out there as early as possible. The Inquisitor had left them in no doubt as to the need for secrecy, and it had also impressed firmly upon them that they'd used up its entire stock of mercy and patience. "Please don't ask us any questions, because we won't be able to answer them."

"I know," James lifted his hand to stop Tristan, then dropped it to grip Dylan's knee. "I know there are things you can't tell me, and I know there are things going on between the two of you that I don't understand. Although," he shot Tristan a hard look, "you and I are going to have an uncomfortable conversation sometime in the very near future about physical boundaries."

"Dad!" Dylan spluttered.

James patted her knee. "If you're old enough to do it, baby, you're old enough to talk about it."

"That's— I mean… We are *not*, Dad! And we're not having this conversation. *Ever*." Dylan's voice was a horrified shriek and Tristan shushed her quietly. He didn't want Joan to catch them, to stop them before James could share what was on the tablet. If he didn't want to ask them questions, what did he want?

"Tristan and I *will* be having a talk, Dylan," James repeated firmly.

"But that isn't what you want to talk about right now." Tristan phrased it as a statement, not a question. A not-so-subtle hint for James to get on with it.

"No," James agreed, then he looked down at the tablet screen again, still keeping it angled away from Tristan, who had to fight the urge to grab it and see for himself what had Dylan's dad ready to break the unspoken pact they'd made, to leave the unsaid secrets between them just that: unsaid.

Tristan waited impatiently. Just when he was about to prompt James to speak, the older man sighed.

"So," he said. "Since, you know—"

"Since you decided to let me stay," Tristan said.

"Since then," James agreed. "Since the things I saw that day, things I can't explain... Well, I – no, I know you can't talk about it," he said, forestalling Tristan's interruption, obviously reading it on his face. "But that doesn't mean I can't investigate. Try to find things out for myself."

Tristan kept his mouth shut. James couldn't possibly find any answers to his questions. Not in this world. Not even on the internet.

"I've been keeping an eye out, doing a little digging and... well, there isn't much to find."

Tristan tried not to smirk – and failed.

If James saw it, he ignored him. His attention was once again on the screen, and this time he held it out towards Tristan.

"Then today," James said quietly, "I found this."

He didn't seem inclined to say anything else, to describe the video – Tristan could now see that was what it was – in any way. Tristan waited a heartbeat longer, then pressed play.

It had been uploaded onto YouTube, a site he and Dylan hadn't even thought to look at as they'd trawled through the news websites.

As the file loaded the little circle cycled round for a few seconds, the screen maddeningly black, before kicking into gear. The video was jerky and unfocused. Whoever had filmed it had probably used a smartphone, and the view jumped and spun with every arm movement. Ragged breathing hissed out of the speakers.

"Do you see it?" someone asked. "Where did it go?"

The camera flew almost one hundred and eighty degrees as the cameraman twisted, presumably hunting for whatever 'it' was. It wasn't dark, exactly, but the light was dim and in the few brief moments that the camera held still, Tristan could see trees.

"I think it's scared of the fire," another voice said.

The cameraman obligingly turned around to show Tristan a shot of the campfire they'd set up in a little clearing. Two trunks angled in a V shape behind the fire acted as seating, though there was no one sitting there now. Tristan couldn't see any of the speakers, but judging by the pitch and tone – and the fact that they were messing about in the woods – he figured it was a group of teenage boys. Older teenage boys, he amended, catching sight of several beer bottles balanced on one of the downed trunks.

"Is it gone, d'you reckon?" Whoever held the camera spoke at last. Another male, his voice tight with restrained fear.

"Dunno." The camera swung and Tristan got a view of one of the boys for the first time. He was younger than Tristan would have guessed, small and skinny with pale skin that looked as if it hadn't met a razor yet.

He looked a lot like the idiot boys who went to Dylan's school.

Weak-looking or not, there was a grim determination on his face, and he had a good grip on the stout length of branch in his left hand.

"If you see it, Mark, bash it!" the cameraman advised, and Mark nodded.

"Did you hear that?" Not Mark this time. Maybe the first speaker? It was hard for Tristan to keep track of who was who, or even how many boys were there.

The cameraman turned to the speaker and Tristan saw the back of his head as he stared off into the woods. He, too, had grabbed a makeshift weapon from the woodland floor.

"What did you hear?" the cameraman asked.

"I dunno. A scream? Listen."

The cameraman walked up to stand beside the boy, whose head panned left and right as he searched. The whole group were deathly silent as they listened for another scream. Tristan held his breath as he listened too. The sound quality was terrible – it was hard to hear anything over the cameraman's breathing, the rustle of the trees and the occasional snap of—

Then he heard it. Tristan's breath froze in his lungs as Mark jerked and said, "There! Hear it?"

Yes, he did. He heard it – and recognised it. The unmistakeable scream of a wraith.

"Oh my God," Dylan breathed beside him. She clutched at his arm, her fingernails digging into his skin. Tristan took a moment to lift his gaze from the screen, saw James watching him intently. There was grim satisfaction in the man's face and Tristan knew he'd given something away.

Well, it was too late now. Filing it away for future consideration, he went back to watching the video as the boys shifted nervously. They were waiting for something – he guessed the reappearance of the wraith. They were right, it would be scared of the flames, and that was likely the only reason they were still alive.

For now.

"Dylan, maybe you shouldn't watch this," he said, starting to angle it away from her, knowing she wouldn't go without a fight.

"Not a chance," Dylan replied firmly. Tristan sighed, but if James had presumably seen the whole video and wasn't objecting, perhaps the concluding scene didn't feature the boys' blood and guts strewn around the clearing. Astounding as that seemed, surely if they had, the story would have been splashed all over the news and he and Dylan would have found it.

"There!" The cameraman's squawk erupted out of the speakers and Tristan's world became a blur as the boy spun, trying to focus on something that swooped across the clearing at lightning speed. Like a bat, but ten times bigger.

And ten thousand times deadlier.

"Maybe we should just leave it alone," the as-yet-nameless first speaker suggested.

"Right, Andy. Brilliant idea." Tristan couldn't see Mark on the screen – the phone camera was pointing uselessly into the tree canopy, the thick covering of leaves too dark to see anything – but he recognised his voice now. "And what happens when we've got to go home? Did you see what it did to Danny's arm?"

On cue, the camera turned and a fourth boy was thrust into the spotlight. Tristan could see why he hadn't spoken until now. He looked almost catatonic, his features grey.

"Show me your sleeve," the cameraman ordered and Danny dutifully obeyed.

Dylan sucked in a breath – the boy's jacket was torn to shreds and, given the slick red smear across the cream fabric, so was the skin underneath.

"We need to move away from the fire a bit," Mark said. "Draw it out. I'm not staying here all bloody night."

"You first," Andy commented wryly.

There was some grunting and shoving, and by the time the camera had panned to face the action and adjusted to the light of the fire enough for Tristan to see, Andy lay sprawled across the woodland floor, a mix of anger and terror on his face, scowling in Mark's direction as he tried to scramble to his feet. Fear or the leaves coating the ground had made him clumsy and he'd slipped.

At exactly the same time, a growling snarl started up and the wraith came darting in from the side furthest from the fire. It flew unerringly for Andy, but before it could reach its target, Mark swung the bat, using his whole body to put power into the stroke.

He thwacked the wraith, sending it tumbling through the air into the trees outside the relative safety of the clearing.

"Shit! Did you get it? Is it dead?"

"Can you see it?"

"You must have killed it, you walloped it!"

There was a confusion of movement and shouting as the boys foolhardily ran after the creature. They crashed through the undergrowth, their progress nothing more than streaks of light and dark, gasping and exclaiming.

"That's it! There! There!"

Tristan lost his grasp on who was shouting. He supposed it didn't really matter. A moment later they'd found it and he was looking down on the wraith, nestled amongst a pile of leaves. It writhed, clearly trying to get up, to face the threat that hovered above it.

"It's moving! Batter it!"

As Tristan watched one of the boys stepped forward and pummelled the wraith, again and again, choked little sobs escaping the wielder with every swing. The rest stood in silent witness until at last one of the boys – Andy? – said, "All right, Danny. That's enough. You killed it."

Danny stopped at last, then stepped back. Tristan saw the wildness in his face, heart-wrenching fear rendering him completely frenzied, manic.

"Look! Look what it's doing!" The shout had Tristan tearing his eyes away from Danny and down to the wraith, which was smoking, preparing to disappear in a cloud of gas.

There was more to the video, but Tristan stopped paying attention as the boys began debating what it was they'd killed, where it came from, and how it managed to evaporate out of existence at the end. Instead, Tristan watched James – who watched him.

"They were so lucky," Dylan breathed. "That thing could have killed them all. If they hadn't had a fire—"

"They'd all be dead," Tristan agreed.

"I'm going to take it," James said quietly, "that you know what that thing is."

"I know what it is," Tristan confirmed.

"You've seen it before?"

"Yes."

"And?"

Tristan just looked at him. James waited a heartbeat, then another. Seeing Tristan wasn't going to bend, he gave up. Letting out a tired sigh, he reached over to take the tablet back. Tristan considered holding on to it – he wanted to watch the video back, again and again – but if it was on YouTube he would be able to find it himself and, really, there was nothing to be gained by picking over every detail. He'd watched closely enough, had taken in all the film had to tell him.

Except…

"You've watched it a few times?" he asked James.

Switching the tablet off so that only the muted glow from the table lamp lit up his features, Dylan's dad nodded sombrely.

"Can you see enough to work out where they are?"

If James said no, Tristan would simply pore over the clip himself, see if he could find clues, but that would mean letting

Dylan watch it again, too. The way she was sitting so close to him, leaning in, her hand still wrapped around his arm, he figured she was going to have nightmares enough as it was.

"Doubt that you'll be able to tell from the footage," James said, "but whoever put up the film tagged the location. It was in a wood just outside of Kilsyth."

"Kilsyth?" Dylan jerked slightly. "Near where all those sheep were attacked?"

Tristan watched James put two and two together as the man nodded. He could have cursed Dylan for pointing that out, but there seemed little harm in the information. It wasn't as if James was going to call the farmer and tell him what happened.

And it wasn't as if James had any idea that the creature was a mutated soul who'd snuck through from the wasteland.

Wanting to make sure no more secrets snuck out, Tristan stood up.

"Thank you for showing me that," he said. Then, "It would be best if you pretended you didn't see it." James said nothing, his expression thoughtful. "Most people will dismiss it as clever CGI," Tristan went on. "You should too."

"Just answer one thing," James said. He took a deep breath, seemed to brace himself. "Are there more of those… things?"

"Here?" Tristan asked, and James looked momentarily taken aback before nodding. "I hope not. Come on, Dylan," he held out his hand and tugged Dylan to her feet when she automatically grabbed it. "We need to work on that essay for English."

James let them go, the tablet tucked tight under his arm, a slightly lost expression on his face.

Tristan could feel Dylan's anxiety beside him, knew she was practically bursting to talk about the wraith in the video, but mercifully she held her tongue until they were back in her room.

Tristan swiped at the map, sending it sliding to the floor, and then drew Dylan down onto her bed. She came willingly, pressing herself into his side then tilting her head up to pierce him with her gaze.

"This is good, right?" she whispered. "If that was the wraith that killed the sheep and the horse, then it's dead now."

"It was *possibly* that wraith," Tristan amended.

"Probably," Dylan fired back.

Tristan didn't argue, wanting to believe that it was. But that still left one very problematic question to which they had no answer.

"How did it get here, though?" he murmured.

"I don't know." Dylan shrugged helplessly.

"It couldn't have come from where we went through, or Susanna and Jack," Tristan reasoned. "It's too far away, for one. We closed both holes, but even if one of them managed to reopen, there's no way a wraith would pass so many populated areas without feeding."

"I don't know," Dylan repeated, a little more quietly. Tristan almost didn't hear her, lost in his thoughts.

"And I'm sure, absolutely sure that no other ferrymen have come through. I'd feel them."

He shut his eyes and reached out with his senses, just in case, but all he felt – all he'd felt the dozen other times he'd tried – was an emptiness, a quiet. He was alone here.

Dylan looked up at him. "You said the veil was thinner on the edge of the wasteland. A wraith couldn't just have clawed its way through?"

Tristan shook his head, immediately dismissing the idea. "The wasteland doesn't work like that," he said. "The veil doesn't just break, or crack. It's held for an eternity."

"As far as you know," Dylan contradicted carefully.

Tristan opened his mouth to tell her that he did know, that he could feel it… but he'd told her that he couldn't follow her back through, could never exist in the real world, and yet here he was. There was, he supposed, a first time for everything.

And just because he'd been conditioned to believe an idea as truth, it didn't mean that it necessarily was.

"It's possible," he had to admit.

"All right." Dylan dropped her head down to rest in on his shoulder. "What do you think we should do, then? How are we supposed to make sure no more wraiths can get through if we can't even work out how this one did?"

Resting his chin on the top of her head, Tristan grimaced. "I don't know," he said, pulling Dylan tight against him. "Strange things are happening, and I don't understand it. Not at all."

CHAPTER 11

"I'm going to miss you, you know."

Susanna rolled over onto her front on the lumpy sofa and stared at Jack, who was standing by the front door again. This time, at least, he had a decent view. The valley they'd made it through by the skin of their teeth stretched out beyond the safe house doorway. It was terrifying, a funnel thrusting them into the path of more wraiths than Susanna had ever seen gathered in one place, but now that they'd crossed it, she could admit that the vast sweeps of hillside, the sinuous, slightly shimmering black of the narrow pathway and the burning hue of the sky had a strange kind of majesty.

If she never saw it again, though, that would be absolutely fine by her.

"Are you talking to me, or the wasteland?" she teased.

"Mostly the wasteland." Jack grinned out at the valley before turning to face her. "But you as well, I suppose."

"Right." Susanna rolled her eyes at him. "Thank you *so* much."

"You're welcome." He smiled at her fake disgruntlement, crossing the room to absently run a hand over the surface of a rickety kitchen table. "I wish there was something to eat."

"You're hungry?" Susanna asked, surprised.

"No." Jack shook his head. "I just… I could really go a bacon roll right now. Or a bag of chips."

"Healthy fare," Susanna commented dryly.

"Yeah well." He shrugged. "My mum never let me have that sort of thing. Meals had to be old-fashioned, with veg and crap, or else my stepdad—" Jack broke off, suddenly shoving at the kitchen table. One of the spindly chairs tucked beneath it toppled loudly to the floor, but Jack ignored it, coming over to sit on the sofa.

Looking at the hunched curve of his spine, the tightness in his shoulders, she sat up and swivelled until they were sitting side by side.

"I've never had chips," Susanna said quietly. "Or a bacon roll."

Jack made a non-committal sound, rubbing his hands through his hair.

"Or chocolate," she added. "I've heard a lot about chocolate." She wished she'd had the chance to taste some while she was in the real world, but with everything that had happened, sampling foods had been the last thing on her mind.

"You should have said," Jack told her. "My mum has loads." His voice took on a caustic edge. "Stashed away where my stepdad can't find it. He's always telling her she's getting fat."

Susanna didn't know what to say to that. She reached out hesitantly and put her hand on Jack's knee. She'd seen him try to act the protector in memory after memory, knew it must be gnawing at him that he couldn't step in between them any more. Make himself the target for his stepdad's cruel words.

For his punches.

"Did I kiss you?" Jack said suddenly.

"What?" Susanna blurted, totally wrong-footed by the abrupt change of direction.

Jack turned his head ever so slightly, giving her a view of his sheepish expression and burning cheeks. "Did I kiss you?" He shifted on the sofa, their positions close enough that he knocked her elbow. "I feel like I remember... the first time we were in the wasteland, we walked to a flat." Jack scrunched his face up, searching memories Susanna knew would be blurry. "You said it belonged to a pal or something. She had a stupid name…"

"Marcy," Susanna said.

Jack snorted. "I should have figured it out right there and then. What kind of a name is Marcy?"

"Lots of people are called Marcy!" Susanna protested.

"Fifty years ago," Jack countered.

"It's hard to keep up with the times," Susanna muttered, resisting the urge to stick her tongue out at him. "And I was under pressure – you were being a nightmare!"

Jack laughed, a loud, hoarse sound. Rusty, as if he hardly used it, which Susanna knew to be true.

"In my defence, I thought you were Sammy," Jack said.

"I know." Susanna nudged him gently with her shoulder. "Do you miss her?"

"I'm not… I mean, I feel like I should." He shrugged. "But I don't, not really."

"Oh." Susanna was surprised. Sammy had been a rock for Jack, a steady presence in the tumult of his life. Susanna knew he'd had strong feelings for her, that's why she'd taken on that form. "Well, that's OK," she added somewhat lamely, feeling the need to fill the awkward silence that had somehow settled on them.

"I did kiss you, didn't I?" Jack asked. He was carefully not looking at her.

"Well…" Yes, he had. He'd lain over her, kissing her neck, tried to slip his hand under her shirt to feel her up. "You thought I was Sammy," she reminded him.

There was a moment of tense silence that Susanna didn't know how to break. She couldn't even guess what Jack was thinking, but he suddenly seemed to find the floor very interesting.

For Susanna, it was hard to think about the memory, fresh as if it had happened only moments ago, without feeling odd. Jittery. The Jack that had kissed her then had been a stranger. But now...

"I'm sorry," he blurted, breaking the silence and fixing his eyes on Susanna's. "For the way I acted, I mean." A pause. "Was that your first kiss?"

"What kind of question is that?" she retorted. She felt heat start to creep up her cheeks and it was a struggle to hold Jack's unrelenting gaze.

"Was it?" he asked, doggedly pursuing an answer.

"No," Susanna said tartly, then, because Jack was looking so skeptical, "and it wasn't the best kiss I've ever had either!"

This time his laugh was so loud it seemed to rock the safe house.

"Now I know you're lying," he said with a wink.

"Hmmm." Susanna sniffed, arching an eyebrow at him. "Anything else you'd like to know? My deepest darkest secrets?"

"Like you've got any!" he shot back.

"I do so!" She smacked his arm. "And I'm not telling you!"

He grinned, then he blew out a breath and looked towards the door. It was near dark, and the wraiths were thick in the air, screaming and wailing, but the magic of the safe house dimmed a lot of the noise, even with the door open, and the terror of the wall of tortured sound had lessened with time.

"Are we nearly there?" he asked, any traces of laughter now gone.

"Yeah." The word came out scratchy and Susanna had to clear her suddenly tight throat. "Yeah, there's not far to go. One more big obstacle, one more safe house, then we'll be at the line. You'll be able to get out of here."

"And you?"

"I'll..." Susanna didn't really know. "I'll probably be sent to ferry another soul."

She hoped. Because if the Inquisitor left her here, alone, with the heat and the desert dryness and the ever-present wraiths, she thought she might lose her mind.

"Right." A pause. "What's the last big obstacle, then?"

"A lake," Susanna said. "We row across it." Then she made a face. "*I* row across it."

"A lake?" Jack asked, and Susanna nodded. "How big is it?"

"Well, I don't really have anything to compare it to, but it's too big to walk around, not before the sun sets."

"Oh." Another pause. "Is it deep?"

"Yeah," Susanna said, "It's pretty deep. I've had the joy of swimming in it a few times." *That* was an understatement. "I've never been able to reach the bottom."

"I can't swim," Jack announced. He fidgeted. "Like, at all."

Susanna already knew that.

"Don't worry, Jack. We'll stay in the boat. I promised you, remember? I'm going to get you out of here. In less than two days, I'll have you across the line."

And didn't that just stab her in the heart.

"I really am going to miss you," Jack repeated quietly, reaching out and pulling her towards him. This time, Susanna didn't make any sort of smart comment. She just rested her head on his shoulder and waited for the dawn.

CHAPTER 12

"Annabelle, would you just sit down!"

The girl with the long black hair ignored her, too intent on the picture she was taking. Jennifer Moffat sighed. She loved netball, and she loved coaching, but dealing with teenage girls she could do without.

She needed a pay rise.

"Annabelle!"

When the star goal attack ignored her once more, Jennifer levered herself out of her seat. Using the headrests for balance, she walked carefully up the narrow aisle of the bus, past the six empty rows to where the majority of the team were seated. Annabelle stood with her back to her, legs slightly bent as she angled her phone to perfectly capture the grinning faces of her two friends, who were leaning dangerously out of their seats.

Done with subtlety, she tapped firmly on Annabelle's shoulder.

"What?" Annabelle spun so quickly her swathe of hair whipped Jennifer across the face. The girl eyed her petulantly. If she wasn't so much better than the reserve goal attack players, Jennifer would have thrown her off the team long ago.

Unfortunately, Annabelle was. And she knew it.

"Sit down," Jennifer said firmly. "Put your seatbelt on."

There was a brief power struggle as Annabelle stared at Jennifer, waiting to see if she could intimidate her into scurrying back to the front with the other coach, old Mrs Halliday, who liked to pretend she was deaf and dumb as soon as the bus started going. Jennifer held her nerve. She might be four inches shorter than Annabelle, but she wasn't going to be intimated by too much hairspray and attitude.

Or at least, she wasn't going to let Annabelle know that she was.

"Sit down, Annabelle," she repeated, the growl in her voice telling the girl this was her last warning.

Just when Jennifer thought she was going to have to pull out the big guns – the bluff that she'd pull Annabelle from the team – Annabelle folded. Huffing, she threw herself into her seat, rolling her eyes at Steph Clark, her seatmate and partner in crime.

"'Sake!" she said, loud enough for Jennifer to hear but sufficiently under her breath for Jennifer to pretend she couldn't (which she did). "I was just taking a picture."

"Seatbelt, Annabelle."

Another roll of her eyes, another extravagant huff, but Annabelle did as she was told, slinging the seatbelt across her hips and buckling it.

"Thank you." Jennifer smiled sweetly at Annabelle and turned her back on her, waiting until she was almost back at her seat before muttering, "Little cow."

She sat back down across the aisle from Mrs Halliday, who was knitting something unidentifiable in a garish red wool.

"Anything wrong, dear?" The old woman raised her eyebrows questioningly, an innocent smile painted across her lips.

Jennifer offered a similarly fake smile in return. "No, no. Everything's fine. They're just excited about the game."

"I don't know how you deal with teenagers." This from the bus driver, a large man who'd given Jennifer his name as he'd lectured her on not letting the girls eat, drink or touch anything while on board his bus. What was his name again? Davey, that was right.

"It has its challenges," Jennifer agreed.

"Oh, goodness no," Mrs Halliday squawked. "Our girls are lovely!"

Jennifer just turned towards the window, thinking her cheeks might crack if she had to force another smile. Making the decision to check the job-search websites that night while she enjoyed what was going to be a well-earned glass of wine, she stared out at the countryside as the bus chugged on towards Falkirk and—

"Did you see that?" she asked.

"See what, dear?" Mrs Halliday asked, looking up from her knitting.

"Davey?"

But the bus driver had his head thrown back, his attention off the road, as he stretched his mouth open in a huge yawn.

"What did you say?" he asked a second later.

Jennifer stared hard at the view out of the window, but what she thought she'd seen had disappeared. It looked exactly as it should: green fields, a few sheep. An industrial unit in the background…

"Nothing," she said slowly. "I just thought I saw—"

There! She was positive this time. A flicker of red, the whole landscape awash with it as if she was seeing through coloured lenses. She paused, waiting to see if it would happen again. After just a couple of seconds it did, only this time the countryside disappeared, replaced with a sweeping burgundy vista.

And this time, it wasn't just for a second or two.

This time it stayed red.

There was a sudden chorus of crying and shrieks of panic from the girls at the back of the bus.

"What in the hell?" Davey's shout was all the warning Jennifer had before the bus started careening wildly. She looked through the windscreen to see that the motorway they'd been travelling on had disappeared and the bus was shuttling at 70 mph across sand. The uneven terrain threw the bus from side to side, and Jennifer was tossed from her seat as it skidded and slid to a halt. The bus's front left wheel was stuck in some hidden crevice, making the vehicle tilt at a dangerous angle.

Jennifer held her breath, terrified, but after rocking for a few moments the bus seemed to decide that it wasn't going to tip completely.

"OK." Jennifer picked herself up shakily, fairly certain no bones were broken, though she ached all over. "Girls, are you all right? Is anybody hurt?"

More shouts and terrified screams, but as Jennifer made her way to the back of the bus, she didn't see any blood – just petrified faces staring back at her. Waiting for her to take charge and tell them what to do.

"OK," Jennifer said again, trying to stay calm. A quick glance back told her that Davey and Mrs Halliday were out of their seats, standing unaided – and looking to her for guidance. Brilliant. "We're all right, nobody's badly injured, so let's just—"

A scream cut her off.

Annabelle stood, her arm shaking as she point out of the window.

"What *the hell* are those?"

Jennifer turned to look out of the window. She saw at once what Annabelle was pointing at.

As the screams echoed around her, Jennifer could only stare as a flock of creatures – much larger and more terrifying than any bird she'd ever seen – flew straight at the bus. As they got closer she could see fangs, claws. Absolute evil in their pitch-black eyes.

Attacking as one, the creatures crashed into the side of the bus. Jennifer watched, frozen, as the windows started to crack.

CHAPTER 13

Dylan knew there was something wrong as soon as she and Tristan stepped into the maths classroom. The atmosphere was quiet, subdued. Everybody was doing what they were meant to be doing – taking off jackets, getting jotters and pencils out of bags, settling into seats – but there was almost a furtive feel to the room. Like they were all waiting for something.

She realised what that was a minute later when Cheryl McNally walked in. She was leaning heavily on Dove MacMillan – who she'd been seeing and then not seeing in dramatic fashion over the course of the previous term. The last Dylan heard, it was very definitely off, but Dove's arm was firmly slung around Cheryl's shoulder.

Then Cheryl lifted her head.

Dylan had never seen Cheryl without absolutely perfect make-up. There was too much of it, and if you asked Dylan it was about four shades too orange for Cheryl's natural skin tone, but it was always flawlessly applied. Now it was sliding down her face, orange streaks across her cheeks as if she'd been scrubbing at them, and eyeliner smudged in dark blotches under her red-rimmed eyes. There was a collective gasp from the class and the expression on Dove's face went from stoic to furious in the space of a nanosecond.

"What the hell you all looking at?" he growled.

Everybody very quickly became absorbed in something else, anything else.

"Perhaps you should go to the office?" Mr Campbell, their maths teacher, suggested. "Ask to go home?" Cheryl shook her head, the gesture just a shimmy of hair since she'd dropped her gaze to stare at the floor. "Maybe for a walk, then? Get some fresh air?" Cheryl shook her head to each suggestion and Mr Campbell made a face, stymied and clearly uncomfortable.

Dylan was too – she'd no idea Cheryl even had emotions. And here was Dove, being protective and supportive, like an actual human being.

"I think the world must be ending," she whispered to Tristan. "Strange things are happening."

He just looked from her to Cheryl and back again, a perplexed expression on his face, and Dylan waved the joke away.

"Right, well… let's start then," Mr Campbell said. He glanced again at Cheryl, then seemed to give a mental shrug and picked up a textbook. "Open up to page seventy-two, folks. We're going to look at how you use sine and cosine to find the angle in a triangle—"

But he didn't get any further than that, because the classroom phone rang. Its shrill intervention didn't garner the usual cheers, but taking in the way Mr Campbell looked at Cheryl again – who was cosseted quietly at the back of the class, as far out of the spotlight as possible – Dylan thought he might be cheering on the inside, thinking the call was to summon her.

Except it wasn't. Dylan watched his expression go from hopeful to slightly annoyed as he barked out, "What, right now?" Sighing, he slammed down the phone and turned to the class. "It seems we have an assembly."

Nobody turned to look at Cheryl – Dove was still there beside her, skulking menacingly – but everyone in the room heard the quiet hiccup as she tried to strangle a sob.

Out of respect for Cheryl, and a healthy respect for Dove's fist, no one spoke as they left the room, but once the class mixed with the rest of fourth year leaving the maths corridor, and then third year as they approached the assembly hall, speculation was rife about the reasons for an unscheduled assembly. Nobody seemed to have any idea what had actually happened, but general concensus seemed to be that it involved Steph Clark, Cheryl's best friend.

She hadn't been in school yesterday, Dylan remembered. She'd been bragging about being picked to be part of the Glasgow City Netball Team, and had been out for the whole day at some game in Falkirk. Dylan had had the misfortune of hearing all about it as she shared a table with Steph in Modern Studies, where the teacher took a sadistic pleasure in assigning seats.

Dylan thought about the genuine grief of Cheryl's face, the way she'd tried to hide herself away, and found herself in a position she never, ever thought she'd be in: feeling sorry for Cheryl McNally.

For once, the headmaster had no trouble establishing quiet in the big assembly hall, even with all of third and fourth year crammed in there together. Everybody shut up as soon as he indicated he was ready to speak – they knew there was juicy gossip heading their way and were eager to hear it.

"All right, boys and girls," the headmaster started. "You'll be aware that this assembly was unscheduled. We've had some bad news as a school, and I thought it was important to talk to you all about it personally rather than let gossip spread half-true and hurtful stories." He paused, cleared his throat. "Yesterday afternoon, a Kaithshall pupil, Stephanie Clark, went missing. She was selected to play as part of Glasgow City Netball Team and was on a bus heading to their match in Falkirk. We know that the bus left Glasgow on time, but it did not arrive at its destination. As of yet, the police have been unable to determine what happened to the bus—"

An outbreak of hushed whispers swept across the hall, building in volume until it sounded like the throbbing buzz of a swarm of bees. The headmaster held up his hands for silence, but this time he was forced to wait as a ripple of shock and conjecture circled the room.

"That's so bizarre," Dylan heard a voice behind her half-whisper. "How can they not find it? It's a bus for God's sake!"

Stunned herself, Dylan looked to Tristan, whose face was furrowed in thought. His eyes seemed a darker shade of blue, shadowed with consternation. He swallowed twice, like he couldn't make his throat work, then opened his mouth to speak. Dylan got in there before he could.

"No," she hissed. "No way. Not everything bad that happens is our fault!"

"Come on," Tristan muttered. "Can you explain it any other way?"

"No, but that doesn't mean that it's the right explanation!"

"A bus doesn't just go missing—"

"Yeah," Dylan whispered furiously, "but if it was wraiths there would still *be* a bus, wouldn't there? Along with a whole netball team's worth of bodies!"

"It might not have been wraiths."

"Well, what then?"

Tristan opened his mouth, but he didn't get the chance to answer her. The headmaster, tired of waiting, started shouting for quiet.

"Obviously," the headmaster stressed, his voice lined with more annoyance that solemnness now, "this is a very upsetting time for Stephanie Clark's family, and all of her friends here at Kaithshall Academy, so I ask you to be sensitive and sympathetic to each other during this difficult period." A soft noise from the side of the assembly hall had the headmaster glancing over towards Mrs Mallaghan, head of pastoral, and he hurriedly added, "If any of you are struggling emotionally or feel overwhelmed by this news, make yourself known to your pastoral teacher – or any teacher – who are all here to support you."

"Are you shutting the school?" a male voice shouted from somewhere amongst the seated pupils.

The headmaster scowled in the general direction the call had come from, but there were too many possible culprits for him to work out who had interrupted him, so he settled for squashing the air of optimism that had suddenly sprung up from the Kaithshall faithful.

"No," he said sternly. "School life will go on as normal. While we are saddened by the situation involving Stephanie," he didn't sound very saddened now, Dylan thought, "your education is too important to disrupt." He ignored the low chorus of boos. "We will of course keep you updated on any developments, and we are very hopeful that Stephanie will be found safe and well. Now," he checked his watch, "there are only a few minutes left of final period, so I think we'll just keep you all here until the bell goes."

This was met initially with cheers, and then outrage and panic as pupils realised that they hadn't brought bags and jackets down to the hall with them. When the headmaster was forced to reverse his decision, sending the third and fourth year pupils back to class with an ill-advised instruction to 'move quickly', there was general madness as everyone tried to get back to their classroom as soon as possible – God forbid they had to remain in the school a moment after the end-of-day bell rang – whilst also discussing the bombshell that had just been dropped.

"What did you mean it might not have been wraiths?" Dylan hissed as soon as they were clear of the hall. "If not wraiths, what?"

"Later," Tristan murmured, eyeing the bodies crushed close to them as everybody pushed and shoved down the corridor. "Too many ears."

Dylan gnashed her teeth with frustration as she was carried along by the crowd and back up to the maths classroom. It possibly said everything that needed to be said about Steph that, despite the fact that everyone in the room knew her, and had at least one class with her, no one seemed particularly upset by her sudden and strange disappearance.

Cheryl hadn't returned to class, deciding, Dylan presumed, that she didn't care enough about her stuff to face the speculation that was rife in the room.

"She's dead," one girl said with a matter-of-factness that made Dylan wince. "She must be."

"Yeah," her seating partner replied, "but where's the bus then? It's like one of those constable theories."

"What?" Her friend looked blank.

"Constable theories."

Dylan tried to tune the pair out as she packed things back into her bag, but their voices floated into the silence between her and Tristan.

"What the hell are you talking about?"

"You know, where people are sold a lie and there are all these theories about what the truth really is."

"You mean…" a disbelieving pause, "a conspiracy theory?" Another pause, then, quietly and disgusted, "Seriously, Mandy."

Normally Dylan would have laughed, but she was too tense. Too impatient. She checked her watch, not trusting the clock on the wall which seemed to be grinding along at half-speed.

Tristan was just as eager to get out of there. Desk already clear and bag on his back, he actually started bouncing on the spot, so strong was his desire to leave.

"The bell hasn't gone yet, Tristan," Dylan reminded him gently. "We can't go until it does."

"Nobody will care," Tristan retorted, his eyes on the door.

Dylan was about to tell him that their maths teacher might have something to say about that, but when she looked over towards his desk, he wasn't there.

She guessed the teachers were as morbidly fascinated with Steph's disappearance as the pupils were – he was probably in the staff room discussing his own 'constable' theories.

"Go on, then," Dylan said, heaving up her bag and sliding out from behind her desk, but before they could cross the threshold, the bell rang, clanging obnoxiously right above their heads. Caught up in the stampede, they were jostled and shepherded through the building.

The crowd thinned as they began walking away from the school and, at Tristan's urging, they took the shortcut through the park even though it meant traipsing across a wide stretch of sodden grass.

As soon as they passed through the gate, splitting off from everyone else, Dylan grabbed Tristan's arm, forcing him to slow.

"All right," she said, glancing around to check there was no one within hearing distance. "Tell me."

Tristan pressed his lips together, then gave a little shrug. "I don't know," he said at last. "I just…"

"Go on," Dylan prompted, when he tailed off.

"We tore a hole in the wasteland—"

"We closed that!"

"And Jack and Susanna did, as well—"

"But we dealt with that one, too!"

"Just, hear me out," Tristan pleaded. He waited a moment to ensure Dylan wasn't going to interrupt again before continuing. "We don't know how that other wraith got through; I'm absolutely positive no other ferryman has travelled through with a soul."

"Which means?"

"Maybe it made its own hole."

Dylan stared at him, incredulous. "But… how? We managed to tear the veil because I had a body to go back to. The wraith didn't."

"No," Tristan agreed, "but maybe it didn't need one. Maybe…" He blew out a breath. "Maybe we've weakened the veil, made it possible for breaches to occur. Like the wraith."

"And the bus? You think it just barrelled right on into the wasteland?"

"It would explain its disappearance."

"Be reasonable, Tristan." Dylan shook her head. "If a bus had careened into the wasteland, the kind of hole it left would have been enormous. Swarms of wraiths would have come through! There would be carnage!"

"Unless the holes don't last," he replied quietly. "Think of it like your skin. If you puncture it, it works to reseal itself."

"And in the meantime, things bleed through," Dylan finished sombrely, the idea beginning to take hold. "But," she scrunched up her nose, "but every other thing to cross over has come from the wasteland to the real world: us, Jack and Susanna, the wraith. If you're right, the bus went from the real world into the wasteland. How is that possible?"

"It's possible if the veil is weakening." Tristan sighed heavily.

"And if that's true, it means there could be more of this. A lot more."

Dylan tried to imagine it: wraiths appearing in the real world at random, anywhere and at any time. People being sucked from their lives into the afterlife, with no ferryman to protect them and get them safely to the line. She paled, horrified.

"No," she croaked, instinctively rearing away from the idea. "No, it can't be." She didn't sound confident, and she didn't feel it either.

"What do you think happened, then?" Tristan asked as they left the park and turned into Dylan's road. "Where'd the bus go?"

"I've no idea," Dylan replied. She racked her brain for a different explanation, a less terrifying explanation. "Maybe the bus driver's gone nuts and driven them away somewhere, to hold them for ransom or something."

Tristan raised an eyebrow. "Right," he said sarcastically.

"I'm not saying that's definitely what happened," Dylan snapped, feeling defensive.

"I know," Tristan reached out and tugged on her ponytail, a familiar gesture that had her smiling ruefully at him, her temper melting away. "I just want to be sure. I'm trying to protect us. I don't want the—"

He stopped short. And he stopped walking.

"The Inquisitor?" Dylan prompted. Tristan ignored her.

He never ignored her.

"Tristan?" She gave him a little shove. "Tristan!"

He was frozen, just like he had been when...

Just when her concern was giving way to panic, he suddenly surged forward in a rush of motion and grabbed Dylan by both arms.

"It's here," he told her. "The Inquisitor, I can feel it. Here."

Unable to draw out of Tristan's grip, Dylan looked round, but all she could see was her street. Two long lines of tenement flats, parked cars lining the road. An old woman walking slowly with her shopping on the opposite pavement while a black cat tiptoed daintily across the road.

"Where?" she asked.

Tristan didn't answer, he just started running.

CHAPTER 14

"Susanna." Jack mangled her name, the syllables coming out a garbled rush. He took a deep breath, visibly steadied himself, then whispered, "I can't swim."

"It's all right," Susanna said. "We're not swimming, remember. We're rowing."

"Are we rowing an invisible boat?"

Susanna smirked. The sarcastic edge to Jack's tone wasn't quite enough to mask his panic. And it was a reasonable question, she supposed. Looking across the lake, her eyes carefully unfocused, the world was a blur – particularly the darting shadows, which didn't seem to be getting easier to ignore with practice, unfortunately. Even so, there was clearly no boat waiting for them on the shoreline.

"That building over there's a boat shed," she said. "Our boat's inside."

"It can't be much of a boat," Jack said dubiously, no doubt eyeing the size of the shed.

Susanna made her way over by feel and memory – the wasteland might be blood-red and burning, but the slope here was pretty much the same. She wished she could say the same for the water.

It looked like it was breathing. Black and viscous, it undulated like some great sleeping monster. Breathing slowly in and out…

just waiting for some idiot to try rowing across and start poking it with oars.

Nothing good came of poking a sleeping monster with a stick.

"Help me with the door?" Susanna asked, hefting at the beam lodged in two couplings. The whole thing had swollen shut – though Susanna couldn't see how, not with the heat sucking all the moisture in the air – and wouldn't budge. Together, she and Jack managed to wrestle it free and Jack tossed it to the side. It landed with a satisfying thunk and then an eerie hiss as it skidded on the stones.

"Hey," Jack said quietly, making Susanna pause, a hand on each door, ready to haul them open. "There's not a tonne of wraiths in there, is there? Ready to pounce on us?"

"It's the kind of place they'd like," Susanna agreed, "but there shouldn't be. It looked rickety but it's sealed pretty well. There aren't any holes for them to sneak in."

Smiling reassuringly (though she doubted Jack would see, he'd be carefully *not* looking at everything, just like she was), Susanna threw her weight back, tugging on the doors. There was a screech and a scrape, the doors resisting, but then they gave way, opening in a sudden rush that had Susanna stumbling backwards, struggling to keep her footing.

Less than a second later, she lost the battle completely as Jack's fears came true and wraith upon wraith came flooding out of the shed. Susanna gaped at them, surprised into staring, and the wraiths pounced on her mistake, diving for her prostrate form.

"Shut your eyes!" she screamed to Jack, throwing her arms up over her face, both to protect herself and so she wouldn't be so stupid as to look at them again. She hissed out a breath as pain radiated up both her forearms, the wraiths clawing at her skin and screeching gleefully as the iron scent of her blood filled the air and sent them into a frenzy.

They battered her, slicing past her body, diving at her head close enough to tangle their talons in her hair and rip chunks from her scalp. Susanna lay still, ignoring the pain that demanded she move, demanded she defend herself against the onslaught. Harder still was ignoring the way Jack was calling out to her, asking if she was all right, how badly she was hurt.

"Just stay put!" she yelled. "If we ignore them, they'll settle and it'll be OK. Just… don't open your eyes yet. Not when they're so crazed. Jack?" No answer. "Jack, tell me you hear me! Tell me you understand!"

It took a moment to come, a moment which sorely tested Susanna's determination to keep her eyes shut and her face covered, but Jack's strained "All right" reached her over the cacophony coming from the wraiths.

Susanna waited. She forced herself to breathe deeply and evenly. Counted to a hundred and then the same backwards. Still, it seemed like the wraiths weren't giving up. They'd been close, the ambush stunning her enough to drop her focus. They'd drawn her blood, and now they were desperate to taste it. The lull in ferocity that Susanna was waiting for might never come.

But she couldn't take Jack across the lake like this. Though she'd checked on him often enough to know that he was still there, that he was all right, she could hear little pants and gasps. She knew he was terrified. That he was frustrated and angry he couldn't protect her, help her. If they went out on the water, his own emotions would be enough to toss them into a storm the little wooden boat couldn't handle. The creatures that lived beneath, that skulked and waited in the deep, wouldn't have to do anything. Jack would doom himself.

"Jack," Susanna called. "Sing me a song."

Again, he made her wait for a response. Then it came.

"What?!"

"A song," Susanna repeated. "Sing something for me." She waited, but nothing happened. "Do that one I like, the one about the boy on a train."

"Seriously?!" Jack's tone dripped incredulity.

"Yes," Susanna replied. "Seriously." She was no singer, but she did her best to belt out the opening couple of lines.

Mercifully, Jack took over after that, and Susanna just listened, trying to pretend that the wraiths didn't exist, that Jack's 'life' wasn't dangling precariously over the abyss. Because Jack had a beautiful voice. It had taken him a long time to reveal that to her, and he'd been hideously embarrassed, but he'd taught Susanna several songs that he knew anyway. And this one was her favourite.

She joined in with the chorus, the lyrics not as uplifting as usual, but hopefully doing the job of giving Jack an anchor, something to focus on other than the fact that he very likely might die.

The song ended and Susanna quickly prompted, "Another."

She thought she caught a grumbled complaint – something about being 'off her head' – but another song soon started up and Susanna was sure that Jack's voice was stronger, the tremble fading away. He sang about a man, a rambler, and the woman who waited behind for him. It was a beautiful song, one Susanna hadn't heard before, and it almost brought her to tears. She tried to listen hard to the lyrics, to remember them.

If she could, she'd sing it to herself in the future. Something to remember Jack by.

"OK," Susanna said when he was finished, the words serving to steady her now more than him. "OK, keep your eyes closed. We're going to feel our way to the boat. We don't need to see to get it in the water."

Susanna wasn't sure, but she thought the wraiths might be less demented, less angry, as if the music had soothed them as well. Do they recognise the music? she wondered, but just as quickly she dismissed the idea. There was nothing human left in the wraiths.

It didn't matter anyway. It was time to move.

"And what are we going to do then?" Jack demanded. "Don't tell me you're going to row with your eyes shut?"

"One problem at a time," Susanna snapped.

She froze, halfway to her feet, and drew in a deep breath. She needed to stay cool. *They* needed to stay cool.

Her searching fingers found the rough, uneven wood of the boat, small splinters slicing into her skin as she ran her hands along the prow, looking for good handholds but really just centring herself. Once she was sure that she wouldn't be distracted by the wraiths, she opened her eyes and focused hard on the bleached silvery-grey wood. Taking a deep breath, she leaned back and heaved. The boat skidded several feet then Susanna had to stop and catch her breath before preparing for another pull.

"Here," Jack said, his shoulder brushing past her as he moved to the back of the boat and put both hands on it. "Let me help."

Together, they dragged and pushed the boat out of the shed and along the beach a short way before shoving it back down towards the shore.

"Get in," Susanna told Jack. "You don't want to stick your feet in that. I'll push the boat the last little bit. It'll be easy enough now."

She didn't want to put her feet in that oozing, oily liquid either, but they had to get the boat afloat one way or another.

Jack didn't argue, climbing inside, but she noticed that his movements were stiff and stilted, as if he wasn't at home in his body. He kept his face carefully blank, but she could feel the tension vibrating off him.

"Find something to stare at," she advised. "Out on the water, it's going to be harder to ignore the wraiths."

He did find something to stare at: her. His grey eyes fixed on her face like she was the one thing tethering him to life (which, she supposed, she was) and Susanna grimaced, a little uncomfortable with the close scrutiny. She didn't want Jack to catch her own nerves, her own hesitation. He needed to stay as calm as possible.

Please, Susanna thought, *please don't let me have to go swimming*.

She shoved, hard, and the little rowing boat sliced into the gloopy, tar-like water. She had one foot in the stuff – which was hot against her ankle instead of freezing like it should be – when she felt the boat begin to glide freely, the lake supporting its weight. Not wanting to walk any further in, she vaulted, landing with a thump into the boat and making it rock wildly.

Jack let out a wordless protest, flinging his hands out to grip the edges.

"Sorry," Susanna muttered. She took her seat but ignored the waiting oars. "It's all right," she said. "We're fine. We'll just let the boat settle and then we'll get going."

The boat had already settled; it was Jack Susanna was worried about. He was bone white and looked like he was going to throw up. He needed to calm down – Susanna did not want to see what a storm looked like in the real wasteland.

Surprisingly, the wraiths didn't follow them out onto the water. Susanna couldn't understand it – there was nothing holding them back, no barrier that she could see – but they remained on the shore. When she risked a glance over her shoulder to look at them, she saw the whole horde that had been lurking in the boathouse, waiting to ambush them, darting to and fro, obviously agitated but unwilling – or unable – to cross the shoreline onto the open water.

"Jack!" she gasped. "Look!"

It went completely against the advice she'd given him thus far, but Susanna was staring right at the wraiths – she almost felt as if she locked eyes with one or two of them – and they still weren't coming after the boat.

"I don't think they can cross the water," she said. "I don't understand it, but I can't think of any other explanation."

"Is it not like that normally?" Jack asked.

"I don't know," Susanna answered honestly. "I've never encountered wraiths on the lake before. It's always too early in the day; the light traps them."

Of course, there were other things to encounter on the lake – or more specifically *under* it – but Susanna thought it was best not to mention those. Jack was shaky enough as it was.

"Shall we go?" Jack asked. He was fidgety, still not comfortable looking directly at the creatures as they wove along the shoreline. "I mean, it's not going to take them too long to realise the lake's circular, is it? They can just go round."

That was a point. Galvanised, Susanna reached forward and grasped the oars. They were down by her feet and for a second she paused, reached out to touch the toe of her shoe – the one that had been in the lake. It should be wet, yes, but not covered in… Susanna pulled her hand away and stared at her fingertips, rubbed them together. An oily, foul-smelling coating clung to her skin.

The lake was not simply water here in the real wasteland.

"Let's go," she said, to herself more than Jack. It didn't matter what the lake was made of, so long as neither of them needed to go in. And Susanna fully intended to stay in the boat.

She manhandled the oars into position and, after a bit of fussing to get the angle of the paddle right, she started to row.

"No, that's fine," she said, already slightly out of breath and sweating heavily under the burning sun. "I don't need any help. Honestly."

"What?" Jack jerked his head towards her, pulling his eyes away from the bubbling blackness beneath them. He stared at her for a moment, lost, then he coloured and swallowed thickly. "Oh, sorry…" He reached out, as if to take the oars from her, then hesitated. "I don't actually know how to row," he admitted. "I might capsize us. Didn't you say—" He peeked at her hopefully, "didn't you say it was your job to row across?"

Susanna laughed, the sound more a release of tension than anything else. The relief of not having to concentrate on her every glance was heady and she felt slightly off-balance – although that could be the rocking of the boat.

"It's fine," she said, then, more seriously, "Don't do that, though. Stare at the water. It can be… mesmerising."

And there was always the chance that he'd see something lurking under there. Something to freak him out. Susanna needed him calm. Cool.

"I spy with my little eye," she said suddenly.

"What?" Jack blinked at her. Then he grinned. "I spy? Seriously? There isn't much to spy around here. All right, I spy with my little eye something beginning with O."

"Oars?" Susanna guessed.

Jack gaped at her, eyes wide with exaggerated shock. "Wow. I can't believe you got it right. Out of all the possibilities."

"I spy with my little eye, something beginning with S," Susanna shot back.

"Smart-arse?"

Dammit. How'd he get that? Susanna's irritation was obviously plain on her face because Jack laughed.

"I've got a much better game," he said. "Ever played 'I've never'?"

Susanna shook her head. Her rowing had slowed and, if it wasn't so hot, it might actually be quite peaceful out on the lake. A quick glance behind her told her that the wraiths weren't as smart as Jack thought, still hadn't worked out that they could race round the edge and be waiting for them on the other side.

"It's simple," he said. "I say something I've never done and if you have, well, usually you have to drink—"

"Just drink?"

"Something alcoholic," Jack clarified.

"Are you old enough for this game?" Susanna asked tartly.

"I've never played it," Jack admitted, explaining why it didn't ring a bell to Susanna: she had his memories, after all. Memories which *did* include underage drinking – though that had been a recent development. "Anyway, we'll just say that if you haven't done it, you score a point. First one to ten wins."

"All right." It was surreal, this peaceful moment, but Susanna wanted it to last as long as possible; she didn't have much time left to make memories with Jack. Plus, since she had knowledge of everything he'd done in his life cached in a corner of her mind, it should be easy to win.

"You go first," she said. Might as well give him a fighting chance.

"I've never…" he tilted his head at her, watching her with careful calculation, "eaten shellfish."

"Point to me!" Susanna crowed. She rolled her eyes at Jack. "I didn't eat food until I went through with you, so I've only had what you fed me."

"And that certainly wasn't shellfish!" Jack laughed. "Damn, I didn't think of that. Your turn."

Susanna dipped her oars and pulled, but gently, barely propelling them forward. "I've never… puked."

She'd seen it, countless times in people's memories, and it seemed gross. Regurgitating half-digested food, some of it coming out of their noses. Yuck!

"Everybody's puked!" Jack protested.

"Not me. Remember my limited eating experiences? Hard to puke when there's nothing in your stomach."

Jack considered her shrewdly. "I don't think I thought this game through."

"You want to give up?"

"No!" He folded his arms, looked thoughtfully out towards the shore.

Perfect, Susanna thought. *Just perfect.* He was relaxed and composed, not thinking about the wraiths or the deep, deep water or anything that might cause a sudden tempest to sweep up and topple them into the lake.

"Hmmm," he drawled. "I've never worn a bra!" He grinned triumphantly.

"Yes you have!" Susanna shot back. "You traded clothes with a girl at a party, bra and all, for a dare. Don't you remember? She was wearing a pink chiffon blouse and a white mini skirt." Susanna smirked. "You looked particularly fetching in her shoes."

Jack looked poleaxed and Susanna's grin faltered. "I forget," he said quietly, "I forget that you have my memories."

She didn't know what to say. She should never have told Jack that, but he'd guessed, really. One long night in that first safe house, when he'd turned to her and asked how she'd known to be Sammy, Susanna had been at a loss what to tell him. Jack found the truth in her silence.

Still, Susanna didn't think the full extent of what that meant had dawned on him until now.

"I'm sorry," she told him. "I can't help it."

A slight nod that told her he understood... but that didn't make it any better. Susanna couldn't blame him; if Jack's memories were hers, she wouldn't want anyone else to see them either.

A wind crept up, lifting the hair that hung, lank and sweaty, around her face. Susanna suddenly realised that she didn't feel as hot as she had before – the air was suffocating rather than burning, blistering – and a glance upwards revealed ugly black clouds skidding across the umber sky.

Shit.

"Is it my turn?" she asked desperately.

"You know what," Jack replied, not looking at her, "I don't think I want to play any more. You win."

"Jack," Susanna pleaded. "Look I'm sorry, I—"

Something thumped the bottom of the boat.

"What was that?" Jack's eyes slammed into Susanna's, wide with sudden fear. That was *not* better than the stomach-churning mix of shame and discomfort in his eyes that had killed their game. The wind picked up again, rocking the little boat, but Susanna knew the change didn't register with Jack, because whatever was beneath them thumped again – harder this time.

"It's OK," Susanna croaked to Jack, because he was teetering on the edge of panic. It wasn't OK, though, and she knew Jack wasn't fooled, particularly when she changed her grip on the oars and started pulling through the water with all her strength.

She heaved and tugged and strained the muscles in her back, arms and legs, but they were barely moving faster. What had been a gentle sighing of lapping water was now a frothing, tumultuous rollercoaster of waves. The boat thumped twice more, the first a shove to the side which seemed an attempt to overturn the vessel and the second a hard, sharp punch that cracked one of the boards in the hull. Both Susanna and Jack stared hard at the splintered fissure but no water poured in. This time.

"Faster," Jack rasped. "We need to go faster!"

"I'm trying!" Susanna panted. "Jack, try to calm down. If you're calm, the water will calm."

"I *am* calm," Jack argued, not sounding calm at all. "I don't think—" he paused as another thump rocked them, "I don't think that's me!"

No, that wasn't him. That was something else – something new. Susanna had been forced to dive into the lake countless times as she ferried souls, and she'd fought the creatures that lurked in the water each and every time. They were wraiths, but sleeker, slicker. Like eels, they wound round their victims and pulled them down and down until…

But this was no water wraith. They were small, attacked in numbers. Whatever was beneath them seemed to have the power to smash their little boat to pieces.

Tug. Heave. Pull.

Tug. Heave. Pull.

Susanna concentrated on the rhythm, rowing as hard as she could, but her eyes she kept fixed on Jack. He sat in the middle of the little bench, his arms stretched out so that he could grip the boat on each side, anchoring himself. His grip was white-knuckled, his jaw clenched tight. He was staring at her, but Susanna thought he wasn't really seeing. Instead he seemed to be held in stasis, just waiting for the next—

Thump!

This time the rear of the boat lifted up, so much Susanna thought she was going to topple overboard. Letting out a little scream, she dropped the oars and reached out, grabbing Jack's thigh with one hand and the side of the boat with the other.

The boat slammed back down and she dropped with it, landing hard on her knees, her face full of Jack's T-shirt.

She scrambled, trying to right herself, but she was too slow. The oars ripped free and disappeared.

"No!" she screamed.

"They didn't fall," Jack whispered, utter terror in his voice. "They didn't fall, something grabbed them. What the hell is under us?!"

"I don't know," Susanna cried. She was panicking now, because they were sitting ducks. Without the oars, they were stranded. The only way off the water, the only way to reach the 'safety' of the shore, was to—

"Susanna, I can't swim," Jack reminded her. He looked like he was hanging on to his sanity by a thread, fear threatening to turn him mindless. Susanna wanted to say something to him, to make it all right, but she felt helpless.

They were stuck.

Another bone-jarring thump from beneath them, hitting right on the already fractured plank. It couldn't handle the pressure, snapping in half. Susanna stared down at the bottom of the boat in horror, watching as water started bubbling up.

They were going to sink.

"Jack," she said, "we need to—"

"No!" He didn't even let her get the words out. "No, no I can't, Susanna. I can't!"

"I'll help you." She stood, her foot splashing when she took a step forward, but Jack scuttled back out of reach. His quick, frantic movements unsettled the boat and Susanna crouched as they tilted and—

"Jack!"

Something erupted out of the water. Not an arm; a tentacle? Susanna didn't know what the hell it was, but it wrapped around one of Jack's arms… and pulled. Jack was wrenched backwards, his free hand reaching desperately for any kind of grip on the boat, but his searching fingers failed to find purchase.

Between one heartbeat and the next, he was gone.

"No!" Susanna screamed. "No, no, no. Jack!"

The water was black and turbulent. It roiled and rolled.

Susanna didn't even think about it. She threw herself over the side, plunging into the glutinous depths.

It burned. That barely registered, though. Susanna pulled herself through the water, its oily consistency making every sweep of her arm, every kick of her leg, that much harder. Where was he? Where was Jack? Where was the creature?

They had to be here, they had to.

Her words to Jack – the ones she should never have said – echoed in her brain. *I promise, Jack. I'll get you through this. I swear it.* She wouldn't break her promise, she wouldn't.

Where was he?

Susanna's hands found nothing but the thick, viscous water. Her eyes saw nothing but the dark. Whispering shadows sliced through the gloom, but Susanna ignored them. The wraiths were nothing. They could only hurt her, hold her down here till her lungs screamed. She couldn't die, but losing Jack would break her.

Susanna's head tore through the surface, dragged in one, two, three breaths, then dived again. He had to be here, he had to be. She refused to believe otherwise.

The water was so, so deep. She swam down as far as she could, but she didn't reach the bottom. She twisted left and right, forced her eyes open even though whatever was polluting the water felt like acid. Nothing. Nowhere.

No. No, please!

Susanna surfaced once more. The water was quiet now, the only violence her flailing movements as she rotated, blinking the foetid drops from her eyes, scouring for any kind of ripple, any kind of sign.

Nothing.

"Jack!" she screamed. "Jack!"

The wraiths answered her. She could hear them all the way from the shore, hissing and cawing. Shrieking. It sounded like laughter.

Like they knew Jack was gone and they were mocking her.

"No!" Susanna yelled. She'd swallowed water and her throat felt raw, her stomach ready to hurl. If it would bring Jack back, Susanna would welcome the sensation. "Jack, where are you?"

Hauling in as deep a breath as possible, Susanna jackknifed on the surface, plunging into the darkness, but even as she did so, the black started to bleed into grey. The water lost its burn and became cool, lighter than air. The real wasteland was fading; the hell that Susanna had wished herself out of a hundred, a thousand times was slipping away.

Susanna knew what that meant.

"No," she whispered, finding herself on her hands and knees in a vastness of white. "No, please. Jack! Jack!"

Unable to rise, to face whatever new world, new soul, awaited her, Susanna dropped her head into her hands and wept.

CHAPTER 15

She had a stitch in her side and her legs were burning, but Dylan barely noticed. Her every thought was focused on Tristan running in front of her, and it took everything she had to keep up with him. Whenever he pulled ahead, the pain of their stretched bond reverberated around her body, and she had to force herself to pump her legs and pick up speed. Tristan reached their building a good few metres ahead of her, but Dylan was grateful. By the time she careered down the little path that led to the front door, Tristan had it unlocked and she was able to barrel straight through to the stairs.

They were nearly the death of her, but she used the handrail to haul herself up each step, each flight. By the time she'd reached their landing, though, Tristan was inside the flat. Dylan paused, leaning heavily on the railing, and stared at the open front door. Stars were exploding in front of her eyes and she thought she might topple over if she left the safety of the banister. She did it anyway, wobbling across the landing into the flat.

"Tristan?" she gasped out. "Tristan, where are you?"

He appeared a moment later, a silhouette at the end of the hallway. His hands were clenched into fists, but because of the light streaming in from the living room behind him, she couldn't see his face. She felt it, though, the ominous atmosphere that shrouded the flat. Something had happened, something bad.

"Is it here?" she whispered, lingering near the door, afraid to move. "Is the Inquisitor here?"

Tristan shook his head slowly and Dylan sagged against the wall with relief. That seemed to spur Tristan into motion and he walked down the hallway towards her. His steps were slow, measured. Reluctant.

"What is it?" Dylan asked. "What's wrong?"

Tristan didn't answer. He didn't say anything until he'd closed the remaining distance between them. Then he reached out for her. "Dylan—"

Something in the way he said her name had her dodging back, out of reach. He was being hesitant with her, careful. That frightened Dylan.

"What's wrong?" she repeated. She shifted to the side slightly, trying to see further into the flat, but Tristan blocked her. "What is it?" she demanded. "What are you hiding?"

"Dylan—" Tristan gently took hold of her hands and tried to ease her backwards. "Let's go and sit out on the step for a little bit, OK? We'll just sit and—"

"No!" Dylan wrenched herself away from him. She set her feet and stared at him, willing him to see her determination. "Tell me what's wrong. Has the Inquisitor been here?"

A slow nod. Tristan's face was like stone, except for his eyes. They were pained, full of sympathy, of pity. Not for himself, she realised. For her.

"What has it done? Has it done something to the flat?" No, as soon as she said it, Dylan knew that wasn't right. Tristan wouldn't act like that if it was only things, only belongings…

"Mum! Dad!" She tried to explode forwards, her thoughts turning into one single, panicked scream, but Tristan was there, in the way. Blocking her. "No." She shoved at him. "Move! Move!

Mum!" She pushed and shoved and kicked at Tristan. "Dad!"

She was dimly aware of a door opening in the landing behind her, but it didn't matter who came out, what they said. All that mattered was finding her parents and—

Tristan cursed quietly and then he was helping and restraining her both as he eased her down the hallway a little so that he could close the front door. Dylan took advantage the moment he took one hand off her to slide the lock across, twisting free of his hold and falling down the hallway.

There was nobody in the living room, and nothing amiss.

She turned to her parents' bedroom, put her hand on the doorknob.

"Dylan, stop." Tristan's hand covered hers, held her there. It wasn't forceful this time, wasn't imprisoning her in his grip. For some reason, that was the thing that made Dylan pause, made her stop.

Cold dread settled in her stomach and she was afraid to open the door, afraid of what waited for her.

"Please," Tristan whispered. "You don't need to see."

He was wrong. She did. She did need to see.

When Dylan had been beyond the line and Eliza, the old woman, had told her how to get back to the wasteland, back to Tristan, she'd said that anyone could do it, they just had to have the strength, the bravery, to open the door. To know that they were risking their lives, their very souls, by going back there. Dylan had stood in front of her chosen door and thought she'd have to summon every ounce of her courage, to stand there for hours, searching within herself, but to her surprise it had opened easily in her hand.

This door would open if she simply turned the handle, there was no magic holding it closed, but Dylan found she couldn't do it. She couldn't make her fingers squeeze, her wrist turn.

Tristan tried to lead her away. "Let's go and sit down in the living roo—"

Dylan opened the door.

Her parents were lying in bed. They looked like they were sleeping, James on his side, Joan cuddled into his front, both of them facing Dylan where she stood in the doorway. They could be resting, taking a nap, except for the stillness in the room. The quiet. The fact that the duvet wasn't shifting with the rise and fall of each breath.

Dylan took a step inside. She felt Tristan behind her, his body almost touching hers, standing with her in silent support.

There was no blood, no claw marks or gaping holes that would indicate a wraith attack. Their expressions were peaceful, their skin unmarked. Dylan could see their hands, just visible beneath the duvet, were entwined together. Her mum's wedding ring glinted slightly in the low light from the bedside lamp. It was like someone had snapped a picture of a perfect, loving moment.

A picture, unmoving and immobile. A life together, frozen.

Dylan wasn't aware of her legs collapsing beneath her, but Tristan caught her round the middle. He lowered her gently to the floor and folded himself down behind her, his arms wrapped around her, his chest against her back. It seemed like his embrace was the only thing holding her together. She floated somewhere outside her body. Screaming, she was screaming – but that couldn't be right, because her lungs didn't have air to breathe. The sound echoed in her head, though, reverberating on and on and on.

They were gone. Her mum and dad were gone. No, not gone. Dead. Joan and James, her parents, her *family*, were dead.

"Why?" she wheezed, still unable to haul in air. "Why would

it do this? Why?" She tried to go on, to give voice to the questions that were racing round her brain, but all that came out was a wordless keening, like an animal caught in a trap.

She didn't know how long she sat there. Time lost meaning as Dylan drowned. Grief overwhelmed her, until she was nothing but her tears. Tristan kept up a steady stream of words, muttering quietly in her ear, but she had no idea what he was saying. It didn't penetrate. Nothing could.

After a while she realised Tristan was trying to get her to stand. She didn't protest: she didn't care what happened to her or where she went, so she let him manoeuvre her up onto her feet. Pins and needles stabbed at her legs as blood rushed back into her lower limbs but the burn was nothing. Insignificant. She stood where she was, staring blindly, until Tristan started urging her to turn. She did so, unresistingly, until her mum and dad slipped out of sight. Then she came to life in a blaze.

She tore free of Tristan and stumbled to the bed. From here she could see the lines on Joan's face, the slight peppering of grey at her dad's temples. Tiny markers of age, signs of a life half-lived.

It wasn't fair.

"Why?!" she asked again, this time in a voice edging on a shout, edging on hysteria. "Why would the Inquisitor do this?" She whirled to face Tristan, who looked like he couldn't decide whether to be relieved that she'd resurfaced from the dwam that had gripped her or nervous of the heat in her eyes.

He regarded her solemnly, his throat working. "I don't know," he said.

"No!" she said, the word a strangled scream. "It's isn't right, it isn't fair! It can't, it can't take them!"

"Angel—" Tristan advanced on her, his hands reaching, but he stopped before he was close enough to draw her in to him.

"They're *mine!*" Dylan shouted. Grief was being subsumed by a haze of red rage inside her mind. "Mine! It can't just come in and take them. It can't!" Her whole body was shaking with adrenaline, with fury. She screamed, hands clutching at her head, fingers tunnelling in her hair and gripping, pulling. Twisting until it hurt.

"Dylan." Tristan's hands were on her then, tugging at her wrists. "Don't. Please don't."

She jerked away from him. "Is it still here?" she demanded. "The Inquisitor, can you sense it? Is it here? Is it watching?" She tore her eyes from Tristan and looked up, to the ceiling and the sky beyond. "Can you hear me, you f—"

"Dylan!" Tristan barked her name, drowning out Dylan's curse.

"Do you sense it?" she demanded again. She waited, pulling in short, sharp breaths as she fought the urge to start tearing things about, smashing things, breaking things. Destroying anything she could get her hands on.

Her back was to her mum and dad and she needed to keep it that way. She couldn't look at them and hold on to her anger, and she needed her anger to stay on her feet. She needed her anger to keep breathing.

Tristan closed his eyes and she watched a tiny crease appear between his brows as he concentrated. Suddenly he snapped them open and Dylan didn't even need to ask. She knew.

"Show yourself!" she screamed. She tore past Tristan and into the living room. She stopped in the middle of the floor space, needing the room because she felt like the walls were squeezing in on her. "I know you're here!" she yelled.

"Dylan!" Tristan sounded afraid. Dylan didn't care. She'd say worse than that if it would get the Inquisitor here, in front of them. It was damned well going to give her parents back! She and Tristan had done *everything* it asked of them; it had no right to punish them like this. To punish her mum and dad, who'd done *nothing*!

"I'm talking to you! Show yourself!"

Tristan blindsided her, wrapping her in his arms from behind and clapping a hand over her mouth.

"Dylan, I'm sorry," he breathed. "I'm sorry, but you can't do that! It can send us back to the wasteland. It can separate us, make you a wraith. It could make me disappear, Dylan!"

She didn't care. Fury and heartache boiled up inside her, making her irrational and nihilistic. "Show yourself!"

Tristan's grip on her suddenly tightened. He drew her back against him, imprisoning her with his arms. His entire body was strung tight. "It's here," he hissed. "The Inquisitor is here!"

Just like that, the fire snuffed out within Dylan. Her anger disappeared and all she was left with was pain. Pain, and fear.

"Where?" she whispered.

She didn't see it… then she did. Between one blink and the next it stood before them. It looked exactly as Dylan remembered: the slight blur that made it hard to fully focus on, the eyes that seemed to see right down to her soul. A creature of nightmares, it exuded menace. It didn't move, just stood there, watching and waiting.

It was almost impossible to break the silence, but Dylan forced her mouth open with grim determination. She would fix this. Her parents would not pay for what she'd done.

"Why?" she said.

She felt Tristan's tension behind her, knew he wanted her to exercise caution, but Dylan needed answers.

The Inquisitor didn't speak, it just inclined its head in a slight tilt, as if it didn't understand the question.

"Why would you take them? They didn't do anything!"

The Inquisitor didn't seem fazed by the heat in her voice. It considered her, then answered calmly, "I took them because of you."

Dylan gaped.

"We did everything you asked of us!" she said. "We upheld the bargain." She shook her head, both in denial of the Inquisitor's words and the tears that wanted to start up again. "We closed the holes, we killed the wraiths. We made a deal with you and we haven't broken it! You had no right to take them!"

"You have not fulfilled your bargain," the Inquisitor disagreed.

"But we have!" she shouted.

"Dylan," Tristan murmured warningly, then, to the Inquisitor, "Is this because of the wraith that got through? The one that killed the animals? Because it's dead. We couldn't find a tear in the veil, but the wraith is dead."

"Not by your hands," the Inquisitor said mildly.

"Please," Tristan pleaded, echoing the desperation Dylan felt. "Don't do this to Dylan's parents."

"It's done."

"But you can undo it," Dylan gasped. "You can bring them back!"

It had to be able to. It had to. She couldn't accept anything else.

"I'll do *anything*," she said.

The Inquisitor stared at her for a long moment, as if considering it, then it slowly shook its head. "You have upset the balance," it told them. "There is no tear in the veil, no other ferryman has tried to come through with their soul, but the wasteland is not holding. This is because of you. A wraith managed to claw its way through, an entire vehicle of children was swallowed by the wasteland and thrown to the mercy of the wraiths. And that is not all. The safe houses are failing, a ferryman was lost amongst the mists." For the first time Dylan heard emotion in the Inquisitor's voice. Fear: she heard fear there. "You have upset the balance and it is my job to reset the equilibrium. I made a bargain with you, and I will hold to it. But if your souls are to be allowed to remain here, then I must take two others with me. I chose." It looked towards the bedroom where the bodies of Dylan's parents lay.

"But why them?" Dylan gasped. "You could have taken anyone! Murderers or paedophiles. You didn't need to take my mum and dad, they were good!"

She should feel ashamed, she realised, trying to barter other souls to be taken in her parents' stead, but had been serious when she'd told the Inquisitor she would do anything.

"You would steal the life of another for your gain?" the Inquisitor asked. It shook its head. "No."

"Please," Dylan begged. "Please, there has to be something."

"There is only one choice," the Inquisitor said. "Your parents or yourselves."

She didn't give herself time to think.

"We'll do it," she said. "We'll go back to the wasteland in their place."

The Inquisitor fixed her with its unnerving gaze, reading her. She let it. It could look right down to the bottom of her soul and it would see the same thing: absolute resolve.

"Take us," she told it.

CHAPTER 16

There was a carpet beneath her knees. Susanna was dimly aware of it and she knew that meant she was in someone's house. Someone's world. She'd been given a new soul to ferry. Something deep within her was urging her up, commanding her to get on with her duty, but she ignored it.

The urge became pain. Her nerves spasmed as tiny electric jolts shocked her system, until her whole body felt like it was in agony. Still Susanna fought.

She'd lost him. She'd promised Jack she'd see him safely across the wasteland, and she'd lost him. Susanna sobbed, one hand clutching at her chest as if that would help ease the ache in her heart.

She had failed him.

"I'm sorry, Jack," she whispered, over and over again. "I'm so, so sorry."

He didn't answer. He'd never answer her again.

"Dylan? Dylan, is that you crying? Are you all right?" The voice was slightly muffled, as if it was coming from another room, but the name was enough to penetrate Susanna's paralysis. She lifted her head and saw she was in a child's bedroom. A teenager, she amended, seeing the posters on the wall and the smattering of make-up on a dresser. It wasn't a big room, but there was enough space for a bed against the wall, a desk and the dresser. There was a full-length mirror embedded in a narrow wardrobe and the door hadn't closed properly, a piece of purple sleeve holding it slightly ajar and angling the mirror just enough that Susanna could see her reflection.

She was a pitiful sight, on her knees with her hands tensed into claws, gripping her thighs; her shoulders hunched, curling protectively in on themselves. But it was her face that really shocked her. Susanna didn't get a lot of chance to examine her reflection in a mirror, but she'd never seen herself like this. It was still her face; she hadn't undergone a change, but her nose was running and her cheeks were blotchy. Her eyes were bloodshot and there were dark circles under them, like bruises. Her hair clung to her face in messy tendrils. It should still be soaked from the lake, but as the wasteland had disappeared, her hair and clothes had dried.

She looked like hell, like she'd had her soul torn from her body. Susanna wasn't sure that that wasn't true.

The door opened and a man's voice – the same one that had spoken before – called, "Dylan?"

He stopped dead in the doorway as soon as he saw Susanna. Middle-aged, he looked fit and healthy, grey just starting to tease his temples. James. The details of the new soul began to trickle into Susanna's mind as the haze of grief started to fade. His name was James and he had a wife, Joan. His daughter, Dylan, lived with them along with her boyfriend—

Susanna's mouth dropped open as she realised who the soul was.

And the surprises kept on coming.

"James? Is it Dylan?" A woman's voice came from down the hall. Joan. "She should still be at school."

James didn't answer her, he just continued to stare at Susanna.

"James?" Joan's face appeared over James's shoulder. She looked a little older than he was, her face thin but drawn with lines. Her eyes were sharp as they landed on Susanna. "Who are you?"

Susanna opened her mouth, but no sound came out.

What was happening? How could this be? It was impossible, for one thing. No ferryman was ever assigned two souls – the wasteland was too dangerous for that; it often took all of Susanna's skill just to keep one soul safe. So many times, she hadn't been enough. Like today…

She cut that thought off, concentrating on the puzzle in front of her.

There were two souls, and Susanna knew them. They were Dylan's parents. Which meant – she glanced around the room again – this was Dylan's bedroom. What had happened…?

Where the souls' final memories should be was a curious blank spot. Susanna had never encountered anything like it before.

"What are you doing in Dylan's room?" Joan asked. Her tone had a little more edge this time, was laced with suspicion, and she tried to squeeze around James. He held her back with an arm. He still hadn't spoken, was gazing at Susanna with something that hinted at understanding… though that couldn't be right.

"Are you a friend of Dylan's from school?" Joan eyed the room like Dylan would magically appear. "Where is she?"

"I—" Susanna didn't know what to say. She should have transformed into Dylan, she knew – that was the obvious guise, the tie that held the two souls together – but it wasn't as if she'd fought against the transformation. It simply hadn't happened.

"Are you a friend of Tristan's?" James asked quietly.

Shocked, Susanna focused her attention on his solemn face and nodded slowly.

It seemed to be the answer he was expecting, but not the one he wanted. Something close to despair moved behind his eyes. He turned to look at the woman beside him and the emotion deepened until Susanna could feel it, squeezing her already broken heart.

"You know Tristan?" Susanna asked.

It was a stupid question. She knew he knew Tristan; she had his memories. Both of their memories. James nodded.

"Do you… do you know what he is?"

They couldn't, surely they couldn't, but there was something strange happening here.

"What? What are you talking about?" Joan asked sharply. "You still haven't answered my questions!"

He knew something, but Dylan's mother was completely in the dark, Susanna decided. She stood up, her legs wobbly beneath her.

"My name is Susanna," she told them. The truth: this time she would lead with the truth. "I'm a ferryman, like Tristan is. Was," she amended. "Our role is to ferry souls across the wasteland, to deliver them beyond. I don't—" She wrinkled her brow, sifting through flashes of memories from both their lives, but there was still that mysterious missing piece of the puzzle from their final moments. "I don't know how you came to be here, but if you're seeing me – and I'm seeing you – then…" She grimaced. "Then your souls have departed your bodies."

"You mean we're dead." James said. It wasn't a question. There was no stunned surprise. Instead, he seemed resigned, like she'd confirmed his suspicions.

"Yes," she replied. "That's what I mean."

There was a moment of silence before Joan made a noise that was half laughing snort, half derisive exclamation.

"What on earth?" she said. "What is this nonsense?" She fixed

Susanna with a beady look. "What are you doing here and where is Dylan?"

Susanna considered her then felt inside herself, to the core of power ferrymen held that allowed them to manipulate souls, to ensure their compliance – and therefore their safety. It was early in the journey to be digging into her box of tricks, and she'd never had to try to sway two souls before, but—

"Joan," James murmured, turning to his wife and taking her hands.

Susanna paused, pulling back the words infused with compulsion. They tingled on the tip of her tongue, waiting to be unleashed.

"Just listen to what she has to say."

"But—" Another splutter. "Did you hear her? It's nonsense!"

"It's the truth," Susanna said quietly, adding just the tiniest trace of push. She sensed James was going to do most of the work for her.

"James," Joan appealed to her husband. "Surely you can't believe this? Look at us, we're still here, in our flat. For goodness' sake, if we'd—"

"Try," Susanna interrupted. "Try to connect with someone. Phone a friend, or speak to someone on the street. Just try."

They didn't really have time for all this delay – the order every ferryman had was to get their soul moving, to start the journey that would only get more perilous the further along the road they travelled. But Susanna knew instinctively that Joan had to accept her fate before they could begin. She needed to acknowledge what had happened to her – even if it didn't fully sink in yet.

"I'm not going to just—"

"Do it, Joan, sweetheart. Call Great Aunt Gladys – you said you needed to anyway."

"James—"

"Just do it, OK?" A hint of steel that had Joan bristling until James softened it with a quiet, "Please."

Looking like she was humouring a couple of lunatics, Joan whipped out her phone from her cardigan pocket and starting poking at buttons. It was an ancient thing, with a keypad instead of a touch screen, and Susanna chafed at the delay as Joan painstakingly tapped in the number. At last she held the device up to her ear, waiting.

"It's not ringing," she said eventually. "I don't think it's connecting. Maybe I have no signal."

"Use the landline," James suggested. "Dial 999, they have to answer. That'll give you your proof."

Instead of doing as he said, Joan stared at James long and hard.

"Why do you believe her?" she asked.

"I saw something," he told her, eyes full of an old memory. "When I threw Tristan out. It was like... as soon as I separated them he collapsed and Dylan was bleeding and—" James shivered. "There was something holding them together. It reversed when I brought Tristan back to Dylan, and they told me it was the train crash." He shrugged his shoulders. "Something happened – Dylan wasn't the same, and she had Tristan with her. They wouldn't tell me any more than that, said it was dangerous for me to know."

"They were right," Susanna said. She was surprised that James had been allowed to know as much as he did. Although, perhaps that went some way to explaining why he was here, in front of her now.

"But—" Joan shook her head, as if in denial of James's words. The dawning horror on her face said that she was starting to believe, however. Then her jaw firmed. "No."

She spun on her heel and stormed down the hall. James followed with Susanna close behind. She reached the door to the living room just as Joan was lifting the handset of the landline telephone. She pressed a single button three times with her thumb then listened, the handset nestled against her face.

Susanna waited for the inevitable, but Joan wasn't going to be defeated that easily. She yanked the phone away from her head and tried again.

"Joan," James said quietly, but she ignored him. "Joan, sweetheart, please."

"No!" She shook her head, tried once more. Her grip on the handset was white-knuckled, her hand shaking slightly. James left his position in the doorway beside Susanna and crossed the room, gently taking the phone from his wife. She let him, and she made no complaints when he drew her into his arms.

"No." Susanna heard her sob into James's shoulder. "No, no, no. It can't be right. It can't!"

Her denials sounded hauntingly like the cries Susanna had choked out just minutes ago and the ferryman had to lock her knees and steel herself against the wave of grief that threatened to take her under once more. Holding onto the doorway, she heard James murmuring into Joan's ear, too low for Susanna to make out. It didn't seem to help, because Joan just sank deeper into his embrace, leaning on him fully, and the handset clattered to the floor.

They stayed that way for a long, long time. Susanna was loath to intrude, but this flat wasn't a safe house, and the wasteland would be unforgiving if they lingered here any longer.

Susanna couldn't fail Dylan's parents the way she'd failed Jack.

"We need to go," she said.

"A minute," James demanded, looking over his shoulder with a reproachful frown.

"No." Susanna stood firm, shaking her head. "You don't understand. We *have* to go. If you have questions, I'll answer them – when we're somewhere safe."

"We're safe right now," James shot back.

"No," Susanna said. "We're not."

Automatically, she drew down inside herself, ready to compel the pair – would it work on two souls at once? However, James saved her once again, drawing back.

"We need some time," he said. "We need a chance to take it in."

"There's no time for that," Susanna said. "We need to go! We're in the wasteland and—"

"What is this 'wasteland'?" James asked.

"Not now," Susanna said, looking him straight in the eye. "I'll answer your questions when we're safe. Please," she grimaced, "we need to *go*."

It didn't seem real, walking out of Dylan's front door and down the steps of her building. Susanna led the way, with James behind her keeping a tight hold of Joan's hand, urging the woman on. Dylan's mum seemed to be in a state of shock, allowing her husband to tug her along like a child, but Susanna had the feeling that it wouldn't last long. Whether she would return to the sharp, suspicious woman Susanna had first met, or whether grief at losing her life – and her daughter – would overwhelm her and drive her to break down again, was still to be seen.

Joan and James's wasteland started innocuously enough. The street they exited onto was wide and lined with red sandstone tenements. There was nobody around. Susanna led them down their street, away from everything that was familiar. The urban landscape continued for a long time. It was eerie and uncomfortable, even for Susanna. She didn't mind wide-open vistas and sweeping landscapes, but the tall buildings made her feel penned in, and the sheer emptiness of all those doors, all those windows, was undeniably creepy.

The two souls walked close enough behind her that she wasn't worried about them disappearing, but far enough back that she couldn't hear what they were saying. Their heads were bent close together every time she glanced back.

"We're not far from the first safe house," she told them, just to break the silence. "After today, we'll be out in the open."

"And that's bad?" James asked.

Susanna shrugged. There wasn't much difference, to be honest. Here the endless empty buildings meant there were countless places for wraiths to hide, but so long as the daylight lasted, they couldn't come out.

It was a relief to have the rules of the wasteland back in place, though she would trade this urban graveyard for the burning sun and swirling sand in a heartbeat if it meant she could have Jack back.

"So long as we're in a safe house before the light fades, it's fine," she said. "We'll have to move faster than we have been, though. We'll have further to go."

With two souls, if they were caught out in the open by the wraiths, there was no chance of Susanna not losing at least one. Maybe both of them.

The first safe house wasn't a house – it was a ground-floor flat in a block of four. It was clean enough, the building nondescript, but still, Susanna couldn't help thinking of Jack, of the first night they'd spent together. She'd had to work so hard to get him this far. A memory of him kissing her, thinking she was his old girlfriend Sammy, barrelled into her mind, along with the conversation they'd had in the safe house only days ago, Jack teasing her about being her first (and only) kiss.

The memories were bittersweet.

James and Joan didn't really seem to take in where they were. They entered the flat, barely glancing around, and then sat on the grubby couch in the handkerchief-sized living room. They huddled close together, Joan holding tight to James's hand.

"We're safe here," Susanna told them. "We just need to stay inside, OK?"

"Why?" James asked.

"What?"

"Why do we need to stay inside?"

Susanna considered him, deciding how flagrant to be with the truth. He'd handled everything incredibly well so far, though.

"There are... creatures out there. We call them wraiths. They... well, they consume souls, until there's nothing left and you become just like them."

James looked at her, long and hard, and then he nodded. "I think I've seen one."

"I... what?" Susanna eyed him askance. "I don't think so, they only exist in the wasteland."

"I've seen one," James repeated. "There was a video online. I showed it to Tristan and he knew what it was. It was—" He shivered in revulsion, and that, more than anything, convinced Susanna that he had actually glimpsed one.

She wanted to ask how, and when; wanted to hound him with details about what he'd seen. But Susanna had learned her lesson: she needed to stop fixating on the real world and instead live in the one she'd been given. The stakes were too high otherwise. Souls depended on her.

Besides, she had access to James's memories. Skimming through, she hunted through James's recent past, but nothing jumped out at her, just more of those curious blank spots, like bits and pieces had been rubbed out.

It was so bizarre.

Taking a chair, Susanna sat and stared out of a window at the gathering dusk. She didn't like this, being outnumbered by the souls. It made her feel unbalanced, strangely vulnerable. James and Joan weren't speaking either, and the silence between the three of them was so heavy it was almost suffocating.

Apparently, Susanna wasn't the only one to feel it.

"I can't do this!" Joan jumped up, drawing the cardigan she wore more tightly around herself and turning to face the door. "I can't stay here. I can't. Dylan is on her own; she'll be so frightened. She needs me."

She took a step towards the exit and Susanna leapt to her feet. She got in front of Joan as James approached her from the back, laying a hand on her shoulder.

"You have to stay inside," Susanna repeated. "I told you, it isn't safe."

"No." Joan shook her head. "No, it doesn't matter what you say to me. My baby needs me, I have to go!"

"Go where?" Susanna asked. "You're not in your world any more! You can't go back!"

Only Susanna now knew that was a lie. A big fat lie that the ferrymen had fed to endless souls, a lie they'd been fed themselves. The souls weren't *allowed* to go back, and that wasn't the same thing at all.

Although... something about Joan and James's flat had seemed off, not quite right. It hadn't really penetrated at the time; Susanna had been too distraught about Jack, and then too thrown by her latest assignment, but now it whispered at her, demanding attention.

The street had been too quiet. The flat, it hadn't been a ghost of the real world: a hairsbreadth to the left, a step out of time. Normally, when Susanna picked up a soul, she could almost feel, almost touch, the real world. It tickled her skin like the faintest breeze.

The air in the flat had been dead, like someone had slammed the door on the real world, as if whoever had taken Joan and James's life had wanted to thrust them deep enough into the wasteland that they'd never reappear.

How did you die? Susanna wondered.

Now wasn't the time to ask, though.

"I have to try," Joan said flatly. "You don't understand, she needs me!"

"I'm sorry," Susanna said. "I really am." The words were sincere, but they still sounded hollow. "If you go out there, that will be the end of you. You lose your chance of ever seeing Dylan again, once her time comes."

"What's she supposed to do, all on her own?" Joan demanded.

Susanna pressed her lips together; she didn't have an answer.

"She's not alone, sweetheart," James put in. "She has Tristan."

"He's just a boy!" Joan shouted. She whirled, standing so that she could keep the two of them in sight and Susanna knew she was gearing herself up for battle. It didn't matter, and in days gone by Susanna would have just let her rage, but she owed Dylan and Tristan. She'd caused trouble for them, and yet they'd helped her. And Tristan had Susanna's loyalty, always.

"He's not just a boy," she told Joan. "He's a ferryman, like me. He's strong, and he's brave. He loves her, he won't let anything happen to her."

"Can he pay bills?" Joan threw back. "Can he keep a roof over their heads? Can he make enough to keep them both fed? Of course he can't!" She tossed her head. "He can't even get a job without ID. I had a hard enough time getting him enrolled in the school! They'll be out on the streets, vulnerable. I. Can't. Stay. Here."

Susanna thought Joan would storm out, that she'd have to run after her, do her best to save the woman from her own stupidity. Instead, Joan crumpled. The scowl melted from her face as tears filled her eyes, and she just dropped right down onto the faded, threadbare carpet and folded in on herself. Sobs wracked her, and to Susanna's shame, she wanted to flee. She'd rather face a swarm of wraiths than stand and listen to Joan cry over her orphaned daughter.

"I'm sorry," Susanna whispered. It wasn't enough, but it was all she could say.

A thought occurred to her as she stood and forced herself to witness Joan's grief: *Was this how Jack's mother felt? Had she stood in a morgue somewhere, hollow and broken? Had she comforted herself by thinking he'd gone on somewhere, to a better place?*

"Joan, come on. Up you get." James's voice was gentle. He bent down and swept her up in his arms, glancing at Susanna before carrying his wife into the single bedroom of the safe house. He closed the door on Susanna, but not before she saw that his eyes were just as bleak, just as pain-filled, as Joan's.

She was alone.

She should be relieved. Grateful. But Joan and James's grief pierced the wall, crept beneath the closed door, finding an echo in Susanna's heart where she still bled for Jack.

She wished for one brief moment that she could go back to who she'd been – that she could be the cold, cruel ferryman who'd watched Michael, and countless souls before him, break down and cry, throw things and rail, and feel nothing. No pity, no empathy. Just a sense of urgency to get rid of them, to move on to the next.

She wouldn't, though. Even if the chance was offered to her. She owed Jack the pain she was feeling, and she owed it to Dylan and Tristan to grieve for them, for their loss.

Flopping down onto the sofa that Joan and James had vacated, Susanna dropped her head into her hands. Her head was as heavy as her heart, a fierce thumping at her temples impervious to her fingers as they gently massaged. Suppressing her own tears, she slid down until she was lying down, her back up against the cushions. Closing her eyes, she tried to pretend that Jack was there, hugging her. That the cold fabric of the couch was the warmth of his chest, that his arm was draped around her, holding her together.

Before, she'd lived for these quiet moments to herself, had basked in the quiet. The peace. Now, she just felt so very, very alone.

Susanna closed her eyes. Would she drop into one of her 'dreams'? She hoped not, because if she did, she knew exactly what she would see, what she would be forced to relive. Breathing through each hitch in her breath, she concentrated on relaxing her muscles, on inhaling and exhaling… on surviving each moment. Slowly, gradually, her breathing evened out and she drifted.

"Susanna, I can't swim." Jack's voice was thin, frightened.

Another bone-jarring thump from beneath them, hitting right on the already fractured plank. Water, seeping into the boat. Swelling alarmingly fast.

"Jack," she said, "we need to—"

"No!" A terrified shake of his head. "No, no I can't, Susanna. I can't."

"I'll help you." She reached for him, but the boat was tilting and—"Jack!"

Something erupted out of the water. It wrapped around one of Jack's arms… and pulled. Jack wrenched backwards, his free hand reaching desperately for any kind of grip on the boat, but his searching fingers failed to find purchase.

Then he was gone.

"No!" A scream, that went on and on. That came from the depths of Susanna's soul. "No, no, no. Jack!"

The water was black and turbulent. It roiled and rolled.

She didn't even think about it. She threw herself over the side.

Where was he?

Susanna's hands found nothing but the thick, viscous water. Her eyes saw nothing but the dark.

Susanna broke through the surface, dragged in enough air to fill her lungs, dived again. He had to be here, he had to be.

The water was so, so deep.

No. No, please!

Susanna surfaced once more. The lake was calm, a violent contrast to the storm of emotions surging in Susanna.

"Jack!" she screamed. "Jack!"

The wraiths laughed. They laughed at her pain, her panic.

"No!" Susanna yelled. "Jack, where are you?"

She jackknifed on the surface, plunging into the darkness, but even as she did so, the black started to bleed into grey…

CHAPTER 17

Dylan lay quietly in Tristan's arms. They were on the sofa in the living room, the door to Dylan's parents' room firmly closed. It was dark, but neither of them had gotten up to switch on the light. Instead, the room was lit by the glare of the television. It was turned to a sitcom, but Tristan wasn't paying any attention to the actors on the screen and he knew Dylan wasn't either. It was on simply to provide comfort, to cover the silence so that neither of them would have to speak.

They hadn't phoned for an ambulance, or for the police. They hadn't called any of Dylan's family, or knocked on any of the neighbours' doors. They hadn't done anything about the two bodies lying in the flat's master bedroom.

Dylan refused to. They weren't dead, she said. The Inquisitor might have taken their souls – temporarily – but their bodies weren't dead; they were simply waiting for their souls to be returned.

And Dylan was adamant that was going to happen.

She was going to trade her life for theirs; trade Tristan's life, too.

That was why the television was on. Why the silence between them was so thick, so heavy.

The dials of the clock on the wall told Tristan it was well past midnight. They needed to go to bed soon and get some rest, especially if they were going to be thrust into the unforgiving landscape of the wasteland once the Inquisitor returned, but Tristan held off. He knew what he'd see as soon as he closed his eyes: Dylan, begging the Inquisitor to give her parents back. To take her instead. If she'd had her way, they'd already be back in the wasteland. Instead, the Inquisitor had given them the night to think about it, to be sure.

Which meant, unless Tristan convinced Dylan otherwise, he only had mere hours left to hold her and know that they were safe, alive and together. Because once they were in the wasteland, all that would change.

Dylan suddenly sighed and sat up, surprising Tristan, who thought she'd been fading into sleep. She reached over and snagged the remote from the coffee table, muting the television.

"You think I'm making the wrong choice," she said quietly. There was no accusation in her voice, only the hollowness of grief and a hint of disappointment, as if she was upset that Tristan didn't see things the way she did.

"I do," he said. There was no pretending otherwise: he couldn't support anything that would take Dylan away from him. Or anything that would take her life – a life that was just beginning – from her. She'd fought so hard for a second chance; how could she give it up now?

Dylan made a frustrated noise. "It's our fault," she said. "You heard what the Inquisitor said. All these things that have happened, they're because *we've* messed with the balance. *We're* the ones who are responsible, *we're* the ones who should pay the price. Not my parents."

"If you asked them, what choice do you think they would make?" Tristan asked.

"I can't ask them, can I?" Dylan snapped. She caught herself, deliberately pulling in a calming breath. "They didn't get a chance to choose, and that's not fair, but I do."

"They would never choose this." Tristan stared at her, daring her to suggest that her parents, either of them, would ever steal her life so that they could live. She didn't, accepting the truth of his words.

"I won't take their happiness away, Tristan. I won't."

"Do you think they'll be happy, without you?"

"They'll have each other. They deserve a chance to be together. You don't know what it's been like for my mum, being alone all this time."

"I have some idea," Tristan said solemnly.

Dylan opened her mouth, already ready with her next argument, but she paused. Really looked at him for the first time in their conversation.

"I'm sorry," she said at last, her voice cracking. "I offered you a chance at life only to take it away again, but I have to make this choice. Can't you see?"

"You think that's why I'm upset?" Tristan asked, astounded.

Dylan gazed at him, genuinely puzzled, and for the first time it dawned on Tristan that Dylan truly didn't understand the deal the Inquisitor was offering her.

"Do you realise what will happen if we take your parents' place in the wasteland, Dylan?"

"It'll be risky, I know," Dylan agreed. "But you got me to the line once, you can do it again." She reached out and grabbed Tristan's hand. "I have faith in you, you'll get us there. Both of us."

"I would," Tristan choked out.. "I'd get *you* there – and I'd leave you there."

One, two, three heartbeats of silence.

"What?"

She didn't. She really didn't understand the bargain the Inquisitor had offered.

"If we go back to the wasteland, we'll go together." He swallowed. "But we won't *stay* together. I'll be your ferryman, you'll be a soul again. And when we get to the line, I won't be able to cross. You'll have to go on without me."

"No." It was a whisper of denial.

"Yes."

"But—" Dylan shook her head, hair flying across her face. "But it wouldn't do that. Not after everything we've been through."

"It would," Tristan disagreed. "Especially after the trouble we've caused. You said yourself, the problems in the wasteland are our fault."

"You don't know you won't be able to cross over," Dylan argued. "It didn't say—"

"I'm sure," Tristan replied firmly. "So when you make the choice, be clear what you're choosing."

She was quiet for a moment, staring sightlessly at the bright light of the television screen.

"What *I'm* choosing?" she asked carefully.

"Yes." Perhaps it wasn't fair, putting the full weight of the decision on Dylan's shoulders, but it was taking everything Tristan had not to beg, plead, convince, coerce... anything to get Dylan to let them stay here, stay alive. Stay together. He was willing to take her back if that was what she wanted, but he couldn't, wouldn't, do anything to push in her in that direction.

He'd follow her anywhere – and protect her as best as he could – but if she wanted to walk down this path, she had to take the lead.

She took her time, thinking it through. Arguments drifted round Tristan's head, but he held them in. If he tried to sway her, and then later, she regretted the decision...

"I'm sorry," she said eventually. She kept her head turned away from him, staring at the television so that he couldn't see her face. "I'm so sorry, Tristan, but I have to. I can't let them give their lives up for me. I was supposed to die, anyway. If this is the cost of getting a second chance at life, then I don't want it. I know that isn't fair to you—" She broke off, her voice tight and high, and Tristan saw tiny tremors run through her frame. "I brought you with me to give you a chance at life, to give us a chance to be together, and now I'm taking that away. But I *can't* stay here; I can't just carry on, living my life, knowing that they paid with theirs to give me the chance. I couldn't live with myself." She did turn, at last, showing him a face wet with tears. "What if they don't make it? Or what if only one of them does? My mum could become a wraith, or my dad. Can you imagine? My mum, on the other side of the line, alone for God knows how long, maybe for ever if I don't manage the journey when it's my turn." She reached for his hand and squeezed, her eyes boring into his. "They've only just found each other again. They need to have this time. They deserve it."

Don't I deserve it? The question lingered on the tip of his tongue, but he held it in, along with all the other things he was desperate to say. He'd told Dylan it needed to be her decision, and she'd made it.

Now they would both have to live with the consequences.

"All right," he said. "If that's what you want."

"It isn't what I want," Dylan hiccupped, fresh tears trailing down her cheeks. "It's what I have to do." Her lip trembled but she kept on going. "I need you, Tristan. Will you help me?"

What else could he say?

"Yes," he promised. "I'll help you."

Dawn – the last real dawn that they would ever see – came not in a blaze of yellow and orange, but with an ooze of slate grey that slowly lightened until the world was revealed. Tristan watched it from the living room window. Dylan lay on the sofa, watching him. Neither of them had slept, which was stupid. Dylan could feel a heaviness in her limbs, grit in her eyes. They were going to start their journey in wasteland bone-tired, but Dylan couldn't feel sorry about that: she didn't want to miss a second of this, of Tristan.

When Tristan turned to check on Dylan – as he had every five minutes through the night – she sat up, the blanket she'd huddled under during the night slipping off her shoulders. She gathered it to her stomach like she was drawing on its warmth, though it wasn't cold in the flat.

"Hey," she said softly.

"Hey," he replied. He tried to smile at her, but it was a poor effort and after a moment he dropped the attempt, along with his eyes, and stared down at the carpet. "It's morning."

"Yeah," Dylan said, standing up and stretching out. The sofa hadn't been comfortable. Walking over to Tristan, she pressed her front to his back and rested her chin on the top of his head, her arms wrapped around his neck. He reached up and wrapped a hand around her left wrist, anchoring her to him, and together they stared out of the window.

Witnessing the beginning of their very last day.

They watched neighbourhood cats stalk along the pavements, watched lights begin to dot the windows of the tenements on the other side of the street as people got up and started getting ready for the day ahead. Then, a little later, they watched weary heads bow as those people trudged out of doors, on their way to work. The odd car turned into a constant trickle as the clock on the wall ticked on towards 8 a.m.

Life, going on as normal.

Just like it would when they were no longer part of it.

"What time do you think the Inquisitor will come back?" Dylan asked softly.

Tristan could only shrug. "Soon."

Dylan made a face, not liking the vagueness, but the Inquisitor had simply told them that it would give them the night to think about it, to be sure. Now that it was morning, they probably didn't have much time left.

"Do you want breakfast?" Dylan asked.

Tristan shook his head. "I'm not hungry," he said tonelessly.

The resignation in Tristan's voice had tears rising up to sting Dylan's eyes. Dropping her head to tuck it into his shoulder, she squeezed him tighter. How could she do this to him? How could she throw him back into the empty, endless existence he'd lived before her?

Given the situation, how could she not?

It was an impossible choice.

"Tristan, I'm sorry," she whispered. "I'm so, so sorry. I have to."

A little sob hiccupped out at the end, swiftly followed by another. Shifting position in his chair, Tristan peeled himself out of her stranglehold and pulled her down into his lap. One arm curled around her back, his other hand going under her chin, lifting her face until she met his gaze.

"It's all right," he said. "I understand."

That just made things worse. Tristan's face blurred as the tears overflowed, streaking down Dylan's cheeks.

It wasn't all right, not at all. She was doing the worst thing possible to the person she loved most. And expecting him to help her do it.

He'd live an eternity without her, ferrying soul after soul; and she'd spend an eternity in the afterlife, waiting for him but knowing he was never going to come.

She was damning them both to hell.

"I'm sorry," she choked out again.

"Shhh." Tristan wiped the tears from her cheeks, but more kept on coming. Smiling sadly, he kissed the new ones that fell, chasing them down towards her mouth. Little butterfly kisses turned into longer, deeper ones.

Dylan leaned into him, her hands clutching at his shoulders. Her nose was stuffy from crying and her lungs screamed for air, but she would rather have suffocated than pulled away. If the kiss didn't end, they didn't have to face what was coming.

If the kiss didn't end, they didn't ever have to leave this moment.

Dylan's hoped were dashed when Tristan suddenly tore away from her. She whined out a protest, but one look at his face had the sound dying on her lips.

"Is this it?" she asked breathlessly. "Is it here?"

Tristan nodded.

The Inquisitor materialised in the middle of the room. Tristan lurched to his feet, putting a hand on Dylan's shoulder in a vain attempt to push her into the seat behind him, protected. It was a wasted effort. She shrugged off his grip and stood so that they were side by side. Facing it together.

"Your time is up," it said.

"We haven't changed our minds," Dylan replied. She glanced quickly at Tristan, guilt heavy in her chest, but then she turned back to the Inquisitor, her back rigid with determination. "Bring them back. We'll go in their place."

The Inquisitor didn't look surprised, or disapproving. Or pleased. It didn't look like it felt anything. It just gave a low "Very well" and raised a hand.

Dylan felt a pitching sensation in her stomach, like free-falling, and she gasped. "Wait!"

The feeling subsided as the Inquisitor paused.

"I have questions," she said. It waited, and Dylan took that as a sign to ask, continuing, "My mum and dad—"

"I will bring them back," the Inquisitor said. "That is what we agreed."

"Will I get to say goodbye? Will I get to see them again?"

Oh God, she hoped so. She needed to see them, alive and breathing, to wipe out the horrible memory of them lying there in their bed, still and lifeless.

"You will see them," the Inquisitor confirmed. "You will need to, to send them back." It paused and Dylan frowned, not following.

"What do you mean?"

"You must find them, in the wasteland. They will not return until you do. Touch them, any part of them, skin to skin, and I will know you have completed your task. I will bring them back to the real world then."

"Wait – are they together in the wasteland?"

"Yes." The inquisitor nodded. "An exception"

"What if we don't catch them, before they go over the line?" Dylan asked, starting to panic. "Or what if a wraith gets them?"

"If that happens, you will be too late."

"But—"

The Inquisitor cut her off. "This is the deal I am offering you. Whether you reach them or not, you will not be allowed to return here. Not again. If you decide to go after the souls of your parents, you forfeit the bargain we made. You forfeit your life, no matter the outcome."

Dylan sucked in a breath. It could all be for nothing. Hours and hours had passed, giving her parents a huge head start on them. What if they'd already been consumed by the wraiths?

No, she refused to accept that.

They were there, and she would find them.

"All right." Her voice wobbled, her eyes drawn to Tristan, who stood, stoic, at her side.

He must have seen the entreaty in her eyes, because he reached out and grabbed her hand. "We'll do it," he swore to the Inquisitor.

He turned to Dylan, "If this is what you want…" He paused, giving her the chance to tell him that it wasn't… but she didn't. She couldn't. He ploughed on. "If this is what you want, I promise you, I'll make sure we succeed."

Dylan offered him a watery smile.

"We're ready," he told the Inquisitor, never taking his eyes off her.

The Inquisitor didn't wish them luck. It didn't utter any words of encouragement or disapproval, or even of farewell. It simply disappeared.

"Wait!" Dylan cried to the empty air. "What?" She turned to Tristan. "Did it change its mind? What's going on?" She spun in a circle, eyes darting round the living room. "Why didn't it take us to the wasteland?"

Tristan closed his eyes, dropping his head.

"It did," he whispered. "We're here."

Chapter 18

"I knew your daughter." She'd been swithering over whether to say it, but not admitting her connection to Dylan felt like a lie. Susanna had lied to souls plenty of times before, but this one had sat on her shoulders like a devil, whispering in her ear until she had to confess.

It was like a weight being taken off her, her devil spreading tiny wings and taking flight. The steep incline they were struggling up suddenly seemed less of an impossible obstacle – though Susanna still gasped for breath, her legs burning.

"What?" It was James who answered her, his long legs making short work of a hill which, if the angry muttering and heavy panting was anything to go by, Joan too was struggling with. "How?" He frowned. "Here? You were her ferryman here? I thought Tristan…"

He tailed off as Susanna shook her head. She didn't respond at once, pretending to focus on the climb. She wasn't quite sure how to answer the question, how much she was allowed to say.

Which was why she should probably have kept her mouth shut. It was too late now, though.

"I met her, in the real world. I was there with, well—"

Stupid, stupid, *stupid.*

Both her actions at the time and mentioning it now.

"I had a soul that I tried to take back, like Tristan did with Dylan, only we... we weren't successful."

"I see." A pause as James considered her words. "Where is this soul now?"

The words didn't want to come out, but Susanna forced them. "He's gone."

"Is he... where we're going? Across the line?" James waved vaguely, showing a hint of his frustration with Susanna's inability to tell them exactly what lay beyond the wasteland.

"No." Susanna shook her head, struggling to say the words. "He's just... gone. He didn't make it across the wasteland. He's one of the creatures I told you about, the wraiths." She swallowed the darkness threatening to surge up, take her under. "The thing you said you saw? That's what's become of him."

James didn't respond, not for a long time. They were at the top of the hill, halting to catch their breath and let Joan clamber up the final few metres to join them, when James reached out and dropped a large, warm hand on Susanna's shoulder.

"I'm sorry," he said.

Susanna smiled grimly at him, then stepped away. She was grateful for his sympathy – few souls ever bothered to put aside their own feelings and consider hers – but she couldn't accept his comfort. Even the small gesture of touch, connection, had a riot of emotions swirling up inside her again, tears threatening to spill down her cheeks. Any more, and she'd be a sobbing mess – and that was not the ferryman James and Joan needed right now. She had a job to do, and she had to focus on that. Not on her mistakes.

Not on Jack.

But oh, how she wanted to let herself soak up James's kindness, his compassion. To let him hug her. To let him be her parent, and she be the teenage girl that she looked like.

But it didn't matter what she wanted. She was the ferryman, he was the soul. That was that.

Besides, an ounce more sympathy and she'd be confessing everything: how she'd tricked Jack, the lives that had been lost when wraiths snuck through the hole she and Jack tore in the veil, the trouble she'd caused Dylan and Tristan – and the danger she put them in – when they had to step in and help her and Jack to salvage the bargain they made with the Inquisitor. She didn't think James would be quite so kind-hearted once he heard that.

"Your daughter," she said, going back to the reason she'd decided to make the confession in the first place. "She was really brave. What she achieved – surviving the wasteland and fighting her way back to the real world – it was incredible. No one had ever managed it before." That Susanna knew of, anyway. She no longer took the 'facts' of the wasteland at face value any more. "And Tristan," pulling her lips into a smile took a monumental effort, but Susanna managed it, "he really loves her. They're connected, the two of them. They're meant to be together. He'll look after her, I promise. He'd give his life for her."

She addressed her comments not just to James, but to Joan too, who'd crested the hill and now stood just a step back from them, listening. Susanna hoped that her words might provide some comfort, alleviate some of the pair's worries, but she could see that, for Joan at least, it wasn't enough. All she had managed to do was remind them that they'd had to leave Dylan behind.

Susanna waited, sure beyond any doubt that one of them would say it, the thing souls *always* said, at some point or other in their journey.

Undo it. Take me back.

It was worse this time, because Joan and James knew that she could. They knew it was possible – their daughter had done it.

Susanna, the ferryman standing in front of them, had done it. She would not make the same error of judgement again, but they didn't know that. Susanna braced, preparing herself for the inevitable, and the gut-wrenching helplessness of telling them that she couldn't.

But they didn't. Instead, James just reached out and grabbed Joan's hand and they gazed at each other, grief etched across their features. Feeling like she was intruding, Susanna turned her face away.

"How did you die?" she asked.

She could have clapped her hand over her own mouth. She was utterly horrified at herself, but the truth was, she hadn't known the words were going to burst out. They'd been there, front and centre in her brain since they'd started their journey. She just couldn't understand it – what were James and Joan doing here? What had happened to them? The information should have been there in Susanna's head, but it wasn't. That there was nothing but a big empty space, a surge of buzzing white noise when she tried to see. It was driving her crazy.

Still, to *ask*… especially so bluntly. Right after highlighting the fact they'd had to leave their daughter in the real world, effectively alone in their eyes, as Tristan apparently didn't count. *Seriously, Susanna!*

Still, it was out now and there was no taking it back. Susanna waited, heart thumping, for the answer.

"What?" Joan asked blankly.

James, too, looked nonplussed.

Susanna was confused. It was a simple question, wasn't it?

"What happened to you? How did you die?"

"I don't…" Joan looked uncertainly to James, "I don't remember." She turned her gaze back to Susanna. "Should I? I just thought, I assumed that was part of it. Am I supposed to remember?"

Yes. She was definitely supposed to remember. Often, Susanna would hide the soul's fate from them in the early part of the journey across the wasteland. It made life easier, made them less likely to do something stupid through grief or panic, but the truth always came out in the end. And the soul's final memories were always intact. They just might not fully understand what it was that had happened to them until their ferryman explained that they'd left the world of the living behind.

"What do you remember?" Susanna pressed. "What's your last memory?"

Joan coloured, red racing across her cheeks, and Susanna had to scroll through the last memories of the souls that were in *her* head. Oh.

"We were sleeping," James said firmly. "We were having a nap, and when we woke up, we heard you crying."

Two healthy people, dying for no reason. It sounded strange, incredible, but then, Susanna had been around for a long time and ferried countless souls. There had to be an easy answer, something obvious that she was missing.

"A gas leak?" she suggested. "Or carbon dioxide poisoning? That would make sense."

It would make sense, but something told her that that wasn't the right answer, that there was something else – something ominous – at play.

In which case she needed to leave it well alone.

She knew things now, things she shouldn't. There were other creatures pulling the strings in the wasteland, beings with more power than her. If one of those things – an Inquisitor, or something else – had a hand in stealing the lives of Dylan's parents, then Susanna needed to be smart and not stick her nose where it definitely didn't belong.

If there were blank spaces in her knowledge of the souls, then she was just going to have to learn to live with it.

"We should go," she said. "There's a good distance still left to travel today."

⚮

They'd long left the urban landscape behind. Susanna was glad about that, but it also meant that the next safe house was a little more... rustic than the last. It was a tumbledown shack, a bothy. The roof was still intact and there were four solid walls. The door, though, Susanna could see as they moved closer, was ajar and the wood looked rotten, bloated. It hung at a drunken angle, and she doubted it closed.

"Here we are," she told Joan and James wearily.

It wasn't the walk so much as the emotional strain that had tired her out. She felt raw inside, and everything was an extra effort. She was also tense and uncertain around Joan and James – it was harder than she'd anticipated to ferry two souls. And she'd expected it to be pretty hard. Two bodies to protect, two sets of feelings to take into account, and two streams of thoughts and opinions on what was happening. They outnumbered Susanna and she couldn't quite settle into her role.

Of course, the turmoil of Jack and everything that had happened might have something to do with it too.

"Here?" Joan asked. She looked as tired as Susanna felt. She eyed the safe house with distaste, though. A memory nudged at Susanna: Dylan pulling that exact same face in the woods with Tristan as they hunted the rogue wraith just outside a small village. What was it called again? The Bridge of Allan, that was it. Dylan had stared at the little bunker with disgust and now, seeing the same expression painted on Joan's face, it was easy to see they were mother and daughter.

This time, Susanna took the wise decision to keep that thought to herself.

"It's not much," Susanna said, "but it'll keep us safe from the wraiths, and that's all that matters."

At that moment, a shadow passed across the single small window in the front face of the bothy.

Susanna blinked. Had she imagined that? She must have. Still, she watched the window – and the small gap in the slightly ajar door – carefully, hunting for movement. She didn't see anything but then—

"Is there someone else in there?" James asked.

"What?"

"Is there someone inside?" He pointed. "I saw something move."

Crap.

"There… there shouldn't be," Susanna murmured. "It can't be another ferryman, or a soul."

She'd sense them if it was, for one thing. But also, ferrymen didn't share safe houses. They coexisted side by side – on top of each other sometimes – but through a quirk of the wasteland, they each had their own places to wait out the hours of darkness. Like a hundred sheaves of paper in a pad, nestled together.

"Is it one of those creatures?" Joan asked, voice high. "Maybe we should find somewhere else to stay? Another… what do you call them? Safe house. Another safe house."

"There's no other safe house within reach," Susanna told her, creeping closer to the bothy. "It'll be dark soon."

Really soon. The light was dimming and the buffer between safety and danger was paper-thin. They needed to get inside. Susanna shifted another foot forward, then another.

There it was again. Something dark, moving with incredible speed. It was too shadowy inside the safe house and the thing was going too fast to be anything other than a blur, but still, Susanna knew what it was.

"It can't be," she said to herself. But it was. It zoomed past again, close enough to the window for Susanna to hear the scrape of its ragged body against the glass. A low whine pierced the silence, followed by a growl.

How the hell did it get in there? The safe houses were so-called because they were meant to be exactly that: safe.

"OK," she said slowly. "I think there's only one. Think of it like a trapped bird. We just need to get it out."

And hope it stayed out. If there was something wrong with the safe house, they'd be fish in a barrel when night unfolded and the full cohort of wraiths arrived.

Speaking of which, it was getting cooler and dimmer by the second. They needed to get inside.

"But you said they were dangerous!" Joan whimpered.

"They are," Susanna agreed. "But there's only one of them." She hoped. "I can deal with one easily enough. Just… just stay back. But close. Don't go wandering. As soon as the wraith's out, we need to get in there."

"But if it got in—" James said.

Yeah. Susanna had the same thought. But they didn't have a choice.

"If there's something wrong with the safe house, if it's stopped doing its job for some reason, we'll still be safer in there than we would be out here. We'll just have to try and barricade the door, get it totally shut if we can. They can't fly through walls."

That Susanna knew of. Because they weren't supposed to be able to bypass the safe house's charms either.

She edged closer. The wraith wasn't battering at the window or snarling at the door. Susanna didn't think it had seen her; it was too consumed with whizzing back and forth. It reminded her of a trapped fly. How long had it been in there?

Her first thought was to simply yank the door open and hope the wraith would fly out of its own accord, but even before she had a hand on the iron door handle she knew that wasn't going to happen: the wraith wouldn't come out for the same reason the others that were lurking nearby hadn't swooped down on them yet. It was just too light. But if they waited until it was dark enough for the wraith to want to leave, it wasn't going to be just one wraith they were dealing with.

She'd have to grab it, drag it out.

The thought of putting her hands on one, purposefully, made Susanna's muscles convulse in a full-body judder. Wraiths were vicious, mindless things. It would attack her. It wouldn't understand that she was trying to free it, to save it – and wasn't that a laugh?

Like she'd said to Joan and James, she could handle it, but getting scratched and gored and bloodied was never fun.

"Stay back," she reminded them.

Susanna eased the door open. It resisted at first, then jolted loose with an ugly screech. She winced. So much for subtlety. The wraith either heard the noise or caught the movement – or, more probably, both – and it gave a furious shriek. Susanna ducked back as it flew straight at her, and for a hopeful second she thought it might soar out after all, but as soon as it hit the dull light filtering in through the doorway, it veered violently off course, returning to the thicker shadows at the back of the single room. It flew back and forth, hunting for an escape route that wasn't there.

"Easy," Susanna murmured. "*Easy.*"

Was she trying to gentle a wraith? Apparently she was.

"I'm not going to hurt you."

She couldn't hurt it. Same thing, really. Besides, it wasn't as if the damn thing knew what she was saying.

For some reason, the memory of Jack singing to the wraiths at the boathouse popped into her head. That moment had been terrifying, but also surprising. The wraiths had been soothed out of their murderous frenzy by the music, she was sure of it.

Susanna wasn't much of a singer, though. She'd likely just make the thing angrier if she warbled at it, out of tune.

"You need to stay back!" Susanna's sharp tone sent the wraith into a flurry of frantic flying and hissing along the back wall, but James had been steadily creeping closer and she caught him out of the corner of her eye, near enough to the front door to get himself maimed if the wraith decided to make a sudden dash for it.

"I can help," James offered. He took another step, craning his neck. "I just want to see—" He stopped speaking, gaping at the wraith, which chose that moment to make another rush at the exit. It swerved away from the light again at the last second, but the sudden action gave James a much closer look than he intended. He scooted back, catching a foot on the uneven paving slabs leading up to the bothy, almost falling over. "That's it," he said. "That's what I saw on the video before." The wraith snarled in frustration and James paled further. "It's a demon," he whispered.

"It was a person," Susanna said. "Once."

There was nothing remotely human about it now, though.

Although…

The incident at the lake wouldn't leave Susanna's head.

"Can you sing?" she asked James.

"What?" He stared at her, bewildered. Susanna understood, it was a completely random question. Still…

"Can you sing?" She grimaced. "In tune."

"I... well, I'm not bad." James shrugged his shoulders. He turned slightly and looked towards Joan, who was doing exactly as Susanna had asked: keeping well back, but close enough for Susanna to get to her quickly if anything happened. "Joan's the singer."

He lifted his voice enough for her to hear him, and Joan cocked her head slightly as she regarded them quizzically.

"A song," he called to her.

"Are you serious?" Joan took a handful of steps forward but halted when she saw the wraith through the doorway. "What on earth for?"

"It'll settle the wraith," Susanna said. "Hopefully. If we can get it to calm down, I can grab it."

"All right." Joan looked at them as if they were crazy, but another wail pierced the growing dusk and she shuddered at the eerie sound, a look of grim determination settling over her features. She opened her mouth and started to sing. It was very different to the songs Jack had sung Susanna. Softer. Melodic. It clearly struck a chord with James, because he made a sort of choked sound and his face took on an anguished look.

Curious – and keeping one eye on the wraith to check for any lessening of its panicked movements – she sped through James's memories.

There.

Joan, younger, standing with her back to him, something in her arms. She was singing the song, albeit more quietly, and rocking slightly. James called out in the memory and Joan turned, allowing Susanna to see the tiny child in her arms. Baby Dylan.

It was a bittersweet memory to James, and Susanna dropped it as soon as she felt his intense love, his racking guilt that not long after this he'd disappeared from both of their lives. She felt sorry for him, having regained his family just to have it snatched away from him again, but he'd made his choices, the same as every other soul that Susanna had ferried.

"Look!" James whispered, yanking her back into the here and now. "It's having an effect."

It definitely was. As Susanna focused on the wraith she saw that it was weaving, its movements slower, almost drunken. It was meandering towards them, as if the song called to it somehow.

As if it remembered music.

If that was the case… that meant that there was still *something* in there. Some tiny part of the person it used to be. A tiny candle of hope flared within Susanna, but she snuffed it out for now. She wouldn't let herself even think on the possibility… yet.

"Keep singing," she urged Joan when the woman's voice dropped down, indicating an end to the song. "It doesn't matter what. Sing that song again if you want."

She didn't, starting something with a higher pitch that rose and fell in a gentle rhythm. Susanna caught her breath, half-in half-out of the door, waiting to see how the wraith would react. It didn't seem to object to the change in tone; if anything, it shifted closer.

Inching forward, Susanna kept her eyes fixed on the wraith. The things didn't really have faces as such, so it was hard to gauge its expression, but she'd swear it looked calmer, more peaceful.

This was as good as it was going to get. Armed with nothing more than her bare hands, Susanna crossed the threshold into the safe house. The wraith noticed, but it didn't seem to care. It was too busy weaving dreamily, almost dancing in the air. Taking her shot, Susanna grabbed it around the middle, pinning its ragged, wispy coat to its sides. It was similar, she presumed, to trying to catch a crow or a raven. It was too big at first, unwieldy in her grip, but once she had it gathered and snug, it stopped struggling.

Until, that is, Joan stopped singing.

"You've got it?" she asked.

As soon as the wraith realised the hypnotic music had ceased, it started writhing and thrashing, claws extending beneath its body and gouging slashes into Susanna's fingers. Its teeth started snapping down, trying to tear at her knuckles. Susanna had a firm grip on it, but as it struggled it seemed to become less substantial. As tight as Susanna tried to hold it, it managed to find wiggle room – and it was wiggling madly.

It was going to get free.

"Sing!" she ordered Joan. "Quickly! Anything!"

Joan didn't hesitate. She launched straight back into the song she'd been singing as if there hadn't been a break. The effect on the wraith was instantaneous. It slumped into Susanna's hands, almost as if it was sighing with relief.

"You recognise that, don't you?" Susanna whispered to it. "Whatever's left of you, you recognise the music."

Not wanting to push her luck, Susanna walked quickly to the door of the bothy, and both Joan and James skirted sensibly back out of the way.

"Inside," Susanna told them, adding, "but don't stop singing. Not yet."

They were quick to obey. The low wailing from the far shadows that Susanna had been resolutely ignoring was growing to a caterwauling. Soon, the air would be thick with wraiths who'd be delighted with a ferryman foolish enough to stay outside after sundown. Knowing she didn't have much time, Susanna flung the wraith upwards, as she imagined someone might release a bird. There was no flutter of wings, but the wraith took to the air.

It didn't go far, though, rising up and turning to swoop back down almost before Susanna could back hastily across the safe house threshold. Despite the noise from its brethren, it wasn't snarling and Susanna realised that it wasn't the lure of two souls that was drawing it.

"Stop," she called to Joan. "Stop singing now."

Joan's voice – which, now that the song was over, had just been humming the tune – cut off between one breath and the next. The wraith lurched in the air, seeming to come out of the enthralled daze it had been caught in.

And then it dived at them, claws out and teeth bared.

This time it was as hungry as any other wraith, but though Susanna braced to defend Joan and James, she didn't try to shut the door. Not yet. She needed to know if the wraith could come back in, if the safeguards around the bothy had fallen.

Readying herself for pain if the wraith got through, Susanna half turned away and scrunched her eyes shut. *Please, please, please*, she thought.

The wraith slammed into the entryway of the safe house... and was sent somersaulting away into the darkening sky.

The protections held.

Relieved, but still confused – how had it got in there in the first place? – Susanna drew in a deep breath.

"We're safe," she told Joan and James. "They can't come in."

It wasn't a minute too soon, either. The distant wailing was coming closer, turning to hissing and growling and screaming as the last of the light leached from the sky and the wraiths were released from their shadows.

"I don't understand," James said quietly as he came up to stand behind Susanna. "How did it get inside?"

"I don't know," she answered honestly.

Strange things were happening in the wasteland lately, not least of all the fact that Susanna had been given two souls to ferry. She had a niggling feeling that it was somehow linked to what she'd attempted to do – what Dylan and Tristan had succeeded in doing – and she knew that puzzling it out should be first and foremost in her thoughts. She needed to understand all of the nuances of the wasteland to protect her souls after all.

But that wasn't it, though.

There was something else.

Something she hadn't dared let herself hope for.

The wraith had recognised the music, there was no doubt about it. It had wanted to be close to it, had become less beast-like, less ferocious. More… human. It had felt more solid in her hands, too. Susanna rarely touched the wraiths – and never voluntarily. But she had more practice than she'd like grabbing them and tearing them away from souls, hauling them free of her own flesh. They always felt… not quite there. Not quite corporeal. As if, should she squeeze too tight, grip too hard, her fingers might sink right through them.

The wraith she'd held in her hands – while Joan was singing – had felt as solid as Susanna was.

The music had triggered a memory. That memory had pulled the wraith out of the ghost-like, mindless existence it was trapped in. Just a little, but enough to prove that it could be done.

A song, trilled out by a stranger, had caused that reaction. Had reached the wraith.

If it could do that, surely Susanna could reach Jack? Could call out to the human part of him buried deep, deep inside.

It went against everything Susanna had ever been told, but as she stood in the doorway of the safe house and watched the wraiths swirling and swooping outside, Susanna decided that didn't mean anything. Not any more. What she knew, what she'd been told, wasn't necessarily the truth. Or all of it, anyway. There was a possibility that Susanna might be able to help Jack.

And no matter how unlikely it was, no matter how slim her chances of success might be, she was going to try.

She'd made him a promise.

And it might not be too late to keep it.

CHAPTER 19

He was back.

Tristan felt the wasteland settle around him and fought to draw breath. Nothing had changed, not really. They still stood in the flat, he could still see the street out of the window.

But everything was different.

It was the stillness of the air; the eerie silence. It was the feeling of desolation that struck so hard it almost dropped him to his knees.

Get used to it, he thought.

He'd convinced himself he'd never be back here, that he'd left this 'life' behind. He should have known better.

"Come on," he said wearily. "Let's go."

Dylan followed him down the stairs of their building and out onto the street, and then she just stood and stared. Knowing the first day was always a short one, he paused, letting her drink in the subtle differences, the tiny markers that signalled they weren't in the real world any longer.

Standing in the middle of two long rows of three-storey tenements, cars lining the pavement on each side, they were surrounded – and yet the place was completely empty. There were no birds calls, no traffic noises. They could knock on any door, peer into any window. Dylan and Tristan were the only people there.

The Inquisitor had taken no chances that they might attempt to change their mind. It had thrust them deep into the wasteland, where they couldn't even catch a glimmer of life continuing just out of reach.

"This is weird," Dylan murmured. She gave a delicate shudder. "Which way?"

Tristan nodded towards the end of the street and they started off. The sky above their heads was thick with cloud, the undersides drooping heavily. He saw Dylan eyeing them uneasily and almost smiled. He remembered just how much she'd hated being cold and wet the first time they'd travelled the wasteland together, how much she'd complained as she traipsed along behind him.

"Is that me?" she asked. "The clouds, are they my fault?"

Tristan paused for a moment, looking up with a frown on his face. "I'm not sure," he said, "but I don't think so. This isn't your wasteland, it's your parents'. They'll be controlling the weather."

"Oh."

Tristan started walking again, his stride both long and quick, forcing Dylan to hurry to keep up with him. He had to. They needed to catch her parents, *before* they got to the line. He promised Dylan he would get her to them, then get her safely to the line, and that's what he was going to do.

He wasn't angry. He *wasn't*.

He was simply determined to succeed, that was all.

And he didn't have any *right* to be angry. The choice had been Dylan's to make, and she'd made it.

He fought to tamp down his emotions, to rein himself in until he could be the cool, calm ferryman he used to be... but the numbness wouldn't come.

"Tristan, I'm sorry."

The words jolted Tristan, forced him to break out of the ruthless pace he'd been setting. He stopped entirely when he saw how out of breath Dylan was. "Don't apologise," he replied. "You did what you thought was right."

"But it wasn't the choice you would have made."

No, it wasn't.

Unable to voice the thought, Tristan set off again, keeping to a gentler pace this time. They continued along in silence until they were out of Dylan's street and into a nameless road that didn't exist in real life.

"I would have made whatever choice kept you safe," he announced as they crossed the street.

"What?" Dylan hurried to catch up.

"If it had been up to me," he clarified, "I would have chosen anything that would keep you safe, so no. I would never have opted to bring you back here." He scowled at the ominously empty windows that stared down at them. "This place is crawling with wraiths."

"Can they come out?" Dylan asked, glancing around nervously.

Tristan shook his head. "No, they're trapped by the light, remember. We're safe. The Inquisitor had that much mercy, at least." He turned to Dylan when she didn't reply, caught the confusion on her face. "It came to us in the morning, and it's put us in the wasteland at that time, too. That means we have the whole day, which is good."

"Because we'll definitely make it to the safe house," Dylan concluded, but Tristan shook his head.

"Because, if we're going to catch your parents, we need to skip straight over the first safe house and make it to the second."

Dylan paled, clearly thinking about how long they had walked last time on that first day... and then the second.

"Tristan, that's an awfully long way."

"We'll make it," he said. He tried to sound determined, confident, but he was worried. He'd never attempted this before, had always stopped at each and every safe house – and for good reason. The journey was hard. How often had he failed to get souls to the next resting place in time? How many had he lost?

"We'll make it," Dylan repeated, nodding, seemingly trying to muster some confidence. "We will. I won't hold us back, I promise."

"Tell me that after the first hill," Tristan shot back, and he gave her a sideways look, one eyebrow raised in amusement.

Dylan smiled, but it faded as a deeper emotion bled into her eyes. She reached out and grabbed his hand. "I love you," she told him. "No matter what happens, remember that."

"I know it," Tristan replied. "I won't forget, not ever. And know that you'll take my heart with you, when you cross the line. So, in a way, we'll always be together."

She'd take his heart, but he'd cling on to the memories they'd made together. All of them, from the first moment she'd stumbled, frightened and hesitant, out of the tunnel, to the moment she'd reappeared in the wasteland, having faced so much alone, for him. The sight of her broken body on the stretcher, her strength when she faced down a wraith armed with nothing more than a stray branch. The sound of her laugh, even her scowl when he annoyed her. Every expression that played across her face, every word she'd ever spoken to him; he'd keep them locked tight in his mind and use them to drag himself through the rest of his sorry existence.

He hoped they'd be enough.

They kept going all morning. Dylan did her best to match his pace, but he knew she was struggling. By the time he paused outside a block of flats, she was sweating and looked exhausted.

She didn't ask why they'd stopped, simply dropped down onto a stone bollard, one of several decorating the front of the building, breathing heavily.

"This is the first safe house," he told her.

"It is?" Dylan looked at the building with surprise – and indignation. "Is this the luxury version, then? Did I get stiffed?"

Tristan managed to raise a vague smile.

"It's all about where you expect to be, remember?" Hoping to lighten the mood, he formed a mock-scowl. "It's not my fault you had to choose a tunnel in the middle of nowhere to pop your clogs."

"Choose?" Dylan spluttered. "*Choose?!*"

He grinned.

"Are we halfway, then?" she asked hopefully. "Are we making good time?"

He grimaced. No, they weren't. Not even close.

"All right." Dylan read the answer on his face. She stood up and dusted off her jeans. "Let's go then. I'm ready."

Another grimace. Because no, she wasn't. Not even close.

"You need to rest, Dylan. It's no good if we get halfway through the afternoon and you collapse because you've pushed yourself too hard."

Dylan set her mouth, her eyes narrowing. "I'll make it," she ground out. "We're in the wasteland, so this isn't really my body any more, right?"

Tristan nodded.

"Then it's mind over matter. I'll do it." She threw Tristan a look, daring him to contradict her. "Let's go."

He wanted to argue, but she had that glint in her eye, the one that said there was no point arguing with her. He loved that glint, loved that she was so strong, so determined. If she could hold on to that, they might just make it.

The wasteland was starting to take them out of the city and into the barren landscape they'd face for the majority of their journey. It got hillier as they traversed what should have been the second day's journey. The inclines became steeper and longer, and each time they crested a hill it was to see another, bigger version hiding behind it. Tristan kept a careful eye on Dylan, and he could see her strength waning, but she didn't complain. She simply put her head down and ploughed on, one foot in front of the other.

⌇

Though it hurt – really, really hurt – Dylan kept up with the pace Tristan set. Partly to prove to him that she *could*, but also because they were getting closer and closer. Every step was one nearer to the safe house. One nearer to her parents. Joan and James had been taken less than twenty-four hours before the Inquisitor put Dylan and Tristan into the wasteland, and if they were squeezing two days into one, they should meet Dylan's mum and dad at the next safe house.

It was little more than twenty-four hours since the Inquisitor stole her parents' lives, less than thirty-six hours since Dylan had spoken to them, and yet it felt like for ever. Like the reunion they were about to have had been years in the making. Lifetimes.

She was near giddy with excitement, thinking only about seeing her parents and not about the separation that was going to happen soon after. Or the second, more painful and more permanent parting that was going to happen just a couple of days after that.

One thing at a time, Dylan told herself. Just get there.

Get to the safe house and see with her own eyes that her parents were fine. That their short stay in the wasteland – something that was entirely Dylan's fault – hadn't hurt them.

"Are we nearly there yet?" Dylan asked. It was getting darker and if Tristan said no, she knew they were going to have to run. Dylan had always maintained that she would only run if she was being chased… she hadn't meant being chased by wraiths.

"Yeah," Tristan grunted. "Just about. We'll make it before it's dark."

Each word came out on a pant and Dylan was so surprised she nearly tripped on the stony path they were following. Tristan was out of breath.

Tristan was out of breath.

The thought buoyed her enough that she practically floated up the hill. Their entire previous journey through the wasteland, Dylan had huffed and puffed and panted and gasped (and complained). Tristan had been insufferable, ignoring her moans and mumbles, and refusing to look so much as winded.

She couldn't resist teasing him about it.

"You must be getting out of shape," she said, looking at him slyly out of the corner of her eye. "It's all those crisps and chocolate."

"Your fault." Tristan scowled at the ground. "Are you allergic to vegetables?"

Dylan laughed and paused, bracing her hands on her hips. They had reached the top of a dip between two higher peaks (that Dylan had been delighted to hear they didn't have to scale), and the wasteland lay spread out before them in a sprawl of hills interspersed with patches of flat ground that Dylan knew from experience would be boggy and difficult to wade through.

"There it is!" She pointed a finger down the hill. There, where the land flattened out, was a bothy. It was small, but looked fairly intact. The door hung slightly open, and though she couldn't see any light spilling out of the sliver of entryway or the small window that might indicate a fire blazing inside, Dylan took it as a sign that her parents were there, waiting for her.

She grinned, relief bubbling like champagne in her blood.

"We made it!" she said to Tristan, then she started down the hill, half-running, knowing he'd follow.

There was still no sign of movement when she reached the bottom of the slope, or when she started down the path – really running now – but Dylan still expected to see her parents in the safe house… right up until she burst through the door.

They weren't there.

She skidded to a stop and looked around in confusion. The safe house was nothing more than a single room: there was nowhere to hide. That didn't stop her calling out for them.

"Mum? Dad?" She turned in a circle, taking in the space: the low bed, the small table and two three-legged stools. The old-fashioned sink and the fireplace – cold and empty, nothing but ashes that could have been left yesterday… or years ago.

A sound from the doorway had her spinning, heart in her throat, but it was only Tristan, easing the door closed as he slipped inside.

"They aren't here," Dylan said. "Why aren't they here? They were only a day ahead of us, we should have caught them by now!"

It was a stupid question, Tristan didn't know any more than she did, but Dylan felt cheated. After everything she'd put herself through today, all the stupid hills she'd climbed without a word (or many words, at least) of protest – where was her reward?

"Why aren't they here?" she repeated, more quietly this time, and to herself, but Tristan answered anyway.

"Time doesn't work the same way in the wasteland. You were gone for days last time, but when you fell back into your body, it was like no time had passed, remember?"

Dylan nodded. She couldn't look at him, trying to stop her lower lip from trembling but failing miserably. She felt like a small child who'd just had their treat taken away.

"OK," she said, working to get a hold of herself. "OK. So tomorrow, we just try harder. We can do the same thing again, right? Skip over a safe house and turn two days into one?" She'd phrased it as a question, but Dylan assumed that would be what they'd do, so she was totally unprepared for the slow shake of Tristan's head.

"It's too far," he told her. "The first day, it's a short one, to make sure the soul makes it, to give the ferryman a little extra time in case they run into difficulties. After that, though, the distances increase. We'd never make it to the valley tomorrow. Not before dark."

"I'll run," Dylan promised. "I can run."

Mind over matter. She'd do it, someway, somehow. She'd bleed if she had to, push her muscles until they screamed.

"No, Dylan." Tristan crossed the distance between them and pulled her into a hug. "I'm sorry, it's just too far. Too dangerous."

Dylan's heart squeezed in her chest, the hope and jubilation she'd felt just minutes ago crumbling into ash as cold and dead as the burnt-out remains in the fireplace.

"We're not going to make it, are we?" Dylan asked him quietly. "We're going to be too late."

Tristan didn't reply; he just squeezed her tighter, his hand wrapped around hers, resting right over her heart.

CHAPTER 20

"I need to ask you something." Susanna stared at Joan and James, who were sitting side by side on the worn-out sofa in the safe house, and grimaced. "Actually, I need to ask you for a favour."

"A favour?" James frowned. "What do you mean?"

Susanna took a deep breath, and held it. Was she really going to ask? Was she going to try? It was a fool's errand, she knew. The chance of success was so miniscule, and yet… there *was* a chance.

She breathed out. "A favour," she repeated, her course decided. "I want you to stay in this safe house for a day. Just one day."

"Why?" Joan asked.

It was a fair question.

"There's something I need to do. Something I need to try." Susanna broke eye contact, looking down at the floor, but she knew the two souls were still sitting there, watching her. Waiting. "I lost a soul here." She gestured out the door at the wasteland. "At the lake."

"Lake?" Joan asked, her face paling. "We have to cross a lake?"

"There's a boat," Susanna explained. "It's safe—"

"Clearly not if you lost someone in it!"

Susanna took a step back, stung. "That was… different. "Jack…" She struggled over his name, realising this was the first time she'd said it out loud since she'd lost him. "Jack and I… we

183

weren't in a normal wasteland." Susanna moved to stand by the door, gazing out at the valley, covered with the purples and muted browns of heather in Joan and James's wasteland. "What you see out there, it's a… well, it's a skin. A coat over the real wasteland. It's a horrible place. The sun burns your skin and the ground is nothing but sharp rock and gritty sand. And the wraiths are everywhere. They aren't held captive by the sun. They swarm, constantly. It's a nightmare."

"What happened to this… coating last time you were here? Why was it so different?"

"We were being punished," Susanna said quietly. "I can't say any more than that."

The Inquisitor hadn't told her that she had to keep quiet about what she and Jack had done – what Dylan and Tristan had done – but Susanna couldn't bear to tell the story. Not today, possibly not ever.

'Time heals' was an idiom she'd heard from souls many a time, but she wasn't sure that it applied here, in the wasteland, where time didn't mean quite the same thing. Honestly, it felt like the raw, pulsing wound inside of her would never heal.

"When did this happen?" James asked, his eyes narrowed in thought. "The soul you lost – Jack, you said – it was recent, wasn't it? When we found you—"

Susanna tried to cut him off. "Yeah, it was recent."

"When we found you," James went on, oblivious to Susanna's attempt to head off his line of questioning, "you were crying. It sounded like your heart was breaking. That was for him, wasn't it? He's the soul that's one of those creatures now… a wraith?"

Susanna nodded, avoiding both of their gazes, eyes back on the valley. Soon the place would be alive with movement, with death.

"What happened to him?" James pressed.

"He was pulled under the water." Susanna tried to make her voice matter-of-fact, but she cracked on the word 'pulled' and the rest came out as a garbled squeak.

"Pulled under? By what?" James looked confused. "Are there… creatures in the water? Wraiths?"

Susanna nodded again, her eyes filling with tears. She swiped quickly at the one that spilled free and slid down her cheek.

Thankfully neither of them pushed the subject further. In fact, they didn't speak at all, and when Susanna finally turned to look at them, to gauge their silence, she saw them conferring, communicating wordlessly.

It was James who spoke.

"So, you want us to stay here tomorrow – all day – inside the safe house?"

Susanna jerked her head once.

"And while we do that," he said slowly, "what, exactly, will you be doing?"

Susanna flicked her eyes from James to Joan and back again, trying to read their faces. The only thing she could see was pity in Joan's eyes. That was what she had to appeal to.

"You saw the wraith in the safe house the other day," she began. "You saw how it reacted to the music."

"It calmed it," Joan agreed.

"I think… I've always believed that the wraiths were empty shells, that there was nothing left of the person that it used to be, but I think that the wraith recognised whatever you were singing. Or at the very least, it remembered the *idea* of music. It wanted to get closer to you, not to hurt you, just to be nearer to your voice."

"You think your friend Jack is still in there somewhere," James said, cutting to the chase.

Susanna took her time replying.

185

"I don't know that I *think*," she said. "I hope."

"So you plan to... what?" James prodded. "Bring him back? How?"

There was the problem.

"I don't know," she had to admit. "I haven't... well, I haven't thought that far ahead. I just want to see if I can find him. If I can detect any kind of spark, any hint that he's still in there. I promised him, you see. I promised him he'd make it, and I let him down."

"He means a lot to you?" James asked bluntly.

"He does," Susanna said. "He's... special to me. We've been through so much together and, well, to say we're friends really isn't enough. There's no one, in any world, who knows me like Jack. No one who cares about me like he does. And to think of him, trapped under the water, reduced to being one of those hate-filled things..." She sniffed, hard, determined not to cry again. "He was afraid of the water," she admitted. "Now he's stuck there."

James stood up. Ignoring Joan's noise of surprise, he walked the length of the safe house and stood with his back to them, his hand thrust in his hair. Susanna could see his fingers twisting and tightening, but then he let go and spun to face them.

"I feel sorry for you, I do," he said, and her heart sank. She knew where he was heading even before he started shaking his head. "But what you're asking... What if you don't come back? What if something in the water gets you? You said there were wraiths under there, and you'd be diving right in with them!"

Wraiths, and something more, though Susanna didn't mention that.

She'd never encountered it before, the thing that had attacked their boat, and she was hoping desperately that it only existed in the real wasteland, that she wouldn't have to face it again.

"If you don't come back," James went on, "what happens to us?

You said we need you, that you're our guide, so what do we do if something goes wrong? We'll just, what? Sit here for ever? Risk going it alone and having to deal with those creatures?" The look he sent Susanna's way held no small amount of sympathy, but it was also resolute. "I'm sorry, but I can't risk it. For me, maybe I'd take that chance. But—" His eyes caught and held Joan's. "I've already lost my daughter, I won't lose my wife. Not again."

"James." Joan stood up and went to him, throwing her arms around him and pressing her face into the width of his chest. He lowered his head to drop a kiss into her hair.

"You're right," Susanna told him, realisation and disappointment bitter in her mouth. "You shouldn't risk it."

She couldn't die, so there was no chance she'd drown in the lake, but she could be held there. Trapped under the water. Unable to return to the souls in the safe house. And because she couldn't die, it might go on indefinitely. She could spend an eternity, drowning and drowning and drowning. Feeling the viscous, oil-like water of the lake sneaking into her nose, her mouth, her lungs. The pain as wraiths bit and sliced and tore. Her bones threatening to snap as whatever thing had pulled Jack under with a long, thickly muscled tentacle wrapped around her and squeezed until she screamed.

Susanna yanked in a breath to pull herself out of the picture that she could imagine with crystal clarity.

Joan turned in James's embrace so that she could see Susanna. Her expression sombre, she gazed at her, something unreadable moving behind her eyes.

"Promise me," Joan said.

"What?" Susanna frowned, not understanding.

"Promise me you'll come back to us."

"Joan, sweetheart—" James murmured, but she shushed him.

"You made a promise to your Jack, and I see what you're doing to try and keep it. So promise me that you'll come back for us, and we'll wait." She pulled out of James's arms so that she could look him in the face. "She deserves a chance," she said. "I would do it for you, I would do it for Dylan, and you would do it for both of us."

"It's not the same," James protested. "Joan, we could be trapped here. We can't leave without her."

"If we're trapped here, then we're together. Always. That would be enough for me."

James pressed his lips together and Susanna watched, her heart pounding. She could feel the turning of the tide as James folded under his wife's honesty. Under her love.

He didn't answer Joan; instead he lifted his gaze to Susanna and she felt his eyes fix hers with laser intensity.

"Your word," he demanded grimly.

"I promise," Susanna said. "I swear it. I'll come back for you."

⤙

It was strange, leaving the safe house alone. At first Susanna wasn't sure she'd even be able to do it. She kept waiting for some unseen force to haul her back, but nothing did. Step after step, she continued on, until the wide expanse of the lake nestled in the basin of land before her. It looked calm from her vantage point, serene. The dark blue of the water barely rippled, the light covering of grey clouds reflected in its glassy surface.

It was a lot more inviting than the last time she'd seen it, and Susanna cursed quietly, feeling anger stir in her stomach. She and Jack would have had no problem crossing this.

But she knew her wrath could only be directed at herself – if she hadn't talked Jack into going back, he would never have been exposed to the hell of the real wasteland.

She could only hope she wasn't too late.

She jogged down the hill, her movements lithe and graceful, borne of long practice. Once she hit the pebbled beach, she cut across to the boathouse. It was a struggle to get the wooden double doors free, but she managed. Her fingers fumbled, clumsy with nerves and an urgency that told her she had to move faster. Perhaps that was the wasteland, telling her to get back to her souls.

Well, the forces of the wasteland were going to have to wait. Susanna planned to stay out here until she'd exhausted everything she could think of – or until it got too close to dark. She'd sworn to Joan and James, whose worried, uncertain faces had watched her leave, that she'd be with them before the first wraith of the night wailed.

Getting the boat out of the shed was easy enough: one good tug and the bottom slid free of the gravelly, muddy puddle it sat in, then it was just a case of manoeuvring it up the beach a little, then back down towards the water.

It slid into the coolness of the lake like a knife into butter.

Susanna took one, two, three steps forwards and then launched herself up into the boat. It rocked, but she steadied herself and then picked up the oars.

"I'm coming for you, Jack," she said quietly as she started to row. "Just hang on, I'm coming."

Right into the centre; that was where she'd lost him and that was where she intended to begin her search. Of course, she had no way to anchor the boat, but when she reached roughly the right spot, she sent it into a gentle spin to halt its forward momentum and then pulled in the oars.

She fixed her eyes on the water – was that something moving down there? A wraith? Or the other thing? Unlacing her boots, she yanked them off, pulling her socks off too. She baulked at ridding herself of her jeans. They'd weigh her down, make her less agile in the water, but they'd also be a barrier between her and anything else. She shuddered at the thought of a tentacle arm snaking round her, suckers attaching themselves to her thigh and reeling her in.

She mentally shook herself. "OK, Susanna, time to go."

She'd done this plenty of times, thrown herself headfirst into the water, without a care for her own safety, to rescue a soul who'd fallen beneath. This should be no different. Except that it was. This was Jack.

And it was different because he was a wraith now, and every instinct was telling her that it was too late, he was gone.

Well, instinct had told her that she couldn't travel to the real world and she had. Instinct had told her that she couldn't walk away and leave souls stranded in a safe house, and she'd done that too.

She was delaying, she knew, because she was afraid to fail.

But every minute that she lingered in the boat, stalling, was a minute lost in the search for Jack.

Taking a breath, Susanna plunged into the water.

It was cold. That was both a shock and a relief. The lake in the real wasteland had burned. Another relief was that the water... felt like water. Gone was the thick, oily substance of before. Susanna held her breath but opened her eyes. The water was murky, heavy with silt and meandering bits of plant life – and darting figures that were quickly coming closer.

A wraith coiled round her ankle, then another slid around her neck, weaving beneath her hair. Susanna forced herself not to react, not even when the wraith by her foot sunk its teeth into her shin. It was a sharp bite, but she doubted it had even broken the skin and was thankful she'd worn her jeans. They'd bite harder soon, though, she knew. They'd draw blood – and when that seeped into the water, it would throw them into a frenzy.

Satisfied she'd made her presence felt, Susanna kicked and wriggled her way free, clawing her way to the surface. She gripped the side of the boat, gasping. After three quick breaths, she inhaled deeply and dived again. More wraiths had come, but they seemed confused. They were circling her, dashing forward then pulling back. Jerking left and right, as if they were scenting the water. Searching for something – but not finding it.

Souls, Susanna realised. They were hunting for her soul. After all, what would a ferryman be doing here without one?

Thankful that they hadn't launched a full-on attack, Susanna took the opportunity to really look at the lake wraiths for the first time. They were almost exactly the same as the ones who flew through the wasteland's night skies and loitered in its shadows, but these ones didn't seem to be restricted in the same way. Only a midday sun in a cloudless sky could penetrate the depths of the water. There was no bright light to keep them pinned to the lakebed.

There were other subtle differences, too. Ones that made it easier for the wraiths to navigate their watery purgatory. Rather than the wispy, ragged coats of the air-inhabiting wraiths, these ones were sleeker, more streamlined. Black fin-like curves ran down the length of their bodies, rippling as they hovered in place, almost if they were feeling at the water. Tasting it. Their eyes were the same, though, black and small and empty of all but the need to feed. The teeth – well, Susanna didn't want to get too close to them, but she knew from the testing bite to her lower leg that they were there, and they were sharp.

How was she going to do this? How could she draw Jack out? Susanna turned slowly in a circle, assessing the group that now surrounded her. She hunted for something to mark one as different, but they all looked and acted the same.

Despair merged with the burning need to breathe, and Susanna shot for the surface once more. This time, she didn't get the chance to regain her breath. She grabbed one quick, sharp inhale and then something under the water pulled at her jeans and tugged her downwards with surprising force. Driving down panic – she needed another breath already, could feel the compulsion in her lungs to draw in deep – she looked down to see three wraiths working in tandem, dragging her deeper with a strength she couldn't fight.

That wasn't right – wraiths didn't work as a team, they didn't have enough capacity for thought for that – but it wasn't the first time Susanna had witnessed it either. She remembered the way wraiths had ripped her from Michael and buried her beneath a huge snowdrift so that they could have unfettered access to the soul.

Susanna kicked her leg and lashed out with her free foot, knocking one, then two away. The third hung on grimly, but a direct hit to its face meant that she was free again. Not hesitating, Susanna swam hard for the surface and this time was able to grab two breaths before the wraiths pulled her back beneath the water. Again, they were working together, attaching to the denim hems at her ankles, and to her midriff, teeth tearing at the fabric of her jumper, ripping her clothes to reveal the vulnerable flesh beneath. Susanna cried out as she felt those teeth sink in deep and slice through skin.

This was it – exactly what James had been afraid would happen. The wraiths were going to overwhelm her and then she'd be trapped down here…

She fought, but she couldn't free herself from their grip and, just as she'd thought, now that her blood was mixing with the water more and more wraiths were appearing. Horror filled her,

her mind supplying images of what was soon to come, but even now, the one thing she couldn't be was sorry.

Even if there had only ever been the smallest, smallest chance, she'd had to take it. She'd had to do everything she could to save Jack. She just wished—

A wraith swam right at her face, fins slapping against her cheek and making her yank her head back and expel precious air in a flurry of bubbles. Susanna clamped her lips shut and braced for more pain, but the wraith didn't latch on to her free arm or to the other side of her torso. Instead, it swam round and sank its teeth into the body of the wraith that was tearing up her side. Susanna watched, disbelieving, as it twisted its head from side to side, aggravating whatever wound it had caused until the wraith loosed its hold on Susanna's flesh with a screech of anger.

What was happening?

Not understanding, Susanna went back to kick, kick, kicking, trying to free her feet so that she could get up to the surface – and into the damned boat. She wouldn't have managed it – the wraiths who had a grip on her jeans were resistant to her every move – but the wraith who'd turned on its own kind harried and snapped at them until one let go, then two.

The lead weights on her ankles suddenly gone, Susanna was able to shake the two remaining wraiths and swim furiously for the surface. She made it and reached at once for the boat, hauling herself up and in with one monumental effort. Utterly exhausted, she lay where she'd fallen, awkwardly splayed along the bottom of the boat, the cross supports digging painfully into her back. She barely noticed, too consumed with coughing and then dragging air, sweet, blessed air into her chest. Her legs ached from kicking and she was bleeding heavily, but she just didn't have the energy to deal with it, to move.

Her thoughts whirled, even as her body punished her with spasms of pain. What had happened down there? The wraith that had appeared, the one that had turned on its friends... There could only be one reason for it to do that, surely? It seemed like it had been protecting her.

Trying to save her.

Susanna had lost many souls in the lake. But of all of those, Jack was the only one who would care enough to defend her. The only one that would come to her aid. She'd found him, she was sure of it.

Now the only question was, how could she help him?

Susanna lay there for several more minutes, her body simply refusing her orders to move, until she was able to lever herself up and peer over the side of the boat. The water was quiet again, the boat gently rocking. She knew, though, that the wraiths were still there. Just out of sight, waiting for her to return.

Susanna wasn't that stupid. She'd learned her lesson. But what was the next step?

"Jack?" she called down into the water. "Jack?"

No response.

Holding on tight to the boat, Susanna leaned over and trailed her fingertips through the gently lapping waves. The water was cool and pleasant on her fingers—

And then something bit her.

"Ow!" Yanking back, Susanna stared at her hand. Three of her fingertips were bloodied, small puncture wounds in each pad where teeth had gnashed down. Her actions had roused the wraiths, and the boat bobbled as they swirled around her like sharks circling their prey.

"Jack!" Susanna yelled. "Jack, it's me."

If he was there still, and he heard her, he didn't react. Nothing broke the surface. Susanna thought she might have heard a lone, mournful wail, different in pitch to the eerie noise that was coming from the rest of the gathered creatures, but she couldn't be sure.

What to do…

Susanna had never, ever seen a wraith from the lake come above the surface, so she had to work on the assumption that Jack *couldn't* come to her. Which really left only one option.

It wasn't her soaking-wet clothes that made Susanna shiver. She really did not want to go back down there. Into the dark, where she was so outnumbered and there was no air or light or—

Splash!

She threw herself overboard before she could talk herself out of it.

It wasn't like the first time. The wraiths were ready. Before she'd even righted herself , they were grabbing and biting and swirling and dragging her down. Bubbles flooded the water before her face and Susanna struggled to make sense of what was happening. The wraiths moved too quickly for her eyes to track, their black-and-slate-grey skin perfectly camouflaged by the water.

Fighting only enough to keep herself from sinking more than a few feet from the surface, Susanna scoured the water. Where was he? Which one was Jack? He'd been utterly indistinguishable, apart from his actions.

Using all the breath she had left in her lungs – which wasn't much – Susanna screamed Jack's name. She wasn't sure how far the sound carried, probably not far. It was a stupid move, too. No sooner had she done it than she had to make for the surface, had to breathe.

She would, if only she could get herself free.

Once again Susanna felt the panic as the wraiths caught and held her there, like a fish caught in a net. She flipped and twisted, but she was stuck. Her mouth was clamped shut, every rational thought left in her mind fixed on keeping it closed and fighting the need to breathe.

She didn't need oxygen: she wouldn't die.

But knowing that didn't make it any easier to bear the pain, the desperate, clawing need to inhale.

Without warning, a wraith holding doggedly onto Susanna's left forearm was gone. A moment later, her right leg was free. Susanna didn't see what happened, but she was knew: it was Jack. Swiping at a wraith that was flailing in front of her face, she saw him. His jaw was distended, the whole thing latched on to another wraith. Awkwardly moving through the water towards him, Susanna reached out, fingers searching, but the wraith that had to, *had to* be Jack, jerked away from her touch. It let go of the creatures it had been holding and swam at another, one that was clinging determinedly to Susanna's jumper, chewing at it like it was flesh. Perhaps it couldn't tell the difference.

Trying again, Susanna twisted and stuck out a hand, but Jack wouldn't even let her fingers graze him. He – if it *was* him – swam deftly away, but he kept at the wraiths that were attacking her, kept helping her.

Susanna wanted to give it one more go, but she couldn't ignore the need to breathe any longer.

Using her newly liberated limbs, she beat at the wraiths that were trapping her, swimming for the surface as she did so. The higher she rose, the fewer wraiths made the journey with her, until she was alone, treading water, her head above the waves, hands clutching the boat. She drew air into her oxygen-starved lungs and wriggled into the rowing boat, much less gracefully this time.

Two near-drownings was too much.

This wasn't going to work. There were too many of them. Susanna couldn't separate Jack from the rest, and though he seemed to recognise her, he hadn't let her touch him. If she was going to get him in the boat to do... something, anything – whatever she needed to do to bring Jack back to himself – then she had to get her hands on him. But she had no idea how to do that and, looking at the light in the sky, she was running out of time.

Utterly dispirited, Susanna picked up the oars and started to row slowly, painfully back towards the shore, sobbing all the way.

She just couldn't do it – not alone.

CHAPTER 21

Dylan walked with her head down, on autopilot. She was hollow.
Broken.

They'd failed, that was almost a certainty now. They'd gone through the valley and crossed the rugged landscape that lay beyond. Now there was only the lake to go – and there was still no sign of her parents.

Unless they'd been unaccountably delayed, Dylan and Tristan weren't going to catch them. It was just as well this wasn't Dylan's wasteland, that she didn't control the weather. If she did, they'd be facing gales and lightning, black clouds and driving rain.

It had all been for nothing.

She'd given up her life, *Tristan*, for nothing.

Not even the thought of seeing her parents in a couple of days' time, when she reached the line, could lift her black mood, because first she'd have to say goodbye to Tristan.

"Dylan, angel, come on."

"Huh?" Dylan lifted her head, the landscape swimming for a dizzying second before her eyes focused. Tristan stood before her, his expression grim.

"You're slowing," he said. "We're not safe yet, we need to get inside."

Dylan looked over his shoulder at the safe house, just a few hundred metres away. She couldn't feel Tristan's urgency, his fear that the wraiths would catch them. She couldn't feel anything.

She just felt… numb.

"Dylan," Tristan repeated. "Come on, we've got to go."

He reached for her hand and she let him take it. When he started walking again, she trudged along behind him.

One night in this safe house.

One night in the safe house on the other side of the lake.

Then they would be separated. For ever.

Unless… A spark of hope lit a small, tentative fire inside her.

"Tristan," Dylan began.

"I know you're tired," he said, not looking back, resolutely marching forward, "but you can rest really soon. We're almost there."

"No, Tristan, listen." Dylan upped her pace so they were walking side by side, so she could see Tristan's determined expression, his eyes fixed on their safe haven. "What will happen to the wasteland when my parents cross the line? Will it disappear, drop us into the real wasteland?"

"What?" Tristan turned to her, clearly startled by the question. His eyebrows scrunched together as he thought, though he didn't stop moving. "No." He shook his head. "It will still be here as long as I am."

"But you're not one of their ferrymen," she reminded him. "If they cross the line, their ferrymen will disappear, be pulled to other souls, and then what will happen?"

"I should be able to hold the projection," Tristan asserted, but he didn't look as sure as he sounded. His pace quickened, though Dylan didn't think he realised. It wasn't as if they were going to be able to beat her parents to the line; they had to stop here for the night to keep Dylan safe from the wraiths.

"If you can hold the projection," Dylan went on, pursuing the line of thought that was growing in strength with every passing second, "then we don't really need to leave the safe house in the morning, do we?"

Or the next day. Or the day after that.

Or ever, really.

If Dylan couldn't gift her parents life, if it was already too late to beat them to the line, then she could at least steal some more time with Tristan. A day, a week, a year; she'd take *anything*.

"What?" Tristan ground to a halt and stared at her. "Dylan, no. We have to keep going."

"It's too late, Tristan. You know it is. We're not going to catch them."

Tristan started walking again. There was a stiff set to his shoulders, and his grip on her hand tightened, squeezing Dylan's fingers almost to the point of pain.

"You can't stay here," he told her through gritted teeth. "No matter if we catch up to your parents or not, I'm delivering you to the line. It isn't safe."

"But we'd be together!"

"No."

"Tristan!"

"I said no, Dylan! It's non-negotiable. The longer you're here, the more chance there is of something happening to you. I couldn't bear it if you became one of those things. I couldn't live with myself knowing that you were trapped like that, because of my selfishness, because I wanted to hold on to you for a little longer. Every wraith I saw, for the rest of eternity, I'd wonder if it was you." He glanced in her direction, eyes blazing. "Would you do that to me?"

The argument Dylan had ready to throw at Tristan died on her lips. No, she wouldn't, *couldn't*, do that.

"Tristan—"

But she didn't get any further than that.

"Tristan! Tristan!"

Like an echo, his name ricocheted around the valley, but it wasn't Dylan doing the shouting. Taking a step closer to Tristan, Dylan glanced around, hunting for the owner of that strangely familiar voice.

"What the hell?" Tristan spotted her a moment before Dylan, but then she saw Susanna running down the path towards them, the path that led to the lake.

"What… what is she doing here?"

"I don't know," Tristan muttered, then he surged forward, hauling Dylan along with him.

They met at the end of the valley, just a few metres from the safe house. Susanna's eyes were wide with astonishment as she ground to a breathless halt. She looked just as Dylan remembered her: dark hair, dark eyes; a little taller than Dylan, a little thinner. She was also sopping wet.

"What are you doing here?" she asked.

"What are *you* doing here?" Dylan demanded right back, even though Susanna's question had been aimed at Tristan. Or, possibly, *because* the question had been aimed at Tristan. She took a small step forward, positioning herself ever so slightly in front of him.

Susanna's eyes dropped to her, and Dylan half-expected to see amusement there, or maybe ever derision. She didn't expect sympathy. Sadness.

"Dylan—" Susanna said softly.

"Why are you here, Susanna?" Tristan prompted. "Where's your soul?"

"You don't know?" Susanna asked, turning to Tristan, confusion clouding her features. Then she shook her head.

"Of course you don't know, how could you? But then, how can you even be here?"

"What?" Dylan snapped, totally lost.

"You're ferrying one of Dylan's parents," Tristan stated, putting the pieces together.

"You are?" Dylan breathed. She looked stupidly about her, as if expecting her mum or dad to suddenly appear at Susanna's side.

"No," Susanna disagreed. There was a small pause before she added, "I'm ferrying both of them."

"I—" Dylan spluttered to a stop. "You're... what?" She glanced around once more, taking in the empty space around Susanna. "Where are they?" The state of Susanna's clothes and the direction she'd come from suddenly took on a new and horrifying meaning. "Have you lost them, in the lake? Have they... did you let them drown?!"

Dylan advanced on Susanna, horror and rage burning inside her until she felt like a wraith, ready to attack.

Susanna took a step back. "What? No, I—"

"Where are they?" Dylan demanded.

Susanna didn't get the chance to answer. Another voice cut through the haze in Dylan's brain, one she'd recognise anywhere.

"Dylan? Oh my God, baby. What are you doing here?"

Joan. She was there, tumbling out of the front door of the safe house, her cardigan flailing around her as she ran towards them.

"Mum!" Dylan didn't hesitate. She ran, her exhausted feet suddenly weightless. She was almost there, almost within the safety of her mum's arms, when her dad emerged from the safe house, too... and a strong arm wrapped round Dylan's middle and jerked her to a painful stop.

"Don't!" Tristan said, suddenly between Dylan and her mum, holding up a hand to halt Joan's progress. "Don't touch her."

"Tristan!" Dylan struggled in his hold, betrayal an ugly aftertaste in her mouth.

"*Remember*, Dylan," he said quietly. "Remember what it said."

For a second Dylan's brain was too stunned to take in what he was saying, then it came back to her. The Inquisitor, explaining what Dylan needed to do to send her parents back to the real world. One touch, any touch, skin to skin. That was all that was needed. If Dylan threw herself into Joan's arms right now, both of her parents would be whisked out of the wasteland, and Dylan would lose the chance to say goodbye.

"Let go of her!" Joan was saying. "Tristan, stop it! Right now!"

"What's going on?" Her dad, now. Shoulder to shoulder with Joan, looking angry... and scared. "Dylan, what the hell are you doing here?" He shifted his gaze to Tristan. "Why is she here? What's going on?" Not giving Tristan a chance to explain, he looked past both of them. "Susanna?"

"We'll explain," Tristan said. "We'll explain everything, just please—" a pause where a low wailing punctuated the silence, "let's get inside!"

No one argued with Tristan's plea. They hurried into the safe house, Tristan orienting himself so that he was between Dylan and her parents. She appreciated it, because Joan looked like she desperately wanted to hug her, and Dylan didn't know whether she'd be able to resist letting her.

"All right," Dylan's dad said, as soon as they were inside and the door safely closed. "Talk."

"No, please." Tristan ignored him, focusing instead on Joan, who was making a beeline for Dylan once more. "You can't touch her."

"What do you mean I can't touch her? She's my daughter!"

The anguish on her mum's face was like a knife in the gut to Dylan, but Tristan was right.

"Listen to Tristan, Mum," she croaked. "If you touch me – you or dad – you'll disappear. We won't get the chance to... to say goodbye."

"I don't understand," Joan said helplessly. She turned to James, who was glowering at Tristan.

"Explain," he demanded.

"It's my fault," Dylan said. She wanted to get that out there, right from the off. "This was my decision. You didn't die. Not really. You're here because of me. The Inquisitor took you because it made a bargain with us that it couldn't break. It couldn't have us, so reaped your souls instead."

Blanket silence followed Dylan's words, until Susanna whispered, "The Inquisitor?"

"What's an Inquisitor?" Dylan's mum asked.

"It's a being that controls the wasteland."

"Dylan," Tristan warned quietly.

"What?" Dylan shrugged her shoulder at him. "What does it matter what I tell them? Do you honestly think the Inquisitor will let them remember?"

Joan and her dad couldn't touch her, but Tristan could. He drew Dylan into his arms and she sagged against his strength, trying hard not to cry.

"How... how did you come to make a bargain with this... Inquisitor thing?" Joan asked, confusion etched all over her face. "Dylan, I don't understand!"

Dylan opened her mouth and closed it again. How to explain? She'd had all this time in the wasteland, but she'd been so consumed with chasing after her parents that she hadn't stopped to think about how she would break the truth to them.

"I died," she said quietly. "In the train crash, I died. I opened my eyes and I was here, in the wasteland. Tristan was my ferryman, he was meant to take me across to the afterlife, but I came back." She glanced helplessly at Tristan, her voice dropping to a barely audible whisper, "We shouldn't have, *I shouldn't have*, but we didn't know what the consequences would be."

"Dylan," Tristan murmured, holding her tighter.

She cleared her throat, determined to get it all out. "The Inquisitor took your lives to restore the balance, because we were in the real world when we shouldn't have been."

"If the Inquisitor took us instead, why are you here?" her dad asked. He had a hand out, as if he wanted to reach for her, but he stayed at arm's length.

"She traded," Tristan told him. "She traded the Inquisitor her life for yours."

"What?" Dylan watched her mum pale, all of the blood leaching from her face. She swayed, and for a moment Dylan thought she might faint, but her dad was there to steady her. He didn't look much happier, though. Dylan watched his throat work as he tried to swallow.

"No," he said, shaking his head. "You can't do that. I won't let you."

"It's done," Dylan said. She was feeling strangely calm all of a sudden, as if she stood in the eye of a storm. Detaching herself from Tristan, she walked towards her parents. She wanted them to read her sincerity. To understand that this had been her choice – and she'd made it.

"It can't be," her dad denied, shaking his head. "You need to tell it that you've changed your mind. That we didn't accept and—"

"I can't," Dylan said. "The Inquisitor was very clear on that. There's no going back. Not for me."

"Oh, baby." Joan tripped forward towards her but stopped short when Dylan stepped neatly back.

"Not yet," Dylan whispered. "As soon… as soon as you touch me, you'll leave the wasteland, and you probably won't remember any of this. Not the journey, or Susanna. You won't even remember Tristan."

Joan shook her head. "Of course I'll remember."

"You won't," Tristan said quietly. "The Inquisitor will take all of your memories from the day of the accident. It'll be like Dylan died in the train crash, after all."

Dylan nodded. "You'll have each other, though. That won't change."

Her gift to them.

Joan gave a little sob, lifting the hands that clearly wanted to reach for Dylan up to her face to cover her mouth.

"That was a brave, selfless thing to do," her dad said quietly, but then he shook his head. "You shouldn't have done it, though, Dylan. We would have given up our lives for you in a heartbeat if the Inquisitor had given us the choice."

"It's not for ever, Dad," Dylan whispered. "You know there's something afterwards now. And I've been across the line, I know what's there. When it's your turn, I'll be there. Waiting for you."

Joan sobbed again and James folded himself around her, drawing her close. He looked like he was leaning on her as much as he was holding her up, and Dylan had a desperate desire to join them, to make them a family.

She didn't even know if the Inquisitor would grant her a moment to enjoy it before her parents vanished, however, so she held herself back. "It's not for ever," she repeated.

"That's right." Her dad cleared his throat, seemed to shore himself up. "And you won't be alone. You'll have Tristan there to take care of you."

"Actually—"

"That's right," Dylan said loudly, drowning out Tristan's quiet rebuttal. "I won't be alone, so you don't have to worry about me." She turned to stare at Tristan, daring him to refute her.

Joan gave a strangled squawk that might have been at attempt at a laugh. "Not worry about you? Oh God, Dylan. I can't... This can't be right. It just can't." She turned to Tristan, a fire lighting her eyes. "How could you let her do this? You could have stopped her!"

"No, Mum." Dylan blocked her mum's view of Tristan, standing as a shield before him. "Don't blame him. He wanted me to let you go, but I couldn't. It was my choice. If you want to be mad at someone, be mad at me."

All the fight drained out of Joan and she sank down onto the worn and faded sofa that ran along the back wall. She put her head in her hands, her shoulders curled in protectively, and for the first time in Dylan's life she noticed how frail her mum was. How brittle she looked, as if she was ready to shatter. Her skin was grey and her mouth was tight and pinched. It was a look Dylan had seen so often on Joan's face growing up that she'd stopped really noticing it. Then it had faded away when Dylan's dad had come back into their lives until it was nothing but a ghostly shadow.

Dylan had brought it back, and that hurt.

She was doing this for them, though. Giving them a chance to live. And when the Inquisitor manipulated their memories, they wouldn't remember this moment, the choice Dylan had made for them.

And Dylan would wait for them. They'd be a real family, a complete family, eventually. She moved so that Tristan was in her line of vision. No, she realised. They'd never be complete – or at least, *she* wouldn't be – but that was her burden to live with.

"Dylan, you look like you're about to fall down," Tristan commented in a low voice. "Here." He dragged a stool from beneath a rickety kitchen table. "Sit on this."

Now that the worst of the emotional storm seemed to have passed, Dylan felt her adrenaline, and her strength, fading. She gladly took the seat and then watched as Tristan moved into the middle of the space, taking quiet control.

"We didn't think we were going to catch you," he said. "We thought you were too far ahead." He flicked his glance at Susanna, who was shifting a little uncomfortably now. "Why are you still here?"

Thick, uncomfortable silence.

"Because I asked them to stay." Susanna looked like she was torn between shame and defiance. "I asked them to wait for me in the safe house."

"You left your souls?" Tristan asked. Then he frowned. "Wait. Go back a bit. Why do you even have two souls? The Inquisitor said Dylan's parents would be together, but not that they would be sharing a ferryman; it's far too dangerous to try and protect two souls at once."

"I don't know," Susanna said, a hint of belligerence colouring her tone. "I was sent to the flat, and two of them were there."

"That's not right," Tristan argued, then he waved his hand through the air, dismissing it as unimportant. Or at least, a mystery they couldn't solve. "Why did you ask them to wait? What were you doing?"

Susanna didn't answer. She looked away, shame winning the war.

"Did you find him?" Dylan's dad asked.

It went very, very quiet as Tristan regarded Susanna with dawning understanding – and bone-deep disapproval.

Dylan didn't understand. "Find who?"

"Jack," Tristan stated. Susanna's shoulders hunched a hair higher, but she didn't contest him.

"Jack?" Dylan repeated dumbly. "Jack's here? Where? How?"

"He's not here," Tristan said. "He's in the lake."

"The lake?" Dylan scrunched her forehead, struggling to catch up, but Tristan wasn't making any sense. It did explain why Susanna was soaked to her skin, however. "I don't understand, how can he be in the lake?" Then, between one heartbeat and the next, she understood. "He's become a wraith?"

Susanna's reaction told her she was right. Dylan could also tell that she'd hurt the other ferryman, blurting it out like that with all the subtlety of a sledgehammer.

"I'm sorry, I didn't mean that." She bit her lip, still feeling like she was missing something. "If he's become a wraith, what were you trying to do?" There was only one thing that made sense. "Were you trying to get him back? I thought that was impossible."

She looked to Tristan for confirmation, but he was concentrating on Susanna, sympathy softening the condemnation on his face.

"It is impossible," he reminded the other ferryman. "He's gone, Susanna. You risked the safety of your souls for nothing. If he's become a wraith, he's gone and he's not coming back. You know that."

Though Dylan could see Susanna knew she was in the wrong, she still came out fighting.

"We were told we could never, ever cross into the real world, either," she shot back. "Now we know that wasn't true!"

"We shouldn't have!" Tristan replied, just as angrily. "Look at all the trouble we've caused! We meddled in things we didn't understand, with no idea what the consequences might be."

"I made a promise, Tristan!" Susanna replied, half-furious, half-pleading. "I swore to him that I'd get him through the wasteland

and I let him down."

"You should never have made that promise," Tristan said. "You know that. And you're just going to have to live with the fact that you broke your word. Listen to me carefully, Susanna. *He. Is. Gone.* He's a wraith, there's no coming back from that. There's nothing inside them, they're just empty, hate-filled shells."

"That's not true!" Susanna had tears in her eyes now. From her position on the stool, Dylan watched her clench her hands into determined fists. "Jack recognised me in the water. He helped me when other wraiths attacked. If he hadn't, I'd have been dragged under and trapped there."

A quiet gasp from Joan drew Dylan's attention. When she looked back to Susanna it was to see the ferryman looking stricken.

"I'm sorry," she said. "It was dangerous, but I had to try. And I came back."

"You might not have," Tristan retorted. "It was a stupid risk to take."

"You would have done it for Dylan."

Tristan opened his mouth and then closed it again.

"He's not gone," Susanna said, pressing her advantage. "He responded to me, I know he did. And on our way here, in a safe house, we found a wraith trapped inside—"

"Inside the safe house?" Tristan asked, but Susanna ignored him.

"Joan sang to it and it responded!"

"You're imagining things," Tristan retorted. "They're gone, Susanna. There's no humanity left in them. They're—"

"She's telling the truth," Dylan's mum interjected, surprising everyone. "When I sang, it calmed it. Then, as soon as I stopped, it was rabid again. I don't understand it, but I saw the change in the wraith. It recognised the music."

Susanna stared at Tristan beseechingly. A quick glance to her left told Dylan that both of her parents were looking to him, too. Dylan had had a lot of practice watching Tristan's expressions. She could read him like a book and she knew what was coming. He was going to shut this down, tell Susanna it was too dangerous, that she needed to forget about Jack. Stick to her role and stop risking the souls in her charge.

She also knew that he would never, ever have given up on her. No matter what he said, if she ever became a wraith he would try anything to get her back – just like she'd do for him.

"He protected you?" Dylan asked.

Susanna nodded her head, looking to Dylan gratefully. "He stopped other wraiths from attacking me." Her earnest expression twisted. "But he wouldn't let me near him, and I couldn't catch him and fight off the other wraiths, not on my own."

Not on her own…

"But if you had another ferryman…?" Dylan let the thought tail off.

"Dylan, no."

"If I had another ferryman, I think I could get him onto the boat," Susanna answered, very, very quietly. "And then, well I can either do something – call him back to me somehow – or I can't. But at least I'll know."

That was the thing that was really tearing Susanna apart, Dylan thought. The idea that Jack was in there somewhere, trapped and calling for her. Hoping she'd save him.

Dylan hadn't thought Jack and Susanna were all that close – or that they even liked each other – but perhaps their time together had changed that. Susanna seemed genuinely heartbroken. The grief on her face was impossible to deny.

"Don't look at me that way, Dylan," Tristan said. He, of course, could read her face as well as she could read his. "I won't risk you, not for anyone."

Susanna flinched, but if Tristan noticed, he ignored it.

"Imagine it was me," Dylan whispered. "Just one day, one chance. If the two of you work together, it'll be safer, won't it?"

Tristan remained silent, reluctant to agree, but over his shoulder Susanna nodded.

"It's dangerous, Dylan," he said quietly. "If something happens, I might not come back."

He was just trying to scare her, she knew. It was working, but she did her best to keep the worry off her face.

"You'll come back to me," she told him. "I know you will." Then she hammered the final nail into the coffin. "It'll give me a little more time with my mum and dad," she reminded him. "A chance to say goodbye."

The safe house seemed to hold its breath as Tristan deliberated. Dylan knew the very moment he made up his mind, because his jaw clenched and his eyes narrowed dangerously. He drew in a deep breath through his nose and shook his head. Susanna looked crestfallen, but Dylan wasn't fooled. She smiled slowly.

"It's the right thing to do," she said.

"Tristan?" Susanna asked, still not sure.

"One chance," Tristan told her. "But know this: if it comes down to it, I *will* give up Jack – and you – to make sure I get back to Dylan. Be very clear on that."

"I understand," Susanna breathed. "Thank you." Then she turned shining eyes on Dylan. "Thank you!"

If Dylan had been told, back when she first met Susanna in the real world, that one day she'd be actively trying to push the two ferrymen together, she would have laughed. Then swore. Then laughed some more. But this was – quite literally – a matter of life and death, and there was no place for petty jealousy.

Besides, she knew with absolute certainty that Tristan loved her and her alone.

And the lengths Susanna was going to to try and save Jack, the pain in her eyes when she spoke of him, well, those were reason alone to help her.

CHAPTER 22

It was awkward, striding out into the morning light with Tristan. So many nights they'd shared companionable quiet, Susanna wishing she could break that impenetrable barrier and talk to him. Now she could speak as much as she wanted to, and yet she found she had nothing to say.

Well, there was one thing.

"Thank you."

Tristan just grunted. She supposed that was because she'd said the words about ten times since he made the decision last night.

They'd never really had the opportunity to talk about what happened in the real world. What Susanna did. Why she did it. The way Tristan tried to stand up for her, but then relinquished her to her fate to save himself, to save Dylan.

Now they had that time – and the freedom to do it – but Susanna found herself trudging silently along, a step behind Tristan.

"When we get there," he said, not turning to look at her, "I think the best idea is just to row right out to the centre, where it's deepest. That's where the wraiths tend to gather, so we'll have the best chance of finding him there."

"That's what I did yesterday," Susanna answered, trying to keep the note of petulance out of her voice. She wasn't stupid; she hadn't just stood on the shore and shouted on him like she was trying to retrieve a misbehaving Labrador. "I just couldn't fight off the rest of the wraiths and grab him at the same time. Not without being pulled under." She paused as they reached the crest of the hill, the gently lapping lake laid out before them. "If you can keep them off me, I can get him. I know I can."

"I'm not going in the water, Susanna," Tristan told her. "I can't."

She was left scrambling as Tristan began striding down to the pebbled shore.

"What?" She rushed to close the distance between them. "But I need your help! I can't do it without you!"

Susanna caught up with him as he reached the little boathouse. She grabbed him by the sleeve and he stilled, turning to face her. His eyes were icy, detached and a little frightening. Susanna resisted the survival instinct that yelled at her to let go of him. If Tristan didn't help her, she had no chance of getting Jack back. He'd be trapped under the water, for ever.

"Please," she begged.

Tristan took hold of her hand and gently but firmly freed his arm. "I'll help you," he said. "I told you I would. But I can't go in the water. I won't risk being caught by the wraiths. If they manage to pull us both down, what's going to happen to Dylan? To her parents? I'm sorry, but Jack's soul is not worth theirs, not to me."

"You won't be much help to me in the boat!" The retort came out without her permission, and she immediately wanted to call it back, particularly when Tristan bristled at her tone. It was true, though. All he'd be able to do from the boat was watch her drown.

Tristan didn't respond at first, he was too busy hefting up the plank used to keep the doors closed. Susanna realised a moment too late that she probably should have helped, but he handled the heavy, awkward hunk of wood much more easily than she ever had, tossing it aside effortlessly.

"I'm going to be a *lot* of help to you in the boat," Tristan said as he swung the door open and disappeared into the shadows inside. He slipped around the side of the little boat and lifted something from a hook on the wall. He held it up and offered her a small smile. "I'm going to be your tether."

A tether. Tying himself to her so he'd be there to haul her back up, out of the water, no matter what happened. Susanna started at him, dumbfounded. She'd never even noticed the rope was there before.

"I could have used this," she whispered, horrified at her own stupidity. "I could have tethered Jack to me, and they wouldn't have been able to take him. Why didn't I think of that? How many souls have I lost here, and I didn't think of that!"

At her words, shock rippled across Tristan's face and he looked back down at the rope. He closed his eyes and shook his head, then let out a bark of dark laughter. "If it makes you feel better," he said, "I didn't either."

The tiny hint of camaraderie lightened Susanna's mood for a moment, but it didn't last. Hindsight was twenty–twenty, but she cursed herself for not seeing how easy it would have been to prevent what happened, prevent Jack from being taken from her.

"You live and learn," Tristan said, coming back around the boat so that he could begin hauling it up out of its cosy home. This time, Susanna stepped up to help. "We'll know to do it with souls from now on. Well," that hint of darkness back in his voice, "those souls we want to save."

"What do you mean?" Susanna asked, surprised. "You'll be across the line with Dylan."

"No," Tristan said, giving the boat a particularly vicious heave. "I won't."

"But she said—"

"I know what she said. But I can't cross the line. When she leaves, I'll go back to doing what I always did, being who I always was."

The breath rushed out of Susanna as she took in what Tristan was saying. "Does Dylan know?" she asked quietly.

Surely she couldn't; surely she wouldn't do that to Tristan?

"She knows." Stones skittered beneath the boat as the two of them manoeuvred it until it faced the water. "She wanted to save her parents, and this was the price."

Susanna didn't know what to say. She couldn't imagine how Tristan must feel, the hell he was going through. To be offered everything any ferryman had ever dreamed of, and then have it taken away. To have to ferry the soul that was responsible for stealing it from you. And still love her.

"I'm sorry," she offered, though it didn't feel like enough.

"Let's just do this," Tristan muttered.

Tristan took control of the oars once they had the boat afloat, scything through the water with strong, smooth strokes that Susanna could only watch enviously, thinking of every time she'd puffed and panted and sweated her way across.

"Tie the rope around your waist," Tristan said when he'd powered them to the very heart of the lake. "Make sure it's really tight; you don't want to slip free."

He gave her a steady look and she heard what he didn't add: if she did, she was on her own. Shuddering slightly, Susanna reached for the length of rope and wound it round her middle. It was thick and had stiffened with age, but she forced it into a knot, tugging experimentally to make sure it would hold. While she worked, Tristan tied the other end to the bench seat of the boat and held the rope in his hand, ready to take the strain, should she need it.

Knowing time was of the essence – Tristan had been clear that he would give her one chance, and one chance only – Susanna contemplated the water.

"I hope we don't disturb the creature," she murmured.

"The wraiths?" Tristan asked, surprised. "I thought that was the idea. How will you find Jack otherwise?"

"No." Susanna shook her head. "Not the wraiths, the other thing. The big thing."

Silence echoed over the lake.

"There's nothing else down there," Tristan said after a long moment. "It's just the wraiths."

"I saw it," Susanna told him. "It's huge, with long tentacles thick enough to pick up a man. That's what got Jack, that's why I lost him."

"No." He shook his head, denying her words.

"I saw it, Tristan," she repeated. "In the real wasteland. It destroyed the planks in the hull, and then, when we started sinking, it reached up and pulled Jack out of the boat."

"Maybe it only exists in the real wasteland," Tristan offered.

Susanna shook her head. He knew better than that. "If it was there, then it's here."

"Well," he said, shrugging helplessly, "I guess try not to wake it up, then." He reached out and laid a hand on her arm, his skin startlingly hot against hers. "Remember, I won't go in the water. If this thing is there and starts trying to sink me, I'll—" He broke off, grimacing.

"You'll row away and leave me," Susanna finished for him.

"I'm sorry," Tristan said softly. "I *am* sorry, but I will. I've got no choice."

"You do have a choice," she disagreed, "and you've made it. Just like your soul made hers. It's OK, Tristan. I understand." Susanna didn't like it, but she understood. She took a deep breath. "All right, it's time."

"Good luck."

Like before, she toed off her boots, not wanting their weight to impact her mobility in the lake. Then, smiling wanly at Tristan, Susanna gathered her courage, and flung herself into the water.

It took her a moment to adjust to the shock of the cold. She spun under the surface, squinting through the murky, silt-heavy water for signs of wraiths. There was none. Their boat held no soul, and the wraiths could tell.

How was she going to draw them to her?

Swimming lithely up to the surface, Susanna clung onto the boat as she drew in several deep breaths.

"Any luck?" Tristan called from above her.

"Nothing yet," she replied. As she shifted position, she scraped her arm on the side of the boat, which rocked with the little waves she'd made. Wincing slightly, Susanna examined the scratch, seeing little drops of red pooling in several slightly deeper cuts.

Well, that was one way to do it, she thought.

Gritting her teeth, Susanna shoved her sleeve higher up so that the full length of her forearm was exposed, then she raked it down the rough edges of the planks along the side of the boat. Splinters dug into her skin and she hissed against the pain, but when she drew back her arm to look at the damage, droplets of red were already splashing down into the water.

"Are you sure that was wise?" Tristan asked, momentarily blocking out the light as he leaned over the edge to stare down at her.

"I've got to attract the wraiths to me somehow," Susanna replied.

She used the vessel's weight to thrust her back under, the water filling her ears so she didn't have to listen to Tristan's grunt of disapproval. It was her arm, after all, and she'd do a lot worse than inflict a few flesh wounds to get Jack back.

This had to work; she'd never have another chance like this, when there was another ferryman to help her. It was now or never.

The water remained empty, but Susanna knew it wouldn't stay that way for long. She might not be a soul, but she knew from painful experience that wraiths enjoyed the taste of her blood.

There!

Something was swimming towards her, fast. Susanna allowed herself a grim smile as she kept her eyes on the approaching wraith – and the two that were following quickly in its wake. She didn't register the two wraiths darting in from behind, though, not until the last second, when the swoosh of air bubbles in the water tickled her neck. She tried to turn, to lift her arm in protection, but one tangled in her hair and the other took a firm grip on the bottom of her jeans.

A heartbeat later, the first wraith she'd seen reached her, slamming straight into her stomach. The breath wheezed out of Susanna and she jerked and twisted in the water.

Suddenly, pressure around her middle started hauling her upwards. She thrashed, fighting against it until she realised it was Tristan doing as he'd promised and pulling her free.

"No!" she gasped as soon as she reached the surface. "Not yet. I don't see Jack."

Tugging the rope slack again, she let the wraiths, who still had her clenched in their jaws, drag her back under, ignoring Tristan's worried shouts.

Where was he? Where was Jack?

Her lungs were already starting to burn, and her body stung all over as the wraiths worked at her, but Susanna ignored them. Pain was fleeting. It was nothing, just her body's warning system. She needed to focus. Find him.

"Jack!" She used all of her precious oxygen on the shout; she didn't see him, but there was a chance he might recognise his name.

Unfortunately, she now had to breathe. Tugging harshly on the rope, Susanna let Tristan haul her up to the surface where she took two quick, ragged breaths, then dived back down.

The wraiths were growing in number, drawn by the scent as more and more of her blood seeped into the water. They were violent and frantic, tearing at her, yanking her this way and that. A small swarm, determined to bring down their prey.

And none of them was helping her.

Where was he?

Please, please, don't say that she'd imagined it last time. That Tristan was right and he was really gone. He might even be the wraith with its teeth wrapped around her wrist, or the one trying to pull her hair from her head.

A wraith slashed in front of her face, side-swiping several that had been bombarding her in repeated dives. Turning fast in the water, it came back again, a vicious snap of its teeth tearing the back fins off the wraith gnawing at her shirt.

Jack!

Ignoring every wraith attacking her, Susanna concentrated on the darting form intent on helping her. He moved so fast, slicing through the water much better than she could. She'd never be able to catch him, but if she read his path correctly...

Susanna waited. The compulsion to breathe became a torment that was almost impossible to ignore, but she managed it. The need to fight the wraiths that surrounded her made her arms spasm and jerk time and again, but she held them still. Then, as the wraith that had to be Jack came back around, intent on a wraith clinging like a limpet to her thigh, she exploded into motion.

221

Her arms snapped closed and her body folded over, creating a cage to hold him. Using her legs for propulsion, she tugged on the rope, hoping Tristan would read the movement and know she needed to be rescued.

Nothing happened for two long, long seconds, but then Susanna felt the pull of the rope as she was hoisted towards the surface.

Yes! she thought. Jack was going crazy in her arms. Like a fox caught in a trap, he twisted and tore, searching for a way out. Susanna just held him tighter. Now that she had him, she wasn't going to let him go. In just a second or two they'd be at the surface…

Without warning, the wraiths attacking Susanna darted away. She experienced a single, blissful moment of calm before the reason behind their desertion became apparent. Something wrapped tightly around her lower leg, something much bigger than a wraith. A tentacle… Its grip tightened to the point of pain, then started pulling her downwards. Susanna felt herself sinking for a moment before Tristan reacted to the pressure on the rope and started tugging harder.

The rope around her middle; the tentacle around her ankle. Susanna felt like she was being torn in two. The pain intensified as both Tristan and the creature pulled, and Susanna knew her body couldn't handle much more. She screamed as blinding pain raced up her leg. The creature's squeezing grip had snapped her tibia in two.

Hanging onto Jack for dear life, Susanna lifted her free foot and kicked, hard. The tentacle wrapped around her just tightened, the resulting agony making Susanna think she might pass out, but fear and adrenaline kept her conscious and gave her the strength to kick, kick, kick again.

She would not let go of Jack. She would not let the creature pull her to the darkness at the bottom of the lake. Not now, when she was so close.

Come on Tristan, she thought. *Pull!*

He seemed to hear her. A spine-jarring yank on the rope coincided with another of Susanna's furious kicks and suddenly she was free, surging towards the surface.

"Here!" she gasped, as soon as she broke the surface. "Take him!"

A moment later Jack's writhing, wriggling form was plucked from her grasp and Susanna was left to scramble over the side. Her leg screamed with the movement, but she ignored it.

"Quick, give him to me!" She gestured furiously, reaching out with one hand and swiping her sodden hair out of her face with the other. "We have to get out of here, now!"

"What?" Tristan thrust wraith-Jack back at her and slammed himself onto the rowing bench. "What do you mean?"

"The creature! The one I told you about, it's down there!"

As if on cue, a resounding thump walloped the bottom of the boat.

"What the hell is that?!" Tristan exclaimed.

"Just row!"

Thankfully he didn't argue further, snatching up the oars and starting to plough them through the water towards the shore. Another thump hit the boat, rocking it and almost making Tristan lose an oar, but he held fast, grimly rowing harder.

Susanna used her back and her one good leg to wedge herself into the bow of the boat, leaving both hands free to try and hang onto Jack. He was gasping alarmingly, his body flopping around. He looked… well, he looked like a fish out of water. And Susanna was no expert, but she was pretty sure most fish couldn't survive long that way.

"Hold on," she murmured to him. "Please hold on."

They needed to get to the shore, where the creature – Susanna prayed fervently – couldn't follow them.

She shrieked involuntarily as another heavy thump smacked the hull. This time it was accompanied by an ominous cracking sound.

"Tristan!" Susanna cried.

"It's OK," he replied through heavy panting. "We're almost there."

They were. When Susanna lifted her head to peek over the side, the pebbled beach was much closer than she'd thought and the next thump, when it came, struck the very back of the boat, with much less force than the ones that had come before.

Susanna let out a single sigh of relief as the boat scraped along the shallows of the lake.

"Come on." Tristan was already up, vaulting over the side and splashing into the ankle-deep water.

"I can't," Susanna replied, shifting awkwardly into a more upright position. "My leg, I think it's broken. Here, take Jack. I can manage if you hang onto him."

Though he'd grabbed the wraith from her when she'd first burst through the surface, Tristan looked extremely unwilling to put his hands on it once more. He took a small step back, eyeing the writhing black bundle with distaste.

"It's Jack, Tristan," Susanna reminded him. "He's still there, deep inside. I know it."

Reluctantly, Tristan took wraith-Jack from Susanna and, with her hands free, she was able to topple painfully over the side. Using Tristan's shoulder for support, she limped and hopped out of the water onto the shore.

"Give him to me," she pleaded, as soon as they were above the tide-line. She dropped to a slumped kneeling position, leaning heavily on her good side, and reached her arms up for him. Tristan immediately relinquished his bundle, relief apparent on his face.

Susanna didn't have time for his distaste, or his scepticism. Jack was gasping violently now, suffocating in the open air. His movements were feeble and spasmodic, as if he was at the very end of his strength.

As gently as she could, Susanna laid him down on the pebbles. She kept him pinned there with one hand, then stroked the length of him with the other. That was enough to rouse Jack into one last attack, his head lifting up to snap at her fingers with a snarl.

"He's not in there," Tristan murmured from above her. "Look at it, Susanna. It's a mindless thing. It's empty."

"No, it isn't," Susanna disagreed. "It's Jack." She took a deep breath, the air wobbling all the way in and coming out just as jaggedly. "Come on, Jack. Come on. It's me, Susanna." A pause as she evaluated Jack's reaction... or lack of it. If he heard her words, recognised her voice, he didn't show it. She didn't know what she had been expecting to happen, what miracle she thought might suddenly take place once she had him in her arms.

She just knew she had to try.

"Jack, please. I know you're in there. I came for you, like I promised I would."

He'd stopped moving, was lying like a lump of charred wood on the bed of stones. His form was smoking gently, wisps rising up into the air.

"He's dying," Tristan said quietly.

"No."

But he was; she could see that he was. Jack was dying right in front of her eyes, and Susanna had no idea how to help him. How to reach him.

"Please, Jack." Struggling to see through her tears, Susanna leaned forward until her forehead pressed against the motionless flank of Jack's wraith body. It felt slightly slimy and scaly against her skin, and the position sent fire running up her injured leg, but Susanna didn't care. This was the closest she could get to Jack, the last few moments she'd have with him. "I'm so sorry," she said hoarsely, steeling herself against the tears threatening to escape. "I tried, but it wasn't enough."

He was still trembling slightly, the gills where his head met the long, eel-like body fluttering valiantly, but unless she was willing to put him back in the water, he'd be gone soon.

And Susanna couldn't do that to him. The Jack she knew would rather die than spend eternity trapped in the darkness of the water he was so afraid of.

A melody came to her, something Jack used to sing all the time. Susanna could barely hold a tune, but she hummed it quietly to him, hoping it might offer some sort of comfort as he slipped away. As she felt the last tremors leave him, she finally let herself cry. She'd failed him, but at least she'd freed him from the torment of being a wraith. That was something.

"That's… impossible," she heard from above her.

Susanna ignored Tristan, turning away from Jack's body. Tears coursed down her face, blurring her vision. Her whole body shook so badly it felt like the ground beneath her was pitching and rocking, as if she was still on the boat.

"Susanna—"

"Go away, Tristan," she managed to grit out. "Go back to your soul."

"Susanna." A hand came to rest on her shoulder and she jerked her head up, ready to scream at him. Why wouldn't he leave her alone?

But it wasn't Tristan's hand. And they weren't Tristan's eyes she caught and held for an instant before familiar arms wrapped round her and she was yanked into a rib-snapping hug.

They were Jack's.

CHAPTER 23

"You were a terror as a toddler. You used to refuse to get your teeth brushed, running all over the flat. Naked." Joan delivered the last word with gusto.

James coughed out a laugh, his mouth stretched into a grin, but tears were streaming down his face. Dylan's cheeks were just as wet, but she'd given up wiping them a long time ago.

"That's not true!"

"Oh, but it is! You liked running around naked. One time you did it in a supermarket. I was panicking because I'd lost you, and when the shop assistant and I found you, you'd ducked into the toy aisle and stripped all but your knickers off. You were most displeased to be interrupted."

"Mum!"

Joan smiled through red-rimmed eyes. "It's lucky for you mobile phones with cameras weren't around then. I'd have had some crackers of you."

For the thousandth time, Dylan wished she could reach up and hug her parents, and for the thousandth time she had to hold herself back. Not yet. Just a little longer.

She sat cross-legged on the floor in front of the sofa, where her mum sat under the comforting arm of Dylan's dad. Joan was retelling every single memory of Dylan's childhood. Most of them were hazy at best to Dylan, and she was drinking in Joan's words as much as her dad was; to him, they were brand new. Moments in time he'd lost, never to get back.

As she'd done every five minutes as the morning had rolled into the afternoon, Dylan craned her neck round and glanced out of the window.

"Don't look, Dylan," her dad said gently.

"What?" Dylan twisted back round to stare at him.

"It's best not to look," he advised. "I know it's frightening, but we're safe in here. It was like this all day yesterday, but as soon as Susanna returned, it went back to normal."

Oh. He thought Dylan was afraid of the scene outside, the harsh, bleeding underbelly of the wasteland. The jagged rocks and burning sun, as well as the wraiths that crawled over the land even in the height of day.

She was afraid of it, of course, but that wasn't why she was looking.

"It's not that," she told him. "I've seen the wasteland like this before." On that awful, awful day when she'd thought she'd lost Tristan, and she'd huddled, alone and terrified, in the corner of the safe house. "It'll go back to normal, once they come back."

That's what she was looking for. A sign that Tristan was returning to her. Had she been alone in here again, she'd have spent the day at the window, watching for him, but this time with her mum and dad was too precious.

"Of course." Joan's smile was brittle. "I forget that you've more experience of this place than we do." She hauled in an unsteady breath. "Are you sure, sweetheart, absolutely sure, that it can't be undone? Your father and I will happily take your place, Dylan. So don't worry about us."

"It's done, Mum," Dylan replied. "There's no going back. But even if I could, I wouldn't. I was supposed to die in the train crash.

That was what was meant to happen. I tried to change it, and I stole your lives instead."

"You didn't steal them, Dylan," her dad jumped in. "We'd give them to you. We *are* giving them to you."

"It's too late."

"No." Her dad shook his head. "I don't accept that. There must be a way."

"There isn't," Dylan insisted. "I knew the stakes when I accepted the Inquisitor's offer. Please." She took a deep breath, tried to calm herself. "I don't want to argue. Not now."

Her dad looked like he wanted to continue, but Joan laid a hand on his knee. "All right, baby," she agreed. "No more arguing."

"Thank you." Dylan did her best to put on a brave face, but as every moment ticked by, it got more and more difficult. Though she and her mum often didn't get along, she couldn't imagine not seeing her every day. She was the one thing Dylan knew she could always rely on. And her dad – they'd barely begun getting to know each other, and now she had to say goodbye.

Dylan gazed at them, sitting side by side, her dad's arm around Joan's shoulder, her mum's hand on his knee. At least one good thing had come out of all of this.

"I'm so glad you found each other again," Dylan whispered.

That was too much for Joan. She stared at Dylan for one long, glassy-eyed moment and then turned her head into James's shoulder and started sobbing.

He didn't try to say anything comforting – there wasn't anything to say. Instead he held her, his eyes drinking Dylan in.

"I know you said the Inquisitor would take our memories," he said quietly, "but I *will* remember you. I swear it."

Dylan swallowed through a throat made of shattered glass. "I hope so."

He wouldn't, though. But that was all right. Dylan would be on the other side of the line, waiting for him. They'd make new memories then. Hundreds of them, thousands. Enough that Dylan would be able to bury this sad, sad day under an avalanche of joyful ones.

James lifted his eyes from her face to the window, which made Dylan turn to look, too. She drew in a deep breath when she saw it, both relieved and anguished: the muted browns and greens of her parents' wasteland was back. Tristan and Susanna were returning.

Jumping to her feet, Dylan ignored the pins and needles that stabbed at her legs from sitting too long. She stalked to the door and yanked it open, stepping outside now that there was no danger from loitering wraiths. She couldn't see Susanna or Tristan, but the path to the lake wove round the back of the cottage, and by the time she'd rounded the first corner of the safe house, they were in sight. And they weren't alone.

Tristan was walking awkwardly, his shoulder dipped low to allow Susanna to throw her arm around it. On her other side, doing the same hunched lope so that Susanna was effectively being held upright between the two of them, was Jack.

Jack. They'd done it then, they'd got him back.

Dylan rushed towards them, reaching the trio just as they navigated the last of the slope. This close, she could see that Tristan and Jack weren't so much supporting Susanna as carrying her. She was ashen with pain, one leg trying to hop along, the other hanging uselessly. Tristan, too, looked pale, though a quick skim over him reassured Dylan that he wasn't hurt.

Jack looked... like someone had smacked him over the head. Hard. If he'd been a cartoon, he'd have had a ring of tweeting little birds circling above him.

"You did it!" she gasped.

"Inside," Tristan said, jerking his head in the direction of the safe house. "We'll talk there."

Dylan was desperate to know what had happened, but Susanna looked ready to drop, so she followed mutely behind as they limped the last few metres into the safe house.

Dylan's parents were already on their feet when they entered, so Tristan and Jack were able to lie Susanna down on the sofa. She reclined with a feeble whimper, her hand reaching down to grab at her bad leg. Jack immediately knelt by her side, clutching at her arm, his gaze fixed on her face.

"This must be Jack, then," Dylan's dad said quietly. "You got him."

"We did," Tristan answered. He turned to the hearth. "I'm going to start a fire. Susanna's soaked and freezing."

"I'm all right," Susanna mumbled weakly, but Tristan was already hunkered down in the fireplace and quickly had a blaze going.

"We need to bind your leg," he said, straightening up. "We don't want the bone to knit out of alignment."

"Give her a minute," Jack growled from the floor, but Susanna was nodding, using one trembling arm to heave herself up. Jack let her struggle for a moment before guiding her up with a low curse. "Let me," he grumbled at her when she reached forward to start rolling her trouser leg up out of the way.

"Thank you," Susanna sighed. She looked like she wanted to lie back down, but she contented herself with leaning awkwardly against Jack's shoulder while he used gentle hands to ease her jean leg as high above her knee as it would go. When he was finished, he put an arm around her and drew her into a hug, kissing the top of her head.

Dylan blinked, astonished. She'd last seen Jack on the night the Inquisitor had passed judgement on them all. He'd been surly, aggressive, and he'd barely tolerated his ferryman. It was impossible to guess how long Jack and Susanna had spent trapped together in the wasteland – time passed differently here – but things had definitely changed between them.

"This is going to be painful," Tristan warned, stepping close. He'd found a length of fabric from somewhere, and Susanna was staring at it as if he held a weapon in his hands rather than a strip of cotton.

"I know," she said quietly, "but at least I won't be doing it to myself this time."

She visibly braced as Tristan knelt beside her, then Dylan watched her squirm and grit her teeth as he started manipulating her lower leg.

"You're hurting her!" Jack growled. He looked like he wanted to shove Tristan away, but Susanna put a hand on his arm.

"He has to do it," she said. "My leg will heal pretty fast, but if the bone's not right I'll be hampered. That's dangerous here."

Jack still didn't look impressed. "Can't he, I don't know, knock you out with his ferryman powers or something?"

"It's fine, Jack." She smiled at him then turned to Tristan. "Do it."

Dylan didn't see Tristan move, but there was an audible 'snick' and Susanna cried out, clutching at Jack.

"Sorry," Tristan mumbled. He took the cloth and started wrapping it around Susanna's leg.

"No splint?" Joan asked from where she and James stood watching near the doorway. She was a nurse, and Dylan would have expected her to step forward and take charge, but the wasteland must have shaken her too much. She seemed content to let Tristan handle things. Dylan had to admit he worked like he knew what he was doing.

Tristan shook his head. "The bone will mend so fast she won't need it. She just needs to stay put for a couple of hours."

"It's a broken leg!" Joan protested.

"It'll heal," Tristan repeated.

"It will, Mum," Dylan added quietly, "I've seen it. They heal super-fast."

Tristan had been battered black and blue when he'd returned to her that day the first time they'd been here, and Dylan had been horrified. By the time morning came, though, there was nothing but some yellowed bruising and a little swelling.

"Must be useful," James said, trying to lift the tense atmosphere that had gathered in the tight space.

"It is," Tristan replied. He shot Susanna a sympathetic look. "Still hurts, though."

She smiled wanly, then turned to Jack and the smile widened at the same time as tears started pooling in her eyes. "It was worth it," she whispered.

They stared at each other, and Dylan had the feeling she was intruding on a very private, very personal moment. She switched her gaze to Tristan, who must have felt the same as he rolled to his feet and stepped back away from the pair.

"You got him," she said to him. "How?"

"He came to Susanna," he replied. "In the water, he came and helped her when the other wraiths were attacking."

Susanna had said that happened before, but Dylan hadn't really believed her; she didn't think Tristan had either.

"But was he Jack then, or was he a wraith?"

"A wraith. We got him onto the boat, but he was suffocating. By the time we reached the shore, I was certain he wasn't going to make it."

Tristan stared at the back of Jack's head, shaking his head in wonder.

"And?" Dylan prompted. "How did you get him back?"

"I don't know," Tristan admitted. "It was Susanna."

Hearing her name, Susanna looked over towards them. "It wasn't me," she said. Her eyes went back to Jack as if she couldn't bear to stop looking at him. "I didn't do anything. I thought—" her voice died in her throat and she swallowed hard. "I thought he was gone. I thought I'd really lost him."

Jack made a strangled noise and gripped Susanna's hands. Dylan could just make out the white-knuckled grip he had on her over his shoulder.

"It was you," he disagreed. He glanced behind him and seemed to realise that the whole room was listening to him with rapt attention. Dylan could see that it made him uncomfortable, and she waited for the Jack-explosion where he scowled and lashed out, but instead he shifted so that he could face them all, angling his body so he didn't have to let go of Susanna. "I could see you, and I wanted to do what the rest of the wraiths were doing, I wanted to slice and bite at you, but there was something at the back of my head that remembered you, that said you were a friend, not an enemy. Not," he gave her a sheepish grimace, "prey. I tried to help you, but it was like I didn't have full control of my body. Every time I got close to you, it was harder and harder to fight the instinct to attack. And then, when you grabbed me, I couldn't think at all." He took a deep breath. "Did I hurt you?"

"No," Susanna replied at once. "You were just trying to survive, to escape. You didn't hurt me."

Jack gave her a disbelieving look and turned over her hands, revealing the slashes and gouges in both of her palms. Her expression mulish, Susanna ripped her hands away and tucked them under her legs, wincing as the movement jostled her injury.

"That was the other wraiths," she asserted.

"Sure it was," Jack replied, though his tone said he clearly didn't believe her.

"What happened on the beach?" Tristan pressed. "How did you actually break free of the wraith's body?"

"I'm… I'm not sure." Jack scrunched up his face in thought. "I could hear you singing," he said to Susanna, whose face coloured beet-red, making Jack grin. "And then you were crying. I could feel it, where you were touching me. I could feel how sorry you were, how guilty you felt." He dropped his voice, hunching his shoulders slightly against the rest of the room, his eyes glued to Susanna's. "I could feel how much you cared about me…" He stopped to gather himself. "I took… I took a breath and it was like my chest tore open. The next thing I knew I had hands, and I was lying under you." He paused, then turned to Tristan. "I don't know how to explain it any better than that."

Tristan nodded, accepting Jack's words, but frustration clouded his eyes. He hated not fully understanding just how Susanna and Jack had achieved it. Dylan could see him thinking it through, trying to unravel the mystery. Jack, however, had finished telling his tale, and his full attention went back to Susanna.

"You came back for me," he murmured to her.

"I promised I would," Susanna replied just as quietly.

It was a private moment, and Dylan fought not to listen in, but she couldn't help herself. The raw emotion on both their faces drew her like a drug.

"I wouldn't have left you there, in the water. I knew you'd be so afraid. And I promised. I said I'd get you across the line, and I'm going to."

There was a moment's silence before Jack spoke, his voice cracking. "I wish you could come with me."

"I do, too."

At that point Dylan had to turn her back to everyone in the room. She was going to start crying, and she didn't want anyone to see. Part of it was for Jack and Susanna, because she knew just how much the separation was going to hurt them both, could see that they'd grown incredibly close in their time together. Mostly, though, it was selfish. Because she and Tristan were going to face that same thing. A farewell, for ever.

"Are you OK, angel?" Tristan's arms wrapped around her from behind and he tugged her into a hug.

"I'm fine," she said, but the words came out a garbled mush. She sniffed, pulling back the tears. "I just don't want to think about it, having to cross the line. Not yet."

Tristan squeezed her tighter, resting his chin on her shoulder. "Not yet," he agreed.

⌐

The mood in the safe house was subdued after the drama of Jack's arrival. Susanna lay flat out on the sofa, squashed towards the back of the cushions, while her leg healed. Jack had squashed himself into the remaining space, one arm acting as a pillow for Susanna, the other hanging on to her, as if he'd feared he'd slide right back into being a wraith if he let her go. Tristan had taken one of the stools and sat staring into the fire, his arms wrapped loosely around Dylan, who was balanced on his lap. Joan was on the only other chair, James leaning against the table.

The space was much too small to hold six people, and it felt crowded and uncomfortable to Dylan. But it was too late in the day to step outside, and she had no desire to do the only other thing that would help the situation. She was on borrowed time, and part of her wanted to talk to her parents, say anything, while another part of her wanted to stay silent, here on Tristan's knees, in the hope that time would stop moving altogether.

She wasn't sure how long she sat there, frozen, staring at her mum and dad as they stared back at her. Moments, maybe. Or years. But eventually Tristan breathed out a long sigh, drawing her attention.

"I think it's time," he told her, speaking low enough that his words wouldn't carry.

"What?" Dylan grabbed at him, shaking her head. "No!"

"Yes, angel." Tristan placed his hand on her cheek, his eyes full of compassion. "Tomorrow we have to cross the lake. We can't stay here."

"We can! We can stay here for ever if we want to! What's going to stop us? We don't need to eat, or drink."

"It's dangerous," Tristan disagreed. "Strange things have been happening in the wasteland. You heard Susanna say that a wraith got into a safe house. I want you out of here, safely across the line. And if you asked your parents, they'd say the same thing."

"Tristan, please!"

"I'm sorry, Dylan. But I promised I would help you, and that's what I'm going to do. Tomorrow we cross the lake." He looked over towards her parents. "You need to say goodbye."

"Tomorrow," Dylan whispered desperately. "I'll do it in the morning, first thing. We have the whole night to go."

"No." He said it gently, but the word cut Dylan like a knife.

"What difference does it make?" Agitated, Dylan shifted on Tristan's lap, trying to get away from him and his words, but he held her fast.

"Do you remember the last time we crossed the lake?"

Dylan stilled. Did she remember? Of course she did. A storm had whipped up and she'd tumbled out of the boat, into the water and the things that lurked there, ready to feast on any souls that toppled into their territory. She'd nearly drowned, and if Tristan hadn't dived in to rescue her, she'd have suffered the same fate as Jack.

Dylan shuddered, yanking in a breath against the tightness in her chest. She never, ever wanted to feel that drowning sensation ever again.

Tristan nodded, as if he could read her thoughts. "Tomorrow, I need you to be calm. Centred. I don't want to risk another storm whipping up. Dylan, angel, you aren't going to be able to do that if you've just said goodbye to your parents. You need the night to grieve—"

"It's going to take more than just one night, Tristan," Dylan retorted, fear and distress making her snap.

"I know." The tender way he held her and the sympathy in his voice made her anger die as quickly as it had surged. "But it'll give you time let the pain flow. I'll be here, Dylan." He rubbed her back, pressed a kiss to her temple. "I'll be here for you."

For now.

Dylan pushed that thought away, because she couldn't acknowledge it and breathe, not when she knew that Tristan was right.

"OK," she said, gathering herself and standing up. "OK."

It took four steps to cross the tiny floorspace of the safe house and stand before her parents. Each step was like hauling herself through quicksand, her feet dragging, her steps as heavy as her heart.

She stopped just outside touching distance, then made herself shuffle forwards a single step more.

Out of the corner of her eye, she could see Susanna and Jack. Selfishly, she wished they weren't here. This was a private moment, and she didn't want anyone to intrude, but then, Jack and Susanna's heartfelt reunion had played out in full view of everyone, and they were so wrapped up in being reunited that they seemed to hardly realise anyone else existed in the space. Dylan could feel Tristan moving closer behind her in silent support, but he stayed far back enough to give her space. To make this final moment between Dylan and her parents be just that. The three of them, a family for the last time in a long, long time: the rest of her parents' lives.

"Are you all right, Dylan?" her dad asked.

No, she wasn't all right.

"Tristan thinks—" she broke off. That wasn't fair, laying it on him. "We think…"

She couldn't do this. The words died on her lips and she just stood there, helplessly. A tear slipped free, then another.

"It's time, then," Joan whispered. She reached out and grabbed James's hand, clinging to it. "Time to say goodbye."

"For a little while," James amended.

A long while, Dylan hoped – though a secret, selfish part of her wanted to keep her parents with her, take them over the line with her right now. She beat it back. Giving them a chance to live was why she was here, why she was surrendering Tristan. He was giving up everything to give her parents this chance, Dylan couldn't make that sacrifice worthless.

"I'm so glad I got to know you," she told her dad. "I wish we'd had more time."

"We will," he promised. "We'll have all the time in the world, soon." He held out a hand towards her, but Dylan shook her head. She only had the strength to do this once, she wanted to do it together.

"Mum," she whispered.

Joan smiled at her, fierce and strong, just like she always was.

Dylan tried to fix the picture in her head, to store in her memory so she'd always have it there.

"I know we didn't always get on," Dylan said, "but I love you. I hope you know that."

"Oh baby, of course I do! And I love you. You're the most wonderful thing in my world."

Dylan bit back a sob. There was one more thing she wanted to say.

"When it's… your turn…" She hauled in a breath. "If something happens to either of you in the wasteland, if something terrible goes wrong and you become a wraith, I'll come for you. I'll come for you and bring you back. I swear it."

That was too much for Joan. With a cry, she threw herself forwards, drawing Dylan into her arms and surrounding her with love. A moment later, her dad joined them, pulling them together and making them one. Dylan had a single, glorious moment to revel in it, to feel the love pouring out of her parents and enveloping her in warmth…

Then they were gone, and she stood, empty-handed. Empty to the bottom of her soul.

Dylan glanced around, took in the room, Jack and Susanna on the sofa, Tristan gazing sorrowfully at her from near the fireplace. Silence rang in the air until it was deafening. For a second, she felt nothing. Then it started, a ripple in her chest that echoed outwards, magnifying in size and strength as it went. It stole her breath and left her reeling, her nerves tingling with pain. She made an inhuman sound and then she was falling.

Tristan caught her before she hit the floor.

"It's OK," he whispered in her ear. "It's OK. I'm here. Just breathe, Dylan. Just breathe."

Didn't he understand? She couldn't breathe. There was no air to breathe. A dead weight in his arms, Dylan could do nothing but shake and sob and wait for her soul to die – because surely it couldn't survive this.

Dylan didn't even want it to, because then she'd have to face saying goodbye to Tristan.

And she knew she would not survive that.

CHAPTER 24

In and out. In and out. Tristan sat on the floor with his back to the rough stone wall, Dylan cuddled into his front, and concentrated on just breathing.

Watching Dylan fall apart when her parents were pulled out of the wasteland and back to the real world had destroyed something in him. She was hurting inside, he knew, her heart torn open and left to bleed. And there was nothing he could do about it. There was no monster to slay, no bandage he could apply that would fix the wound. He could do nothing but sit here and hold her. Useless.

He couldn't even think of the right words to say to comfort her, because his thoughts were in a blind panic. The moment was coming, moving closer and closer like a high-speed train, and he was helpless to stop it. In fact, he had to actively move towards it, be complicit in his own destruction.

Saying goodbye to Dylan would end him. And then he'd have to go on, day after day, soul after soul. Tristan didn't know how he was supposed to do it.

In and out. In and out.

The sky outside was lightening by degrees. Tristan was aware of it, and of Susanna stirring on the sofa, gathering herself to move from the comfort of Jack's embrace and test her leg. It should be fine, Tristan knew, and if Susanna was feeling anything remotely close to what Tristan was, any lingering pain from the break would be nothing.

In and out. In and out.

Today, the lake. Four of them in the little boat was going to be tight, but as long as Dylan and Jack were able to contain their emotions, it should be all right. This wasn't their wasteland, but now that Joan and James had gone, Tristan wasn't sure how it would react, whether it would feed off either one – or both – of them.

Murmuring from the sofa across the room spurred him, finally, into nudging Dylan back to consciousness. She wasn't sleeping, but she'd retreated deep into herself, to a place where she was protected and safe, and the harsh realities of life – and death – didn't apply.

"Angel, we need to start getting ready to go."

Dylan didn't speak, she just climbed silently to her feet.

Tristan's legs throbbed with relief – Dylan didn't weigh much, but she'd been sitting on him all night and the stone floor wasn't exactly cushioned – but he immediately missed the warmth of her, the comfort of touch. Getting his numb legs beneath him, he stood and immediately reached out, dropping a hand on her shoulder. He needed that connection, that tangible contact that told him he hadn't lost her. Not yet.

In and out. In and out.

It didn't take long for them to get ready to leave the safe house. It wasn't as if any one needed to eat or drink or slip round the side to use a make-shift toilet. A cloud hung over the space as they readied themselves. Nobody spoke much, the quiet punctuated only by Jack's murmured enquiries about Susanna's leg.

"It's fine," she assured him. "Good as new."

Tristan doubted that was true, but it would hold up and, if she could avoid injuring it again today, it would be completely healed after one more night of resting.

Taking the lead, as always, he walked to the door and swung it wide. Dylan joined him there, the two of them staring out at the narrow length of the valley.

"I thought it might have reverted back to the real wasteland," she said, the first words she'd spoken in hours. She glanced at him. "Did you know it would stay like this?"

"I wasn't sure what would happen," Tristan answered honestly. "This is all unchartered territory."

"We've been experiencing a lot of that lately," Dylan offered, a small attempt at lightness. Knowing what it cost her, Tristan grabbed her hand and squeezed her fingers. She squeezed back, the tiny smile on her face wobbling.

"Shall we go?" Susanna asked quietly behind them. She, too, was looking with interest at the skin that still held true in the wasteland. The quiet surprise on her face told Tristan that she hadn't been sure what would happen either. He didn't know if it was the Inquisitor's doing, or if the wasteland was just reacting to the presence of souls, any souls, but he was grateful for it.

"Yeah," he said. "Let's go."

His feet knew the way to the lake and he let them carry him in the right direction, shutting off his mind. If he thought about it, he might just turn tail and run, heading back to the safe house and dragging Dylan with him. Like she said, they could stay there for ever, but, just as he'd said, it was dangerous. A soul wasn't supposed to stay in the wasteland for long, and Tristan didn't know what might happen if they broke the rules.

He'd learned the hard way recently that actions had consequences – and he would not risk Dylan. He thought he might be able to go on, somehow, if he at least knew that she was safe behind the line. She might even be happy there, eventually, when it was her parents' time to join her. A small part of Tristan hoped he'd be the one to ferry them. That way, he'd be able to ensure they made it, and it would be the closest he'd ever come to touching her again, seeing her. He'd have all of their memories – minus the ones the Inquisitor decided they wouldn't be allowed to keep – and that would be something. Something to treasure, to keep him company though the long hours of the endless nights that awaited him.

Finally, the lake came into view. As one, they stopped. Yesterday, Tristan hadn't really thought much about the lake. He'd been more worried about Susanna, about how upset she was going to be to discover that she was mistaken about the wraith, that she'd only imagined it to be Jack, and that he was really gone.

How wrong Tristan had been about that one.

Now, coming back here with Dylan, it seemed more intimidating. More frightening. He'd seen what the lake wraiths had done to Susanna, and felt the ominous strength of whatever unearthly creature had roused itself from the lake's depths. But more than that, he'd almost lost Dylan here last time, and everything in him warred against taking her back out on that open stretch of water. Glancing to the side, he saw Dylan and Susanna staring at the lake with apprehension, but also grim determination.

Jack, though, looked terrified.

"Susanna," Tristan murmured.

He didn't have the relationship with Jack to calm him. He could get him on the boat, he was sure about that, but if Jack's emotions had the ability to influence the currently calm waters, they'd all quickly end up overboard.

Tristan looked up at the sky. A light slate-grey, it refused to reveal its secrets. Perhaps it would react to Jack's fear, perhaps not.

Susanna turned to look at Tristan, then followed his line of sight to Jack. Worry and compassion clouded her face and she reached out for her soul.

"Hey," she said. "It'll be all right. There are two of us to keep you safe now. We'll get across, I promise."

As soon as the words were out, she winced. Tristan did too: she'd promised Jack she'd get him across the real wasteland, and that had almost ended in disaster.

Jack, though, was too lost in panic for her words to penetrate. "I can't," he mumbled. "I just can't."

He was shaking so hard, Tristan could actually see it, tiny tremors racking his frame.

"You can." Susanna gripped his hand tightly. "I'm going to tether you to me, all right? That way we'll always be connected. No matter what happens, nothing will separate us."

Tristan didn't think Jack really heard her, but then he turned towards his ferryman, hope a flicker in his eyes.

"A tether?"

"There's a rope," Susanna said. "I'll tie us together."

Tristan had planned to use the rope to tether him and Dylan together, and he hadn't seen a second one in the shed, but looking at Jack, he realised this was the only way they were going to get him in the boat, short of putting a compulsion on him so hard, they risked shattering his mind. After having lived for days as a wraith, who knew what damage had already been done.

"Shall we go?" he suggested.

Nobody argued, so Tristan took Dylan's hand and started down the slope. He was leading her to safety, he reminded himself when his body fought every single step. When she crossed the line, she would be safe.

That the same journey would lead to his doom was something he was just going to have to live with.

"The boat's already out," Dylan noticed quietly. "I thought you said the wasteland always reset itself, that the boat moved back to the shed each time?"

"It does," Tristan replied, "but we're still in the same wasteland. This is where Susanna and I left it yesterday."

Yesterday, when that creature had smashed at the bottom of the boat. It hadn't leaked then – not much, at least – but they were going to have to take it back out, more heavily laden, today. Tristan could do nothing but hope it survived the trip: there was only one boat, and not enough time to walk around the lake.

"Let's just get this over with," Susanna muttered. She was pale, Tristan noticed, and she kept glancing at Jack, who was looking near catatonic with fear now that they were at the water's edge.

"You all get in," Tristan offered. "I'll push the boat out."

It didn't take long for Susanna to tie a length of the rope around her middle and then lasso Jack in the same way. There was enough left to include Dylan in the safety-line and Susanna held it out to her in silent question, but Tristan shook his head. If Jack and Susanna went overboard, he didn't want Dylan to be pulled in after them. He'd look after her himself.

"Get in," he repeated.

It was harder, getting the little rowing boat afloat on his own with two extra people weighing it down, but Susanna needed to stay in the boat to comfort Jack, and there was no way Tristan was asking Dylan to set foot in the water. He heaved, straining every muscle in his back and shoulders, and the boat had no option but to give way, edging slowly into the lapping waves.

The boat rode lower in the water, so Tristan had to wade in until the lake was up to his knees before he could vault in, sprinkling everyone inside with water.

"Sorry," he said, but no one responded. They were all too tense.

Taking the oars, Tristan sighed then started powering them forward. He kept a close eye on the cracked planks in the hull, but nothing seemed to be seeping through. They weren't in danger of sinking, at least. The weather, too, was holding. Dylan was clearly nervous, and Jack was just about keeping it together, but the water stayed calm, and the monsters stayed beneath, where they belonged.

Stroke after stroke, Tristan took them into the middle of the lake, and then towards the far shore.

It was too quick. Too easy. Though Tristan desperately wanted to get Dylan to safety, a part of him had hoped for disaster, for something ill to befall them so that they'd have to abandon the attempt, return to the safe house they'd just left.

Something to give him just a little longer with Dylan.

The boat nearly unseated him when it hit a sandbank just a metre or two off the shore. On autopilot, Tristan got out of the boat and helped Dylan clamber out after him. Jack was out and on the stony beach before Tristan even had time to turn back to him. Susanna hobbled along beside him.

"Come on, Jack," she said when she reached the shore. "Let's go inside."

Jack didn't hesitate, following Susanna into the safe house. With a long look at Tristan, thick with meaning, Susanna closed the door. She was giving each of them time, he realised. A final few moments of stolen time to spend together with their souls.

Tristan turned to Dylan, opened his arms to her. "Come here," he croaked.

This was it, the end. Tomorrow, Tristan would deliver Dylan to the line. She'd walk through it, and he'd never see her again.

Gathering Dylan to him, Tristan sat down on the pebbles and allowed himself to feel the joy of simply holding her. Of being with her, feeling her breathe and letting the wispy tendrils of her hair tickle his face. This memory had to last a lifetime. An endless lifetime.

As if mocking him and his pain, the sun burst through the clouds as they sat there on the shore. It shined down on them, turning the sprawl of the lake into a thousand glistening sparkles.

⟿

"They're not coming inside?" Jack looked out through the one window of the safe house towards where Tristan and Dylan were huddled together. "Is it safe out there?"

"They'll be safe for a while," Susanna said. "It's only mid-afternoon."

"But they'd be safer in here, wouldn't they?"

Susanna shrugged. "I guess so, but—"

"But?"

She stared at him, willing the burn behind her eyes to hold. It was going to be a long night if she started crying now.

"We're almost there. Tomorrow, Tristan and I will deliver you both to the line, and you'll go through." She swallowed. "We'll never see each other again. I just thought it might be nice, you know…" She shrugged.

"A bit of privacy for them," Jack concluded.

"For all of us." Dammit, the tears just wouldn't stay put. "This is our goodbye too, and I didn't want to share it with them."

Jack smiled then. The slow, warm smile that Susanna hadn't seen on his face until they'd been trapped together in the safe house in the real wasteland, the one that had developed after countless days of warily circling each other. After they made peace with both of their actions and called a fragile truce that morphed slowly into a friendship so strong that no distance could break the bonds that bound them together.

There would never be another Jack.

He crossed the room to her and pulled her into a hug, and Susanna felt herself dissolve. She clung to him, and felt his arms wrap around her waist as he hung just as tightly onto her. Unbalanced, they toppled until they were half-kneeling, half-sitting on the stone floor. Susanna's leg gave a vicious twinge, but she ignored it, unwilling to let go.

"I don't want to go without you," Jack mumbled into her hair.

"It'll be all right," Susanna reassured him. "You don't need to be afraid."

Jack pulled back slightly, dropping his head so that he could glower down at Susanna.

"That's not why!" he told her. "I want you to come because I want you to come!"

Though his words didn't really make sense, Susanna understood what he was trying to say. The words, nonsensical as they were, meant a lot to her.

"I know," she replied. "I wish I could come with you, too."

Susanna had stood in front of the line so many times she'd lost count, and she'd wished it was possible for her to take that step, to see what was beyond, almost every time. This was different, though. This time, for the first time, she wanted to go for no other reason than to be with Jack. If all that was beyond the line was a little cottage like this one, empty of everything and everyone, Susanna thought she could be happy, so long as she had him beside her.

"I want to offer to stay here with you," Jack said, "but I'm too afraid of becoming one of those things again." He gave her a heartbreakingly sad smile. "I'm a coward."

"No, you aren't," she disagreed. "And I wouldn't let you, anyway. It's too dangerous here. I would never forgive myself if something happened to you. Again."

She added the last on a whim, offering Jack a little quirk of her lips, and it worked: he laughed.

"We've been through a lot, you and me," he said.

"We have." That was an understatement.

"You won't forget about me, will you?"

Jack murmured the question into the top of Susanna's head, his tone light and almost joking, but something about the words made Susanna draw back and study him.

"Are you serious?"

To her surprise, Jack blushed, looked away from her.

"Jack?" she prompted. "I mean it, is that a serious question? Look at me, Jack."

It seemed to cost him to turn his head and face her, but he did it. What Susanna saw there took her breath away: vulnerability, and real fear.

"Jack!" she whispered.

He clenched his jaw, but he held her stare.

"Of course I'm going to remember you! You're the only person who matters to me, Jack. The only person who's ever really seen me, who cares about me. And who I care about."

Jack's face reddened and he looked like he didn't know what to say. He hated emotional moments, she knew. She smiled a little sadly and shifted to move away, to give him an escape from the intensity of the moment, but Jack held fast, refusing to let her.

"I'm not sorry," he said gruffly. "About everything that's happened. I'm not, because it meant I found you."

Susanna beamed even as her eyes filled.

"You don't know what that means to someone like me, you can't possibly." She breathed deeply, trying to loosen the tightness in her chest. "I won't forget about you. Not ever." She quirked her lips at him. "Are you going to forget about me?"

"Don't be stupid!"

"Well, then!"

"All right, all right." He pulled her back into a hug so that he could whisper in her ear. "You're my best friend, you know that? You're... special." He shifted his shoulders beneath her hands, the line of his back tense, and Susanna knew he was uncomfortable. "I don't talk about feelings, not since I was a little kid. Not even with my mum." A long, sad pause. "I wish I had, but it's too late now. I can tell you, though, and I don't want to go without making sure you know what you mean to me. I will never, *ever* forget you. And I'm not sorry, about any of it. It was all worth it, to know you like I do."

Susanna closed her eyes and let herself enjoy the moment. When Jack let go, she wanted to cling to him, but she made herself draw back, a smile plastered on her face.

"You'll be able to tell your mum how you feel – you know, that you love her," she told him. "She'll be with you again, one day."

"Yeah." Jack nodded, a look of childlike longing on his face. It quickly faded into sadness, though. "I won't see you, though. Not ever again."

"No," Susanna replied quietly. "You won't."

There was no bed or sofa in the safe house, but Jack helped Susanna up from the floor before moving over to an aged rug that lay in the far corner. The colours had dulled, but the pile was thick enough to look reasonably comfortable.

"Come on," he said, sitting down and then reclining back on one elbow. "Once more, for old time's sake."

Susanna smiled as she followed him down. Leaning her head on his chest, she closed her eyes and listened to him breathe in and out, in and out...

There it was, the line. It shimmered in the air, insubstantial, and yet it was more effective at keeping Susanna out than a steel vault door.

Jack stood beside her, making no move to go.

"Go on," she said. "You just have to take a step, that's all."

"And then what happens to you?"

"I'll go on." To the next soul, and the one after that, and the one after that. An endless cycle that would be so much harder to endure now that she'd had a taste of real freedom, of real happiness. "Go on, Jack. Just step."

He went. Without another look, another word or another touch. He went. Jack stepped across the line.

Susanna watched as he turned and stared at the scene behind him. He wouldn't see her, she knew, he'd just see an empty road.

Something caught Jack's attention and he looked away, towards whatever lay beyond – something Susanna had never seen. He took one step, then another. Susanna stood there watching as the world started to bleed white. Her very last glimpse of Jack was of the back of his head as he left her behind.

"Goodbye, Jack," she whispered.

She could have shouted it and he still wouldn't have heard. He was – now and forevermore – out of her reach. As her entire world glowed a blinding, brilliant white, she closed her eyes and let the loneliness crush her.

Susanna opened her eyes to the sound of Tristan and Dylan walking quietly into the safe house. The light through the door was dim and the hissing and wailing of the wraiths outside cut through the air until Tristan firmly closed the door on them.

Susanna turned her head, burying her face into Jack's T-shirt. She didn't want to talk to anyone, not even Jack, who she sensed was awake, too. She couldn't, not after that dream. Was it just her imagination, or was that how it was going to be? Had she just had a premonition?

She didn't understand why the wasteland was doing this to her, sliding her out of herself and showing her these things. She hated it.

She'd thought the 'dreams' she'd had of Jack's past had been painful. The future, she now knew, would be even worse.

CHAPTER 25

It was quiet in the safe house. Susanna and Jack couldn't be sleeping, but they didn't look up or speak as Dylan and Tristan slid in the door with the last of the fading light. They'd lingered outside as long as possible, soaking in the time together, but the wraiths were gathering. Tristan had hustled her to her feet at the first low hiss and urged her inside.

Neither Jack nor Susanna had lit the fire, and between that and the growing twilight outside, it was dark in the safe house. Dylan was glad for that, because she didn't think she could control her face. Outside, she'd been able to forget, just for a while, what lay in store for them tomorrow, but in here, with the other ferryman and her soul, it was inescapable.

She thought she might cry. Or scream. Or puke.

Instead, she forced herself to follow as Tristan pulled her over to a spot against the wall, as far from the others as was possible, which wasn't very far. There was no bed to lie on, and nothing beneath them but stone floor, but Tristan tugged her down anyway. He let go of her briefly to haul his jumper over his head, laying it down on the floor as a makeshift pallet.

It wasn't comfortable, but Tristan arranged Dylan so that she was mostly lying on him. The hard floor still dug into her hip, but there was no point in complaining. It didn't matter. She tried to relax, something which got a little easier when Tristan started stroking his fingers softly through her hair. She tried to commit the feeling to memory.

"Dylan," he murmured. "Come here."

She lifted her head to peer at him in the gloom. "I am here."

"No." He tugged at her, urging her higher. "Here."

"Tristan!" She hissed the whisper a moment before his lips found hers. Really? He wanted to start kissing now, when Jack and Susanna were just feet away? They'd had most of the afternoon outside, he couldn't have started it then?

Dylan's cheeks burned, but she wasn't going to draw away. This was her last chance to kiss Tristan like this, when the darkened safe house offered a semblance of privacy. Levering herself up so that she could get a little closer, she kissed him back, leaning into his touch when his hand snaked under her shirt and stroked across her lower back.

This was it, all she'd ever have of him. The thought shot through Dylan like a cannonball and turned the kiss desperate, raw.

"Hey," Tristan said, breaking away. "Hey, it's OK."

She hadn't even realised she was crying, but when Tristan's thumbs smoothed across her cheeks she felt the wetness as he wiped it away.

"Tristan, I can't. I can't do this."

He didn't say anything, just sighed and held her.

"You missed your line," she told him quietly.

"What?" The word came out as a puff of breath against her lips.

"Your line." She tried hard to curve her mouth into a smile. "You're supposed to promise to come with me, remember?"

She couldn't read Tristan's expression in the dark, but she felt it when he understood. He didn't laugh, though, like she'd thought he would. Instead he tensed, his muscles drawing tight.

"No," he said. "No lies, not even as a joke. I shouldn't have done that to you, I'm ashamed of myself."

"Tristan—" She hadn't meant that, to break open old wounds. She'd just been trying to find a way to survive the moment.

"Tomorrow, at the line, I'm going to be happy," he told her, "because I'm going to know that you're safe. That nothing can touch you, nothing can hurt you, ever again."

Dylan tried to shush him, to go back to kissing, because she couldn't stand to hear this, but Tristan wasn't done.

"Every single time I deliver another soul to the line, I'm going to stand as close to it as I can get, and I'm going to reach out and imagine that I can touch you. If you ever feel it, a brush of fingers that you can't explain, know that it's me and I'm there."

"Tristan." Nothing else would come out, no matter how hard Dylan swallowed. How was she supposed to manage the walk to the line? How could she walk through, knowing that Tristan couldn't follow? "I can't, Tristan. I can't do it."

"Yes, you can," he whispered. "Because I'll be beside you. Every step until the last."

Until the last. The final step that Dylan didn't know how she'd have the strength to take.

But there was no point wasting precious time worrying about it now. Dylan would face tomorrow when it came. Until then…

"Kiss me," she murmured. "Please, Tristan, just kiss me."

CHAPTER 26

They were there again, at the line. The exact spot on the road shimmered slightly, and the air in front of them was distorted, just a little. Like a heat haze, though the day was cool.

They stood abreast, the four of them. No one spoke, no one moved. Tristan thought they might stand there all day, until the appearance of wraiths would finally force their hand.

He clutched Dylan's hand in his, but he didn't look at her. If he did, he thought he might plead with her to stay. They could be happy here, in the wasteland... right up until his attention slipped and a wraith stole her from him.

So he stood there, and he stared at the line, and he waited.

"This is it," Susanna said unnecessarily.

"What do we do?" Jack asked.

"You just walk through."

Jack nodded, but he made no move towards the line.

"Go on, Jack," Susanna urged. "Go."

She sounded firm, encouraging. Anyone who didn't know her wouldn't hear the quiet edge of desperation, or despair. Tristan did, and he knew Jack did, too. Her soul didn't move from her side.

Tristan clung more tightly to Dylan. This wasn't right. It wasn't *fair*. If he thought it would make any difference, he'd curse the powers that controlled the wasteland, but he didn't dare. Not when anything he did might have consequences for Dylan.

"Why do you think you can't go through?" Jack asked suddenly.

"Because we *can't*," Susanna replied. She sounded exasperated, but Tristan suspected the truth that she, like him, was struggling to keep her composure.

"Have you ever tried?" Jack argued.

"No, but that doesn't matter, we c—"

"I have," Tristan said suddenly. "I've tried. It didn't work."

"When?" Dylan asked quietly beside him.

He looked down at her, offered her a sad smile.

"Oh." She gazed up at him, her heart in her eyes, and he knew she was remembering the moment. She thought he'd tricked her, lied to her and betrayed her. The hurt and agony had been written all over her face as she knelt on the floor in front of him, within touching distance but completely out of reach.

Now, knowing that he'd tried to come with her, to stay with her like he promised, the expression on her face was bittersweet.

"I would have followed you, if I could," he told her quietly.

"You said that you assumed ferrymen could never go to the real world before Tristan did it," Jack reminded Susanna.

"I told you," Tristan growled, annoyed that Jack wouldn't let this go. He didn't want his and Dylan's last moments together to be ruined by a stupid argument. "I tried. It didn't work."

"But that was before you were in our world," Jack went on doggedly. "Maybe things have changed."

"They haven't."

"They might have."

"They haven't."

"We should try!"

"Look—" Tristan rounded on Jack, ready to compel him into shutting his mouth if that's what it took, but Jack was already moving. Grabbing Susanna by the arm, he yanked on her, spun, and then shoved her backwards – towards the line.

Susanna's face was a mask of shock and surprise as she hurtled backwards. She reached out, but the force with which Jack had thrown her propelled her out of Tristan's reach. He winced, waiting for her to slam into the invisible wall… but she didn't.

She flew straight through.

Tristan stared, astonished. Beside him, he heard Dylan give an audible gasp.

"That's impossible," he burst out.

Susanna, utterly thrown, stumbled and tripped, landing heavily on the ground. She spun, twisting from her hands and knees to her back, staring out at them – from the other side of the line. Tristan saw her eyes widen, panic etching itself across her face.

"Jack! Jack, where are you!" Her gaze darted from side to side, moving sightlessly over them.

"She can't see you," Tristan told Jack, but the soul had already worked that out. He stormed forward and the next moment he was kneeling beside Susanna, helping her up and dusting her off. Susanna still hadn't managed to wipe the amazement off her face before she was pulled into a fierce hug. Tristan watched her bewilderment morph slowly into an astonished smile.

Tristan turned to Dylan the exact moment she turned to him, and he knew the shock must be as clear on his face as it was on hers.

How? It wasn't possible.

He knew, he *knew* it wasn't possible, but it had happened.

Jack had to be right – their journey into the real world had to be what was allowing them to cross over.

Dylan grinned at him. "If she can…"

"…I should be able to, as well."

He thought. He *hoped*. God, he hoped.

Jack and Susanna were laughing now, their sounds of relief and happiness ringing crystal clear in Tristan's ears. As if they stood right by his side, and not on the other side of an almost invisible barrier.

"Are you ready?" he asked Dylan. Reaching out, he grabbed her hand, held on tight.

"Yes… I—" But the expression on her face was at odds with her words. She bit her lip. "Tristan, if this doesn't work—"

"It will."

"But if it doesn't," Dylan persisted. She drew in a deep breath, her eyes fixed on his face. "If it doesn't work, I want you to know that I love you. And if… when you're bringing souls to the line," her voice cracked a little, "if you feel someone's eyes on you, it's me, watching over you."

He thought his heart might burst. Drawing her into his arms, Tristan held her close. "I love you, too," he managed. "But it's going to work. I know it." He let her go, her hand still clenched in his, and smiled. "Now?"

Dylan nodded. "Together?" she asked.

"Together." He moved forward, thinking to kiss her in this, their last moment in the wasteland, but she stopped him, pressing a hand to his mouth.

"Wait," she said, laughter in her eyes, her doubts quieted. "Kiss me on the other side."

"No," he replied, sharing the memory from the last time they had stood in this very spot, this moment too joyful to be tainted by the pain of the past. "Now."

She laughed, stepped forward and tugged. Together, they stepped through the veil, out of the wasteland.

Tristan couldn't wait any longer. With one hand he pulled her in closer to his body, with the other he cupped the back of her neck, sliding his fingers into her hair. Letting his eyes slide closed, he pressed his lips against Dylan's. He felt her fingers twist into the fabric of his jumper, her hands shaking slightly against his sides. Her lips parted, moving against his. He heard her utter a tiny moan, and the sound sent a ripple into the pit of his stomach. He squeezed her tighter, mouth pressing harder against hers. His heart was crashing against his ribs, his breathing ragged. The only thing he was aware of was the warmth of her, the softness. He felt her grow bolder, going up on her tiptoes to lean further into him, lifting her hands from his side and gripping his shoulders, his face. He copied the movement, his fingers trailing down her hairline, around her chin—

"Welcome."

Tristan jerked his mouth from Dylan's at the low, musical voice that floated through the air: something had been waiting for them on the other side of the line.

He tensed, thinking the being was an Inquisitor. He waited for his body to lock down, for control to be stolen from him, but it didn't happen.

"Caeli!" Dylan said beside him. Then, more hesitantly, "Are you Caeli?"

"I am." The being inclined its head, and after Tristan's initial moment of panic had passed, he saw that it was nothing like the Inquisitor. If the Inquisitor was made of darkness and terror, this being was light and warmth. It wasn't cloaked, but it still seemed strangely faceless, apart from its welcoming gold eyes. The features were there, but blurred slightly. Tristan couldn't focus on it, couldn't tell if its nose was bulbous or blade-like, its mouth wide or narrow. It hurt, trying to figure it out, so he forced himself to relax his eyes, to let everything stay smudged, just out of focus.

"You have returned, Dylan McKenzie." Tristan felt the being, Caeli, sweep its gaze across the four of them. "This is highly irregular," it said.

That didn't sound good to Tristan.

"Are you going to try and stop us?" he demanded.

"No." The being seemed to smile, a sense of puzzlement crossing its strange face. "I am here to welcome you." It bowed its head. "Welcome home, Dylan, Jack, Tristan, Susanna."

Welcome home. The words rang in Tristan's ears and he scarcely dared believe them.

"Please, come with me." Caeli moved to the side, revealing a metal gate. It was closed, but there was no fence on either side of the gateposts, so anyone could simply walk around. Tristan stared at the gate and then at Caeli, confused, but Dylan started walking.

Of all of them, she was the only one with experience of this side of the line, and she didn't seem afraid. Moving quickly to catch up with her, Tristan followed Caeli, the quiet sound of feet crunching on dirt behind telling him that Susanna and Jack, too, were following. When Caeli reached the gate, it swung it open and Tristan ground to a halt, astonished.

It was as if Caeli had cut a hole in the world. In the space where the gate had been, was now a window onto a whole other place.

"What the hell…?" he heard Jack gasp.

Dylan took Tristan's hand, and when he turned to look at her, her eyes were twinkling.

"I want to show you something," she said.

Walking past the beautiful, glowing being, Dylan led Tristan into the strangest room he'd ever seen. Everywhere he looked the walls seemed to morph and change, expanding, adding nooks and crannies and extra corridors filled with bookshelves.

"This is the records room," Dylan said.

Jack and Susanna were looking around with awed faces, but Tristan only had eyes for Dylan.

"My book," he said. Dylan had told him all about it when she'd come back for him last time.

She smiled, a secret smile, and looked towards the being, who had followed them in. "Can you show him?"

It should have worried Tristan that this creature was shadowing their every move, but he didn't sense any sort of threat from it. On the contrary, it seemed pleased, the warmth emanating from it making Tristan think it was happy to see him and Susanna just as much as it was to see Dylan and Jack.

"What book?" Susanna asked, her curiosity piqued.

"You'll see," Dylan said. She towed Tristan along behind her, following Caeli until they were stood at an ornately carved wooden desk, a faded green leather-bound book with pages gilded in gold resting on the surface. The corners appeared worn, soft, as if a thousand fingers had lifted the cover and leafed through.

Tristan wanted to reach out and flip the cover back, reveal what was inside, but at the same time he also wanted to run away from it.

Dylan took the initiative and opened it to a page at random. There, in tiny writing, was a list of name, after name, after name. All the souls that Tristan had ferried.

"My souls," he croaked. It was incredible, to see them all written down. To see just how many were there. The souls he'd saved... and lost.

Two of the entries on the page, he could see, had been scribbled out, heavy ink almost completely obscuring whatever name had been written there.

"You should be proud," Dylan told him. "Look how many people are here, because of you." She smiled. "But you're finished now. It's time to live, at last. Here, with me."

He huffed out a breath, still not quite daring to believe it. Glancing at the book, he looked again at those crossed-out names. "I'm not sure that I deserve it."

Dylan lifted her hand to the book, her fingers skimming down the list until she hovered over one of those names, a soul who loitered still in the wasteland, turned into a mindless, hate-filled creature.

"You do deserve it," she said.

"What about those souls?" he whispered. "They deserved it, too."

"It's not too late for them," Dylan reminded him. "We know that now. And we can help them: we can figure out who they are, and then we can find their loved ones and let them know." Her gaze turned to Jack, who was watching warily, half his attention on Dylan and half on Susanna, who was staring at the book with a mix of emotions on her face. The same ones Tristan was feeling: triumph for all those names written there, and shame for the ones removed.

"Let them know what?" he asked.

Dylan grinned at him. "Let them know that their souls aren't really gone. That they can be brought back." Her gaze shifted to encompass Susanna, too. "That if they've lost loved ones they really, sincerely care about, and if they're willing to risk their souls for them, that they can go and get them. They can bring them back."

Tristan stared at her, pride filling his chest and a new sense of purpose taking hold of him.

"We're going to let everybody know," Dylan went on, "that nobody's truly gone. They're only waiting to be saved."

"This is why I love you," Tristan told her, reaching up to cup her cheek. "Your compassion, your strength, your determination to do the right thing."

She blushed, her eyes flickering away in embarrassment at the compliment, but a heartbeat later her gaze returned to his. "I hope so," she said, "because now you're stuck with me, for ever!"

"Trust me," Tristan murmured, moving closer so that she was near enough to hold, to kiss, "it won't be long enough."

Feeling, finally, that he was right where he belonged, Tristan pressed his lips to hers.

Acknowledgements

So this is it, the end! Over the last seven years, the *Ferryman* series has changed my whole world. I can't quite believe that I've written the last words and that I'm saying goodbye to Dylan and Tristan, Susanna and Jack. I remember exactly sitting down in my (damp) flat in Peebles, Scotland, and typing out the first couple of lines – what later became the beginning of *Ferryman's* third chapter.

Back then I could never even have imagined the book being read by anyone other than my mum and husband, never mind people across the globe. It's mind-blowing, and has only been possible with the help of the following lovely, lovely people.

Huge thanks are owed to my agent, Ben Illis at the BIA, who found *Ferryman* amongst a heap of manuscripts I threw at him when he was brave enough to take me on. In addition, thank you to Helen Boyle, who guided me through my first editing process and helped shape the book with a sympathetic hand and a lot of patience.

Thank you to my friends and family who were the very first readers of *Ferryman, Trespassers* and now *Outcasts*: Chris, Clare, Ruth and Mum. I admit I'm not the greatest at receiving criticism, but your encouragement and support means a lot to me. Further thanks to the many bloggers and journalists who helped bring the *Ferryman* series to readers.

I need to say thank you, of course, to the team at Floris, who breathed new life into *Ferryman*, and brought *Trespassers* and *Outcasts* into the world. I'm very grateful to you for believing in Dylan the way I do. In the same vein, thank you to

White Horse Time, who discovered *Ferryman* and brought it and the following books to readers in China. The love I've felt there is incredibly heart-warming.

Finally thank you to you, the reader. Whoever you are, wherever you are in the world, I'm humbled that you chose my stories to read out of the millions of books out there, waiting. I hope you enjoyed them.

Claire -x-

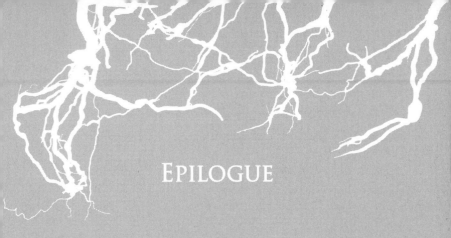

EPILOGUE

She stood in front of the door, her body hunched over with age, her joints riddled with arthritis that was nothing but a ghost her body couldn't shake, a prison her mind had built. Her hair was wispy, hanging limply to her shoulders, and the skin on her face sagged, sinking her chin into her neck. Everything about her was tired and worn, except her eyes, which shone bright and alert. And afraid.

Eliza stood in front of the door and she was deathly, deathly afraid.

She wasn't alone, she knew. Countless souls had come to her, wanting to know the secrets of this place, how to get back, return to the real world. Countless souls, and not one had ever had the nerve to do it, to open the door... until recently. Until one frightened but fierce girl had found the courage to risk her soul for the one she loved.

That girl made Eliza feel like a coward.

And so here she was.

Heart thudding in her chest, hand trembling, she reached out for the doorknob. In her mind's eye she conjured up the vision, the picture she held dear in her heart. Her husband, who she'd thought lost for ever, twisted and warped and turned into one of those wretched beasts. Her husband, who she'd abandoned to that fate. No longer, not with the knowledge those four young people had brought with them. Not with the knowledge that there was a chance.

She gripped the circular handle, took a final breath, and twisted.

Eliza expected nothing to happen. She thought she'd meet an immovable force, a lock she could never unpick. She honestly believed she'd have to stand there for hour after hour, searching for her courage, her conviction, until she was sure, utterly sure, that she wanted to do this.

But the door opened easily in her hand.